It Must Be Love

Other Avon Contemporary Romances by
Rachel Gibson

RACHEL GIBSON

It Must Be Love

AVON BOOKS NEW YORK

This is a work of fiction. Names, characters, places, and incidents either are the product of the author's imagination or are used fictitiously. Any resemblance to actual events, locales, organizations, or persons, living or dead, is entirely coincidental and beyond the intent of either the author or the publisher.

AVON BOOKS, INC.
An Imprint of HarperCollins*Publishers*
10 East 53rd Street
New York, New York 10022-5299

Copyright © 2000 by Rachel Gibson
Published by arrangement with the author
ISBN: 0-7394-0851-8
www.harpercollins.com

Printed in the U.S.A.

This one is dedicated with much love
to my brothers and sisters

Mary Kae Larson
A big heart in a small package
an accomplished driver and bumper rider
You had the best earrings
a younger sister could steal

Keith Reed
Thanks for the 25 bucks so I could get that
makeover in '77 and look like Farrah
When you left, you left a hole in my heart
I miss you every day

Terry Rogers
A beautiful person inside and out
a gifted singer and musician
with a special talent for chicken songs

Al Reed
An avid hunter and a good man
I've always been proud to call you my brother—
except when I found Malibu Barbie hanging
from the ceiling with needles stuck in her eyes

Growing up on Resseguie Street with you all
was the absolute best

Acknowledgments

I would like to express my heartfelt gratitude to the following people for their help with this book: Property Crimes Detective Shane Hartgrove, who helped in the beginning and answered my questions without laughing at me too much; Candis Terry, a talented writer, for helping with my cop questions; Officer John Terry, who let me touch his handcuffs and showed me his bulletproof vest; Dr. Paul Collins, for taking the time to talk to me about gunshot wounds and barometric pressure; and especially to my best buddy, Stef Ann Holm, who tells me the truth—even when I don't want to hear it. And a huge thanks to Lucia Macro, who understood I needed extra time and didn't hesitate to give it to me.

One

D ETECTIVE J OSEPH S HANAHAN HATED
rain. He hated it about as much as he
hated dirt-bag criminals, slick defense lawyers,
and stupid geese. The first were scum, the second bottom feeders, the third an embarrassment to the bird family in general.

He set his foot on the front bumper of a beige
Chevy, leaned forward, and stretched his muscles. He didn't need to see the metal-colored
clouds forming over Ann Morrison Park to
know he was in for a good shower. The dull
ache in his right thigh let him know this just
wasn't going to be his day.

Once he felt the muscles stretch and warm,
he switched legs. Most of the time, the only re-
minder that a 9mm slug had torn through flesh
and changed his life was the five-inch scar
puckering his thigh. Nine months and countless
hours of intense physical therapy later, he was
able to forget the rod and pins screwed to his
femur. Except when it rained and the change in

barometric pressure caused it to throb.

Joe straightened, rolled his head from side to side like a prize fighter, then reached into the pocket of the sweatpants he'd chopped into shorts and pulled out a pack of cigarettes. He pulled a Marlboro from the pack, then lit the end with his Zippo. Squinting his gaze against the flame, he eyed the sleek white goose staring at him from fewer than two feet away. The bird waddled closer, stretched up its long neck, and hissed, angry orange beak wide open, pink tongue sticking out straight.

With a snap of his wrist, the Zippo closed, and he shoved the pack and lighter into his pocket. He exhaled a long stream of smoke as the goose lowered its head and locked its beady sights on Joe's balls.

"Do it and I'll punt you like a football."

For several tense seconds they entered into a Mexican stand-off, then the bird pulled its head back, turned on its webbed feet, and waddled away, casting one last glance in Joe's direction before it hopped up on the curb and headed toward the other geese.

"Pantywaist," he muttered and turned his gaze from the retreating threat. More than rain, shifting air pressure, and even slick lawyers, Joe disliked police informants most. He'd never known more than one or two who wouldn't screw over their wives, mothers, or best friends to save their own sorry asses. He owed the hole in his leg to his last informant, Robby Martin.

Robby's double dealings had cost Joe a chunk of flesh and bone and a job he loved. The young drug dealer had paid a higher price—his life.

Joe leaned back against the side of the nondescript Caprice and took a deep pull off the cigarette. Smoke burned his throat and filled his lungs with tar and nicotine. The nicotine calmed his craving like a lover's soothing caress. As far as he was concerned, there was only one thing better than a chest full of toxins.

Unfortunately, he hadn't had that one thing since he'd broken up with Wendy, his last girlfriend. Wendy had been a fairly decent cook, and she'd looked downright amazing squeezed into Spandex. But he couldn't face a future with a woman who freaked out because he'd forgotten their two month dating anniversary. She'd accused him of being "unromantic." Hell, he was as romantic as the next guy. He just didn't act sappy and get stupid about it.

Joe took another long pull off the cigarette. Even if it hadn't been for that anniversary crap, his relationship with Wendy wouldn't have worked out anyway. She hadn't understood the amount of time he needed to spend with Sam. She'd been jealous, but if Joe didn't give Sam attention, he chewed up the furniture.

Joe exhaled slowly and watched the smoke hang in front of his face. Last time he'd quit smoking for three months, and he'd quit again. But not today. Probably not tomorrow either. He'd just been given a good ream by Captain

Luchetti, and if he was going to get fucked over, he damn sure wanted a cigarette afterward.

Through the smoke, his gaze narrowed, then settled, on a woman with a mass of auburn curls hanging halfway down her back. A breeze picked up her hair and lifted it about her shoulders. He didn't need to see her face to know who stood in the middle of Ann Morrison Park stretching her arms upward like a goddess worshiping the gray sky.

Her name was Gabrielle Breedlove, and she owned a curio shop in the historic Hyde Park district, along with her business partner, Kevin Carter. Both were suspected of using the shop as a front for their other, more lucrative, business—fencing stolen antiques.

Neither store owner had a prior record and might never have come to the attention of the police if they'd stayed small-time, but they had bigger ambitions. A famous Impressionist painting had been stolen the week before from the wealthiest man in the state, Norris Hillard, better known as The Potato King. In Idaho his power and influence were second only to God's. It would take someone with a huge set of cojones to steal The Potato King's Monet. So far, Gabrielle Breedlove and Kevin Carter were the strongest leads in the case. A jailhouse informer had given the police their names, and when the Hillards had checked their records, they'd discovered that six months prior, Carter had been in the Hillard home appraising a collection of Tiffany lamps.

Joe took a drag off his smoke and exhaled slowly. That little antique shop in Hyde Park was a perfect front for a fence, and he'd bet his left nut that Mr. Carter and Ms. Breedlove had the Hillards' Monet tucked away until the heat was off and they could hand it over to a dealer for a wad of cash. The best chance for recovery was to find the painting before it passed to the dealer and went underground.

The Potato King was raising hell with Chief Walker, who'd turned up the heat on Captain Luchetti and the property crimes detectives. Stress caused some cops to reach for the bottle. Not Joe. He wasn't big on booze, and he took another calming drag off his Marlboro as he eyed his suspect. In his head, he ran through the hastily compiled file he had on Ms. Breedlove.

He knew she'd been born and raised in a small town in northern Idaho. Her father had died when she'd been young, and she'd lived with her mother, fraternal aunt, and grandfather.

She was twenty-eight, five feet ten inches tall, and weighed somewhere in the neighborhood of one hundred and thirty pounds. Her legs were long. Her shorts were not. He watched her bend over to touch the ground in front of her, and he enjoyed the view along with his smoke. Since he'd been assigned to tail her, he'd developed an appreciation for the sweet shape of her backside.

Gabrielle Breedlove. Her name sounded like a porno star, like Mona Lot or Candy Peaks. Joe had never spoken to her, but he'd seen her up close personal enough to know she had all the right curves in all the right places.

And her family wasn't unknown in the state, either. The Breedlove Mining Company had operated up north for about ninety years before selling out in the mid-seventies. At one time, the family had been extremely wealthy, but bad investments and bad management had dwindled the fortune considerably.

He watched her do some sort of one-legged Yoga stretches before she took off at a slow jog. Joe flipped his Marlboro into the dew-covered grass and pushed away from the Chevy. He set out across the park after her and stepped onto the black ribbon of asphalt known as the greenbelt.

The greenbelt followed the Boise River and wove a path through the capital city, connecting eight major parks along its way. The strong scent of river water and cottonwood trees filled the morning air, while bits of fuzzy cotton blew on the breeze and stuck to the front of Joe's sweatshirt.

He controlled his breathing, slow and easy as he kept pace with the woman fifty feet in front of him. For the past week, since the theft, he'd been tailing her, learning her habits—the kind of information he couldn't get from government, private, and public records.

As far as he could tell, she jogged the same two-mile loop and wore the same black fanny pack. She constantly looked about her surroundings at the same time. At first, he'd suspected she was searching for something or someone, but she never encountered a soul. He also worried she suspected his surveillance, but he'd been careful to wear different clothing every day, park in different lots, and tail her from different locations. Some days he covered his dark hair with a baseball cap and wore slick jogging gear. This morning, he'd tied a red do-rag on his head and worn his gray BSU sweatshirt.

Two men in bright blue running suits jogged up the greenbelt toward him. The second they passed Ms. Breedlove, they craned their necks around and eyed the sway of her white shorts. When they turned back, they wore identical smiles of appreciation. Joe didn't blame them for straining their eyes for one last look at her. She had great legs and a great ass. Too bad she was destined for a prison uniform.

Joe followed her across a footbridge out of Ann Morrison Park, careful to keep an even distance as they continued along the Boise River.

Her profile didn't fit that of a typical thief. Unlike her business partner, she wasn't in debt up to her eyebrows. She didn't gamble, and she didn't have a drug habit to support, which left only two possible motivations for a woman like her to participate in a felony.

One was thrill, and Joe could certainly understand the pull of living on the edge. Adrenaline was a powerful drug. God knows he'd loved it. He'd loved the way it crawled across his skin and tingled his flesh and raised the hair on his head.

The second was more common—love. Love tended to get a lot of women in trouble. Joe had met more than his share of women who'd do anything for some worthless son of a bitch who wouldn't hesitate to turn her in to save himself. Joe was no longer surprised by what some women would do for love. He was no longer surprised to find women sitting in jail doing time for their men, tears flowing, mascara running, saying shit like, "I can't tell you anything bad about so-and-so, I *love* him."

The trees above Joe's head became denser as he followed her into a second park. Julia Davis Park was lusher, greener, and held the added attractions of the historical and art museums, the Boise Zoo, and of course the Tootin' Tater tour train.

He felt something work free of his pocket an instant before he heard a plop on the pavement. He grabbed his empty pocket and turned his head to see a pack of Marlboros laying on the path. He hesitated several seconds before he retraced his steps. A few stray cigarettes rolled across the blacktop, and he hurriedly stooped to pick them up before they rolled into a puddle of water. His gaze shifted to the suspect, who was jogging at her usual sedate pace, then back to his smokes.

He placed the cigarettes into the pack, careful not to break them. He intended to enjoy every last one. He wasn't worried that he'd lose the suspect. She ran about as fast as an arthritic old dog, a fact he appreciated today.

When he returned his gaze to the path, his hand stilled, and slowly he shoved the cigarettes back into his pocket. All that greeted his well-trained eyes was the black trail as it wove through thick towering trees and grass. A gust of wind blew the heavy boughs overhead and flattened his sweatshirt against his chest.

His gaze shot to the left, and he spotted her cutting across the park toward the zoo and kiddie playground. He set out in pursuit. As far as he could see, the park was empty. Anyone with any brains at all had made a run for it before the impending storm broke. But just because the park appeared empty didn't mean she wasn't meeting someone.

When a suspect deviated from a set pattern, it usually meant that something was about to happen. The taste of adrenaline numbed the back of his throat and brought a smile to his lips. Damn, he hadn't felt this alive since the last time he'd chased a dope dealer down an alley in the north end.

He lost sight of her again as she ran past the

rest rooms and disappeared around back. Years of experience slowed his steps as he waited for her to appear again. When she didn't, he reached beneath his sweatshirt and popped the snap to his shoulder holster. He flattened himself against the brick building and listened.

An abandoned plastic grocery bag tumbled across the ground, but he heard nothing except wind and leaves rattling above his head. From his position he could see exactly squat, and he realized he should have hung back. He stepped around the side of the building and came eye level with the trigger of a can of hair spray. A blast hit him full in the face, and immediately his vision blurred. A fist grabbed his sweatshirt, and a knee slammed between his thighs, missing his berries by a mere half inch. The muscle in his right thigh cramped, and he would have doubled over if it hadn't been for the solid shoulder block to his chest. His breath whooshed from his lungs as he hit the hard ground flat on his back. A pair of chrome handcuffs, tucked in the waistband of his shorts, dug into the small of his back.

Through vision hazed over by Miss Clairol, he looked up at Gabrielle Breedlove standing between his widespread legs. He let the pain cramping his thigh wash through him, and he fought to steady his breath. She'd gotten the jump on him and tried to shove his gonads into his throat.

"Jesus," he groaned. "You're a crazy bitch."

"That's right, just give me an excuse to shoot your kneecaps."

Joe blinked a few more times, and his vision cleared. Slowly his gaze moved from her face, down her arms, to her hands. *Shit.* In one hand she clutched the hair spray, her finger poised on the nozzle, but her other hand gripped what looked like a derringer. It wasn't pointed at his knees but directly at his nose.

Everything within him stilled. He absolutely hated handguns pointed at him. "Put down the weapon," he commanded. He didn't know if the derringer was loaded or if it even worked, but he didn't want to find out. Only his eyes moved as he looked back up into her face. Her breathing was erratic, her green eyes wild. She looked unstable as hell.

"Someone call the police!" she began to yell frantically.

Joe frowned at her. Not only had she managed to knock him on his ass but now she was screaming her head off. If she kept it up, he was going to have to blow his cover, and he really didn't want to do that. The thought of walking into the police station with the number one female suspect in the Hillard case, the suspect who wasn't supposed to know she was a suspect, and explaining how she'd brought him down with a can of hair spray filled him with a sick dread that gripped the base of his skull. "Put down the gun," he repeated.

"Not a chance! You so much as twitch and

I'll fill you with lead, you filthy scum."

He didn't believe there was another soul within one hundred feet, but he wasn't positive, and the last thing he needed was a heroic civilian coming to her rescue.

"Someone help me—please!" she hollered loud enough to be heard in several distant counties.

Joe's jaw clenched. He'd never live this down, and he didn't even want to imagine facing Walker and Luchetti. Joe was still on the chief's shit list for the fallout after the Robby Martin shooting. He didn't have to think too hard to know what the chief would say. "You screwed the pooch, Shanahan!" he'd yell right before he busted Joe to patrol division. And this time, the chief would be right.

"Call 911."

"Quit screaming," he commanded in his best law enforcement officer's voice.

"I need a cop!"

Damn. "Lady," he gritted between his teeth, "I *am* a cop!"

Her eyes narrowed as she gazed down at him. "Right, and I'm the governor."

Joe moved his hand toward his pocket, but she made a threatening motion with the small weapon, and he decided against it. "In my left pocket is my identification."

"Don't move," she warned him once again.

Her auburn curls blew about her head, wild and unruly, looking like maybe she should have used some of that hair spray on her head instead of his face. Her hand trembled as she pushed one side of her hair behind her ear. In an instant he could have her on the ground, but he'd have to distract her first or run the risk of getting shot. This time in a place where he was unlikely to recover. "You can reach into my pocket yourself. I won't move a muscle." He hated tackling women. He hated slamming them to the ground. But in this case he didn't think he'd mind.

"I'm not stupid. I haven't fallen for that trick since high school."

"Oh for God's sake." He struggled to control his temper and barely won. "Do you have a permit to carry a concealed weapon?"

"Give me a break," she answered. "You're not a cop; you're a stalker! I wish there was a cop around here, because I'd have *you* arrested for following me around this past week. There's a law in this state against stalking, you know." She sucked in a deep breath, then let it out slowly. "I bet you have a record for some sort of deviant behavior. You're probably one of those psychos who makes obscene phone calls and breathes really heavy. I bet you're on parole for harassing women." She took a few more deep breaths and tossed the hair spray. "I think you'd better give me your wallet after all."

Never in his fifteen-year career had he ever been so careless as to let a suspect—let alone a female—get the jump on him.

His temples pounded and his thigh ached. His eyes stung and his lashes were stuck together. "You're crazy, lady," he said in a relatively calm voice as he reached into his pocket.

"Really? From where I'm standing, you look like the crazy one." Her gaze never left his as she reached for the wallet. "I'll need your name and address to give to the police, but I bet they already know who you are."

She didn't know how right she was, but Joe didn't waste any more time talking. The second she flipped open the wallet and glanced at the badge inside, his legs scissored around her calves. She hit the ground, and he lunged on top of her, pinning her with his weight. She twisted one way, then the other, pushing at his shoulders, bringing the derringer dangerously close to his left ear. He grabbed her wrists and forced them above her head, using the full length of his body to pin her to the earth.

He lay stretched out on top of her, her full breasts pressed into his chest, her hips pressed into his. He secured her hands above her head and her struggles weakened, yet she refused to give up completely. His face was barely an inch above hers, and her nose bumped his twice. Her parted lips sucked air into her lungs, and her green eyes stared into his, huge and filled with panic and fear as she fought to free her wrists. Her long, smooth legs tangled with his own, and the bottom of his sweatshirt was up around his armpits. Against his stomach he felt the soft warm skin of her lower abdomen and the flat nylon of her fanny pack.

"You really are a cop!" Her breasts rose and fell as she struggled to catch her breath.

He'd get up as soon as he secured her derringer. "That's right, and you're under arrest for carrying a concealed weapon and aggravated assault."

"Oh, thank God!" She took a deep breath, and he could feel her relax, feel her turn all soft and pliant beneath him. "I'm so relieved. I thought you were a perverted psychopath."

A brilliant smile lit her face as she looked up at him. He'd just placed her under arrest, and she actually seemed happy about it. Not the kind of blissful happy he usually put on a woman's face when he found himself in this same position, more like a kind of deluded happy. She was not only a thief, she was ten-ninety six—definitely crazy. "You have the right to remain silent," he said as he pried the derringer from her fingers. "You have the right . . ."

"You're not serious are you? You aren't really going to arrest me, are you?"

". . . to an attorney," he continued, one hand still pinning hers above her head as he tossed the handgun several feet away.

"But it isn't really a gun. I mean it is, but it

isn't. It's a nineteenth-century derringer. It's an antique, and so I don't think it qualifies as a *real* gun. And besides, it's not loaded, and even if it was, it wouldn't make a very big hole anyway. I was only carrying it because I was so frightened, and you've been following me." She stopped, and her brows scrunched together. "*Why* have you been following me?"

Instead of answering, he finished reading her her rights, then rolled off to his side. He scooped up the small pistol and rose carefully to his feet. He wasn't going to answer her questions. Not when he didn't know what he was going to do with her now. Not when she'd accused him of being a pervert, and a psychopath, and tried to make him a soprano. He didn't trust himself to talk to her more than was absolutely necessary. "Are you carrying any more weapons on you?"

"No."

"Slowly hand me your fanny pack, then turn your pockets inside out."

"I only have my car keys," she muttered while doing as he requested. With her keys held high, she dropped them into his palm. His hand closed, and he shoved them in his front pocket. He took the little pack from her and turned it inside out. It was empty.

"Place your hands on the wall."

"Are you going to frisk me?"

"That's right," he answered and motioned toward the brick building.

"Like this?" she asked over her shoulder.

As his gaze moved from her rounded behind and down the length of her long legs, he slid the small handgun into the waistband of his shorts. "That's right," he repeated and placed his palms on her shoulders. Now that he saw her this close, he realized that she wasn't five feet ten inches tall. Joe was six foot, and her eyes met his. He moved his palms down her sides, across the small of her back, and around to her abdomen. He slipped his hand beneath the bottom of her shirt and felt the waistband of her shorts. He felt her soft skin and the cool metal of her belly ring. Then he slid one hand up between the mounds of her breasts.

"Hey, watch your hands!"

"Don't get excited," he warned. "I'm not." Next, he patted down her behind, then knelt to check the tops of her socks. He didn't bother to feel for anything hidden between her thighs. Not that he trusted her, he just didn't think she would have been able to jog with a weapon in her panties.

"Once we get to jail, do I pay a fine and then go home?"

"When the judge sets bail you can go home." She tried to turn and face him, but his grasp on her hips prevented it.

"I've never been arrested before."

He already knew that.

"I'm not really being arrested like with fingerprints and mug shots, am I?"

Joe patted the waistband of her shorts one last time. "Yes, ma'am, with fingerprints and mug shots."

Turning, her eyes narrowed, and she glared at him. "Until this very minute I didn't think you were serious. I thought you were trying to get even with me for kneeing you in your . . . your private area."

"You missed," he informed her dryly.

"Are you sure?"

Joe straightened, reached into the back of his shorts, and brought out the handcuffs. "There's no mistaking something like that."

"Oh." She sounded real disappointed. "Well, I still can't believe you're really doing this to me. If you had an ounce of decency you'd admit this is all your fault." She paused and took a deep breath. "You are creating very bad karma for yourself, and I'm sure you're going to be very sorry."

Joe looked into her eyes and slapped the cuffs on her wrists. He was sorry all right. He was sorry he'd been knocked on his ass by a suspected felon, and he was real sorry he'd blown his cover. And he knew his troubles were just beginning.

The first fat raindrop struck his cheek, and he glanced up at the storm cloud hanging over his head. Three more drops hit his forehead and chin. He laughed without humor. "Fan-fucking-tastic."

Two

FOR SOME REASON, WHENEVER GA-
brielle had thought of a police interrogation, she'd always envisioned Dustin
Hoffman in *Marathon Man*. She'd always pic-
tured a dark room, spotlight, and a crazed Nazi
war criminal with a dentist drill.

The room she found herself in wasn't like
that. The walls were stark white, without windows to let in the June sunshine. Metal chairs
surrounded a table with a fake wooden top. A
telephone sat on it at one end. A single poster,
warning against the dangers of drugs, hung on
the closed door.

A video camera stood in one corner, its red
light glowing, indicating it was in use. She'd
given her consent to let them record her debrief-
ing. What did she care? She was innocent. She
figured if she cooperated, they'd hurry and finish and she could go home. She was tired and
hungry. Besides, Sundays and Mondays were
her only days off, and she still had a lot to get

done before the Coeur Festival that weekend.

Gabrielle took several deep breaths, controlling the amount of oxygen she took in for fear she might pass out or hyperventilate. *Breathe away the tension.* she told herself. *You are calm.* She raised her hand and raked her fingers through her hair. She didn't feel calm and knew she wouldn't until she was released to go home. Only then could she find her quiet center and tune out the static in her head.

Traces of black ink stained the pads of her fingers, and she could still feel the pressure of the handcuffs she no longer wore around her wrists. Detective Shanahan had made her walk all through the park in the rain cuffed like a criminal, and her only consolation was that he hadn't enjoyed the walk any more than she had.

Neither of them had said a word, but she had noticed that he'd massaged his right thigh several times. She assumed she was responsible for his injury, and she supposed she should feel sorry—but she didn't. She was scared and confused and her clothes were still damp. And it was all his fault. The least he could do was suffer along with her.

After being booked for aggravated assault on a police officer and carrying a concealed weapon, she'd been led into the small interrogation room. Now across the table from Gabrielle sat Shanahan and Captain Luchetti. Both men wanted to know about stolen antiques. Their dark heads were bent over a black notebook, and they were in deep discussion. She didn't know what stolen antiques had to do with aggravated assault. They seemed to think the two were related, yet neither of them seemed in a hurry to explain anything to her.

Worse than her confusion was the knowledge that she couldn't just get up and leave. She was at the mercy of Detective Shanahan. She'd known him a little over an hour, but she knew him well enough to know he had no mercy.

The first time she'd seen him a week ago, he'd been standing beneath a tree in Ann Morrison Park. She'd jogged past him and might not have noticed him at all if it hadn't been for the cloud of cigarette smoke surrounding his head. She probably wouldn't have given him another thought if she hadn't seen him the next day at Albertson's buying a frozen pot pie. That time she'd noticed the way his muscular thighs filled out his hacked-off sweatpants, and the way his hair curled up like small *c*s around the edge of his baseball cap. His eyes were dark, and the intense way he'd watched her had sent an alarming shiver of pleasure up her spine.

She'd sworn off gorgeous men years ago—they caused heartbreak and chaos in the continuum of body, mind, and spirit. They were like Snickers bars—they looked and tasted good, but they could never pass for a well-balanced meal. Once in a while she still got cravings, but these days she was much more interested in a man's soul than in his gluteus. An enlightened mind turned her on.

A few days later, she'd spotted him sitting in a car outside the post office, then again parked down the street from Anomaly, her curio shop. At first she'd told herself she was imagining things. Why would a dark, handsome man follow her? But as the week wore on, she spotted him several more times, never close enough to approach, but never far away either.

Still, she tried to dismiss it as her creative imagination working overtime—until yesterday when she'd seen him at Barnes and Noble. She'd been in the store buying more books on essential oils when she'd looked up and noticed him lurking in the women's health section. With his dark, brooding looks and T-shirt-straining muscles, he just hadn't seemed like the kind of guy sympathetic to the anguish of PMS. That's when she finally accepted that he'd been stalking her like a serial psycho. She'd called the police and had been told that she could come in and fill out a complaint against the "unknown smoking jogger," but since he hadn't done anything, there wasn't a lot she could do. The police had been no help, and she hadn't even bothered to leave her name.

She'd slept very little the night before. Mostly she'd lain awake carefully devising her plan. At the time her strategy had seemed good. She'd lure him into a very public place. The chunk of the park next to the playground, in front of the zoo, and a few hundred yards from the Tootin' Tater train station. She'd take the stalker down and scream like crazy for help. She still thought it was a good plan, but unfortunately she hadn't foreseen two very important details. The weather had closed everything down, and, of course, her stalker wasn't a stalker. He was a cop.

When she'd first seen him standing beneath that tree, it had been like staring at her friend Francie's Hunk Of Burnin' Love calendar. Now as she looked across the table at him, she wondered how she'd ever confused him for a hunk of the month. In the sloppy sweatshirt he still wore and with that red bandanna tied around his head, he looked more like some hell-bound biker.

"I don't know what you want from me," Gabrielle stated, switching her gaze from Shanahan to the other man. "I thought I was brought here because of what happened in the park earlier."

"Have you ever seen this before today?" Shanahan asked as he slid a new photograph toward her.

Gabrielle had seen the same photo in the local newspaper. She'd read about the theft of the Hillard Monet and heard about it on the local and national news.

"You recognize it?"

"I recognize a Monet when I see it." She smiled ruefully and pushed the pictures back across the table. "I've also read about it in the *Statesman*. That's the painting that was stolen from Mr. Hillard."

"What can you tell me about it?" Shanahan stared at her through his cop's eyes as if he could see the answer to his question written on her brain.

Gabrielle tried not to feel intimidated, but she couldn't help it. She was intimidated. He was such a big man, and she was stuck in such a small room with him. "Only what everyone else has read or heard about the theft." Which was quite a bit, since it was such a hot story. The mayor had publicly stated his outrage. The owner of the painting was beside himself, and the Boise police department had been portrayed as a bunch of backward hicks on the national network news. Which she supposed was an improvement over how Idaho was usually portrayed to the rest of the country, as a state filled with potato-loving, white supremacist gun nuts. The real facts were that not everyone loved potatoes, and ninety-nine percent of the population wasn't associated with the Aryan Nation or affiliated groups. And of those people who were members, most weren't natives of the state anyway.

The gun nut part was probably true, though.

"Do you have an interest in art?" he asked, his deep voice seeming to fill every corner of the room.

"Of course, I'm an artist myself." Well, she

was more a person who painted than an actual artist. While she could paint a reasonable likeness, she'd never mastered the intricacies of hands and feet. But she loved it, and that was all that really counted.

"Then you can understand Mr. Hillard is quite anxious to get it back," he said and set the photo to one side.

"I would imagine so." She still didn't understand what any of this had to do with her. At one time Norris Hillard had been a friend of her family, but that had been a long time ago.

"Have you ever seen or met this man?" Shanahan asked as he slid another photograph toward her. "His name is Sal Katzinger."

Gabrielle looked at the photo and shook her head. Not only did this man have the thickest pair of glasses she'd ever seen but his face also appeared sallow and rather sickly. Of course, she might have met the man before and just not recognized him from his photo. It hadn't been taken under the best of circumstances. Her own mug shots were probably just as atrocious.

"No. I don't think I've ever met him," she answered and pushed the mug shot back across the table.

"Have you ever heard his name mentioned by your business partner, Kevin Carter?" the other man in the room asked her.

Gabrielle turned her gaze to the older man with graying black hair. The name on his plastic ID card read Captain Luchetti. She'd seen enough movies and watched enough television to know he was playing the "good cop" to Shanahan's "bad cop"—not that it was that much of a stretch for Shanahan. But of the two, Captain Luchetti seemed genuinely nicer. He kind of reminded her of her uncle Judd, and his aura was less hostile than the detective's. "Kevin? What does Kevin have to do with the man in the picture?"

"Mr. Katzinger is a professional thief. He's very good and steals only the best. A little over a week ago he was arrested for the theft of over twenty-five thousand dollars' worth of stolen antiques. While in custody, he indicated that he might know who has Mr. Hillard's painting," Captain Luchetti informed her as he waved a hand at a pile of photographs. "He told us that he'd been offered the job of stealing the Monet, but he turned it down."

Gabrielle crossed her arms beneath her breasts and sat back. "Why are you talking to me about this? It sounds like you should talk to *him*." She pointed to the mug shot across the table.

"We have, and during his confession he turned over on his fence." Luchetti paused, looking at her as if he expected some sort of reaction.

She supposed he meant a fence as in a person who received and sold stolen property, as opposed to someone rolling around on chain-link. But she didn't know what that had to do with her. "Perhaps you should tell me *exactly* what you mean." She nodded in Shanahan's direction. "And why have I been followed by the archangel of doom for the past few days?"

Shanahan's scowl remained embedded in his forehead, while the captain's face remained impassive. "According to Mr. Katzinger, your partner knowingly buys and sells stolen antiques." Captain Luchetti paused before he added, "He is also suspected of being the middleman in the Hillard theft. That makes him guilty of a lot of things, including grand theft."

She gasped. "Kevin? No way. That Mr. Katzinger person is lying!"

"Now, why would he do that?" Luchetti asked. "He's been promised leniency in exchange for his cooperation."

"Kevin would never do anything like that," she assured them. Her heart pounded, and no amount of deep breathing calmed her spirit or cleared her mind.

"How do you know?"

"I just do. I know he would never become involved in anything illegal."

"Yeah?" The expression in Shanahan's eyes told her he was as exasperated as he sounded. "Why's that?"

Gabrielle glanced briefly at Shanahan. Several rich brown curls fell from beneath the bandanna and touched his forehead. He reached for a small notebook and began to scribble inside. Negative energy surrounded him like a black cloud and permeated the air. He obviously had anger-control issues. "Well," she began and switched her gaze between both men, "for one thing, I've known him for several years. I would certainly know if he were selling stolen antiques. We work together almost every day, and I could tell if he were hiding a secret like that."

"How?" Captain Luchetti asked.

He didn't look like the sort of man who believed in auras, so she didn't mention that she hadn't felt any black spots surrounding Kevin lately. "I just would."

"Any other reasons?" Shanahan asked.

"Yes, he's an Aquarius."

The pen flew straight up into the air, somersaulted several times, then landed somewhere behind the detective. "Sweet baby Jesus," he groaned as if in pain.

Gabrielle glared at him. "Well, he is. Aquarians despise lying and cheating. They hate hypocrisy and double-dealing. Abraham Lincoln was an Aquarian, you know."

"No. I didn't know that," Captain Luchetti answered and reached for the notebook. He placed it in front of him and took a silver pen from his breast pocket. "But I really don't think you realize the seriousness of this situation. The charge of aggravated assault on a police officer carries a maximum of fifteen years."

"Fifteen years! I never would have assaulted him if he hadn't been stalking me. And it wasn't a real assault anyway. I'm a pacifist."

"Pacifists don't carry guns," Shanahan reminded her.

Gabrielle purposely ignored the surly detective.

"Ms. Breedlove," the captain continued, "on top of the assault charge, you've got an added charge of felony grand theft. You're looking at thirty years in the state pen. That's a whole heap of trouble, Ms. Breedlove."

"Grand theft—ME?" She raised a hand to her heart. "For what?"

"The Hillard Monet."

"You think *I* had something to do with Mr. Hillard's stolen painting?"

"You're implicated."

"Wait," she ordered and placed her palms flat on the table before her. "You think I stole Mr. Hillard's Monet?" She would have laughed if the situation weren't so singularly unfunny. "I've never ever stolen anything in my life." Her cosmic conscience chose that moment to disagree with her. "Well, unless you count the Chiko Stix when I was seven years old, but I felt so bad I didn't really enjoy it all that much."

"Ms. Breedlove," Shanahan interrupted, "I don't give a rat's ass about some damn candy bar you stole when you were seven."

Gabrielle's gaze darted between the two men. Captain Luchetti looked dazed, while deep grooves dented Shanahan's forehead and the sides of his mouth.

Any semblance of peace and serenity had deserted her long ago, and her nerves were raw. She couldn't stop the tears filling her eyes, and she placed her elbows on the table and covered her face with her hands. Maybe she shouldn't have refused her right to an attorney, but until now she hadn't *really* believed she'd needed one. In the small town where she'd been born and raised, she knew everyone, including the police officers. They were always bringing her aunt Yolanda home after she'd accidentally walked off with someone else's property.

Of course, there were only three police officers in her hometown, but they were more than just three men who drove around in gas-guzzling automobiles. They were nice guys who helped people.

Her hands dropped to her lap, and she looked back up through her tears. Captain Luchetti still stared at her, looking as tired as she felt. Shanahan had disappeared. He'd probably gone to get the thumbscrews.

Gabrielle sighed and brushed the moisture from her eyes. She was in big trouble. An hour ago, she'd felt certain they'd let her go when they realized she hadn't done anything wrong—not really. She never would have carried the derringer if she hadn't felt threatened by Detective Shanahan. And besides, no one got into *real* trouble in Idaho for carrying concealed. But now she realized they thought she was somehow involved in something she wasn't, and neither was Kevin. She knew him too well to believe otherwise. Yes, Kevin had several businesses besides Anomaly; he was a successful entrepreneur. He made a lot of money, and yes he was perhaps a little greedy, and self-absorbed, and far more concerned with money than his soul, but that certainly wasn't a crime.

"Why don't you take a look at these," Captain Luchetti suggested, then slid two written appraisals and a stack of Polaroids across the table toward her.

She felt shaky all over and more frightened now than she'd been earlier.

The antique pieces in the pictures were mostly Oriental in origin; a few were Staffordshire. If they were true antiques, and not reproductions, they were also very expensive. She turned her attention to the insurance appraisals. They weren't reproductions.

"What can you tell me about those?"

"I would say this Ming bowl is closer to seven thousand than eight. But the appraisal is fair."

"Do you sell this sort of thing in your store?"

"I could, but I don't," she answered as she read the descriptions of several more items. "These things generally sell better at auctions or stores dealing strictly in antiques. People don't come into Anomaly looking for Staffordshire. If one of my customers picked up this little cow creamer here, they'd go into sticker shock and put it right back on the shelf where it would probably stay for several years."

"Have you ever seen these items before today?"

She pushed the papers to the side and looked at the captain across the table. "Are you accusing me of stealing them?"

"We know they were stolen from a home on Warm Springs Avenue three months ago."

"I didn't do it!"

"I know." Luchetti smiled, then reached across the table to pat her hand. "Sal Katzinger already confessed. Listen, if you're not involved in any illegal activity, then you have nothing to worry about. But we know for a fact that your boyfriend is up to his bal—er, eyeballs in selling stolen goods."

Gabrielle frowned. "Boyfriend? Kevin isn't my boyfriend. I don't think it's a good idea to date your business partner."

The captain tilted his head to the side and looked at her as if he were trying to sort pieces of a puzzle that didn't quite fit. "So, you never dated him?"

"Oh, we dated a few times," Gabrielle continued with a dismissive wave of her hand, "that's how I know it's not a good idea, but that was a few years ago. We found we just weren't compatible. He's Republican. I vote Independent." It was the truth, but it wasn't the real reason. The real reason was far too personal to explain to the man across the table. How could she tell Captain Luchetti that Kevin had very thin lips, and as a result, she found him physically un-appealing? The first time Kevin kissed her had ended any amorous feelings she might have felt for him. But just because Kevin didn't have lips didn't mean he was guilty of any crimes or he was a bad person. Shanahan had wonderful lips, which proved that appearances were de-ceiving, because he was a real jerk.

"Will you agree to take a lie detector test, Ms. Breedlove?" Luchetti asked, interrupting Ga-brielle's silent contemplation of men and their lips.

Gabrielle's nose wrinkled with distaste. "Are you serious?" Even the thought of taking a test to detect a lie was abhorrent. Why should she have to prove she was telling the truth? She never lied. Well, not on purpose anyway. Some-times she evaded or skirted the truth, which wasn't the same at all. Lying created bad karma, and she believed in karma. She'd been raised to believe it.

"If you're telling us the truth, then you have nothing to fear from taking the test. Look at it as proving your innocence. Don't you want to prove you're innocent?"

The door swung open before she could an-swer, and a man Gabrielle had never seen be-fore entered the room. He was tall and thin and had a white comb-over covering his shiny pink head. He had a manila folder under one arm. "Hello, Ms. Breedlove," he said as he shook her hand. "I'm Jerome Walker, chief of police. I've

just spoken with Prosecuting Attorney Blackburn, and he is willing to offer you complete
immunity."

"Immunity from what?"

"Right now the charges against you are carrying a concealed weapon and aggravated assault
on a law enforcement officer."

That law enforcement officer part of the aggravated assault charge had her worried. They
obviously didn't think she'd been justified in
carrying the derringer, no matter what she'd believed. Fifteen years was the maximum sentence. She wondered what the minimum was,
but she guessed she really didn't want to know.

She had two choices. She could hire a lawyer,
go to court and fight the charges, or she could
cooperate with the police. Neither option held
an ounce of appeal, but she supposed she could
listen to their offer. "What would I have to do?"

"You would sign a confidential informant
agreement, and then we'd place an undercover
detective in your store."

"As a customer?"

"No, we thought he could pose as a relative
who needs work."

"Kevin won't let my relatives work in the
store any more." Not since she'd had to fire her
third cousin, Babe Fairchild, for scaring customers with her stories of levitation and thought
transference. "And besides, I don't think I'll be
much help to you. I won't be in the store this

Friday and Saturday. I'll be at the Coeur Festival in Julia Davis Park."

Chief Walker pulled out the chair across the table from her and sat. He placed the folder on the table in front of him. "Coors Festival?"

"Coeur. Heart. I have a booth to sell my essential oils and aromatherapies."

"Will Carter be in your shop while you're at this heart thing?"

"Yes."

"Good. Now, how about if you hire a handyman to work for you?"

"I don't know." Actually, she and Kevin had discussed hiring someone to move a shelving system to a bigger wall and building more storage shelves in the back room. And she needed new countertops in the back, too, but the store hadn't done as well during the past holiday season as they'd hoped, and he'd rejected the idea as an unnecessary expense.

"Kevin's tight with money right now," she told them.

Chief Walker took out two papers from the folder. "What if you offered to pay the cost yourself? The department would reimburse you, of course."

Perhaps she was looking at this whole informant thing from the wrong angle. Kevin wasn't guilty, but maybe if she agreed to help the police, she really would be helping him. She was certain the police would find nothing incriminating in her shop, so why not let them search?

If she played it smart, she'd get the government to pay for the renovations she wanted. "Kevin really doesn't like to hire employees out of the newspaper or off the street. I'd have to pretend to know this handyman."

The door opened and Detective Shanahan entered. He'd changed out of his shorts and taken the bandanna off his head. His hair was wet and slicked back except for one lock that escaped and curled over his forehead and touched his brow.

He wore a shoulder holster over a white dress shirt that fit him snug across his wide chest and tapered to his waist, where it was tucked into a pair of khaki pants. The sleeves of his shirt were rolled up his forearms, and he'd strapped a silver watch to his wrist. On his breast pocket, next to his blue-and-beige tie, he'd clamped his ID. His brown eyes stared into hers as he handed Chief Walker a third piece of paper.

The captain glanced at the paper, then slid it across the table and handed her a Bic pen.

"What's this?" She turned her attention to the document and tried to ignore Detective Shanahan.

"The confidential informant agreement," Walker answered. "How about a boyfriend?"

"No." She shook her head and kept her eyes on the document before her. She hadn't had a serious relationship for some time. Finding an enlightened *and* physically appealing man was proving to be extremely difficult. When her spirit and mind said yes, her body usually said no way. Or vice versa. She ran her fingers through her hair as she studied the papers before her. "I don't have one."

"You do now. Say hello to your new boyfriend."

An awful foreboding brushed up Gabrielle's spine, and she glanced at the front of Joe Shanahan's crisp white shirt. Her gaze moved up the stripes on his tie to his tan throat, over his chin to the finely etched lines of his mouth. The corners of his lips slid upward into a slow, sensual smile. "Hello, sweet cheeks."

Gabrielle straightened and set the pen aside. "I want a lawyer."

Three

GABRIELLE PHONED HER BUSINESS AT-
torney, who gave her the name of a
criminal defense lawyer. She envisioned Jerry
Spence. Someone in a buckskin coat to kick butt
on her behalf. She got Ronald Lowman, a cocky
young guy with razor cut hair and a Brooks
Brothers suit. He met with her in a holding cell
for ten minutes, then left her alone again. When
he returned, he wasn't so sure of himself.

"I've just spoken with the prosecutor," he began. "They're going to proceed with the aggravated charges against you. They think you
know something about Mr. Hillard's stolen Monet, and they're not going to let you just walk
out of here."

"I don't know anything about that stupid
painting. I'm innocent," she said, frowning at
the man she'd hired to protect her interests.

"Listen, Ms. Breedlove, I believe you're innocent. But we've got Prosecuting Attorney
Blackburn, Chief of Police Walker, Captain Lu-

chetti, and at least one detective who aren't convinced." He let out a deep breath and folded his arms across his chest. "They're not going to go easy on you. Not now that you know you and your partner are suspects. If we refuse to assist them in this investigation, they'll proceed with the aggravated assault charge. But they really don't want to do that. They want Mr. Carter, his private books, and his contacts. They want Mr. Hillard's art back, if possible. They want your cooperation."

She knew what they wanted, and she didn't need an attorney just out of law school to tell her. In order to save herself, she had to participate in an undercover police investigation. She had to convince Kevin she'd hired her *boyfriend* to work as a handyman in their shop. She had to keep her mouth shut and look the other way while Detective Doom gathered evidence to convict her good friend and business partner of a felony.

For the first time in her life, her beliefs and her desires counted for nothing. No one seemed to care that what they were asking her to do conflicted with her morals, those bits and pieces of morality she'd assembled from different religions and cultures throughout her life. They were asking her to break principles that demanded honesty, asking her to betray a friend.

"I don't believe Kevin has stolen anything."

"I'm not here to represent your partner. I'm here to help you, but if he is guilty, he's implicated you in a serious crime. You could lose your business, or at the very least, your reputation as an honest businesswoman. And if Kevin is innocent, you've got nothing to lose and absolutely nothing to fear. Look at it as helping to clear his name. Or we can go to court. If we request a jury trial, you probably won't serve time. But you will have a felony conviction on your record."

She looked up at him. The idea of a felony conviction upset her more than she'd ever realized it would. Of course, she'd never thought of herself as a felon before. "What if I say yes and they come into my shop, tear it up, then leave?"

He stood and glanced at his wristwatch. "Let me talk to the prosecutor and see if we can't get a few more concessions. They want your cooperation pretty badly, so I think they'll work with us."

"So you think I should sign the agreement?"

"It's up to you, but it would be your best option. You let them work undercover for a few days, then they're gone. I'll make sure they leave your store in the same condition it's in now, or better. You get to keep your right to vote, and you even get to keep your right to own a gun. Although I would recommend that you get a license to carry concealed."

It seemed so simple, yet so horrible. But in the end, she signed the agreement that would make her a confidential informant. She signed it along with a consent-to-search form and wondered if they'd give her a code name like a Bond Girl.

After she was released, she went home and tried to lose herself in the pleasure she usually found blending essential oils. She needed to finish her basil and neroli massage oil before the Coeur Festival, but when she tried to fill the small blue bottles, she made a mess and had to stop. She wasn't much more successful at placing the labels on, either.

Her mind and spirit were divided, and she had to try and relax, to bring them in sync. She sat cross-legged in her bedroom and sought to find her quiet center before her head exploded. But Joe Shanahan's brooding face kept popping into her brain, disturbing her meditation.

Detective Shanahan was the exact opposite of any man she would ever consider dating. He had dark untamed hair, dark skin, and intense brown eyes. Full, unsmiling mouth. Broad shoulders and big impersonal hands. He was a real throwback . . . but there had been those few days, before she'd decided he was a stalker, that she'd found his dark, brooding looks wildly sensual. When he'd looked at her from beneath those black lashes and she'd melted a little right there in the frozen foods aisle. His size and presence reeked of strength and confidence, and no matter how often in her life she'd tried to ignore big, bulky he-men, she wasn't always successful.

It was her height. Her height always caused her eyes to wander to the biggest man around. She was five eleven, although she would never admit to being an inch over five ten. For as long as she could remember, she'd had height-related issues. All through school she'd been the tallest girl in her class. She'd been clumsy and bony and had grown taller each day.

She'd prayed to every god she could think of for intervention. She'd wanted to wake up petite with small breasts and feet. Of course, that had never happened, but by her senior year, the boys had caught up with her, and a few had passed her enough to ask her out. Her first boyfriend had been the captain of the basketball team. But after three months, he'd dumped her for the head cheerleader. Five foot two Mindy Crenshaw.

She had to remind herself not to slouch when she stood next to short women.

Gabrielle gave up on finding balance and drew a warm bath instead. She added a special oil mixture of lavender, ylang-ylang, and rose absolute to the water. The essential blend was reputed to aid in relaxation. Gabrielle didn't know if it worked, but it did smell wonderful. She slipped into the scented bath and leaned her head back against the edge of the tub. Warmth enveloped her, and she closed her eyes. The events of the day raced through her mind, and only the memory of Joe Shanahan, laying on the ground at her feet, his breath knocked from his lungs and his lashes stuck to his eyelids, brought a smile to her lips. The memory succeeded in relaxing her where an hour of meditation had failed.

She held on to the memory and the hope that maybe someday, if she were real good and her karma chose to reward her, she might get the chance to blast him with another can of super-hold.

Joe entered the back door of his parents' house without knocking and set the pet carrier on the kitchen counter. He heard the television from the direction of the family room to his right. A cupboard door sat propped against the front of the stove, and a drill lay next to the sink. One more project forgotten before it was finished. Joe's father, Dewey, had provided a comfortable life for his wife and five children off his income as a homebuilder, but he never seemed to complete anything in his own house. Joe knew from years of experience that it would take his mother's threatening to hire someone else before the job would suddenly get done.

"Is anyone home?" Joe called, even though he'd spotted both his parents' cars in the garage.

"Is that you, Joey?" Joyce Shanahan's voice could barely be heard over the sound of tanks and gunfire. He'd interrupted one of his father's favorite pasttimes. John Wayne movies.

"Yeah, it's me." He reached into the carrier, and Sam scrambled up his arm.

Joyce walked into the kitchen, her black-and-white streaked hair pulled back from her face with a stretchy red headband. She took one look at the twelve-inch gray African parrot perched on Joe's shoulder and stopped in her tracks. Her lips disappeared into her mouth, and displeasure lowered her brows.

"I couldn't leave him at home," Joe began before she could voice her distress. "You know how he gets when he doesn't get enough attention. I made him promise to behave this time." He shrugged and glanced at his bird. "Tell her, Sam."

The parrot blinked its yellow-and-black eyes and shifted from one foot to the other. *"Go ahead, make my day,"* Sam cried in a shrill voice.

Joe turned his gaze to his mother and smiled like a proud parent. "See, I substituted his Jerry Springer tape for Clint Eastwood."

Joyce folded her arms across the front of her Betty Boop T-shirt. She was barely five feet tall, but she had always been queen, king, and dictator of the Shanahan household. "If he starts with the potty mouth again, he has to leave."

"The grandkids taught him those swear words when they were here for Easter," he said, referring to all ten of his nieces and nephews.

"Don't you dare blame that bird's bad behavior on my grandchildren." Joyce sighed and dropped her hands to her waist. "Have you eaten dinner?"

"Yeah, I grabbed something on my way home from work."

"Don't tell me, greasy deli chicken and those horrible potato wedges." She shook her head. "I have some leftover lasagna and a nice green salad. You take some home with you."

Like a lot of families, the Shanahan women showed their love and concern through food. Usually Joe didn't mind—except when they all decided to show him at the same time. Or when they discussed his eating habits as if he were ten and living on potato chips. "That'd be great." He turned to Sam. "Grandma made you lasagna."

"Humph. Since he's likely to be the closest thing I get to a grandbaby out of you, I guess he's welcome. But you just better make sure he's cleaned up his language."

Talk of grandbabies was Joe's cue to retreat. He knew that if he didn't escape now the con- versation would take an inevitable turn toward the women who seemed to enter and exit his life on a frequent basis. "Sam's reformed," he said as he slid past his mother and moved into the family room, decorated with his mother's most recent garage sale find—a pair of iron wall sconces and matching shield of armor. He found his father relaxed in his brown La-Z-Boy, remote in one hand, tall glass of iced tea in the other. A pack of cigarettes and lighter sat on a

lamptable separating the chair from the matching sofa. Dewey was in his late sixties, and Joe
had recently noticed something odd happening
to his father's hair. It was still thick and completely white, but in the last year it had started
to grow straight forward as if he were sitting
with a strong wind at his back.

"They don't make movies like this anymore,"
Dewey said without taking his eyes from the
console television. He turned down the volume
before he added, "All those special effects they
use these days just aren't the same as the real
thing. John Wayne knew how to fight and make
it look good."

As soon as Joe sat, Sam hopped off his shoulder and gripped the back of the sofa with his
scaly black feet. "Don't go too far away," Joe
told his bird, then reached for a cigarette. He
slid the Marlboro through his fingers, but he
didn't light it. He wanted Sam to breathe as little secondhand smoke as possible.

"You start smoking again?" Dewey asked, finally pulling his gaze from the Duke. "I
thought you quit. What happened?"

"Norris Hillard," was all Joe said. He didn't
need to elaborate. Everyone in the free world
knew about the stolen Monet by now. He
wanted everyone to know. He wanted the people involved to be nervous. Nervous people
made mistakes. When they did, he'd be right
there, ready to take them down. But he
wouldn't be taking down Gabrielle Breedlove.

It wouldn't matter if she were involved up to her sweet little behind. It didn't matter if she'd cut the painting from its frame. She'd been given complete immunity—not only from the assault charges and any subsequent indictments stemming from the Hillard case but she also wouldn't be prosecuted for any of the antique thefts, either. That lawyer of hers might be young, but he was a sharp little weasel.

"Any leads?"

"A few." His father didn't ask the obvious questions, and Joe didn't offer any explanations. "I need to borrow your drill and a few of your tools." Even if he could, Joe didn't want to talk about his confidential informant. Not only did he distrust informants but his latest was as flaky as a box of Post Toasties, and that stunt with the derringer had nearly cost him another demotion. And this time, they wouldn't pussyfoot around and call it a transfer. After the nightmare that had taken place in the park that morning, he had to deliver Carter's head on a platter. He had to redeem himself. If not, he feared they'd bust him so far down into the patrol division that he'd never see the light of day. He didn't have anything against uniformed police. They were the frontline guys, and he couldn't do his job without them, but he'd worked too long, and put up with too much crap, to let a gun-toting redhead screw up his career.

"Joe, I picked up something for you last

weekend," his mother informed him as she breezed through the room on her way toward the back of the house.

The last "something" his mother had "picked up" for him had been a matching pair of aluminum peacocks that were supposed to hang on the wall. At the moment they were beneath his bed next to a huge macrame owl. "Ah, geez," he groaned and tossed the unlit cigarette on the lamptable. "I wish she wouldn't do that. I hate that garage sale shit."

"Don't fight it, son, it's a sickness," his father said and returned his attention to the television. "It's a disease like alcoholism. She's powerless over her addiction."

When Joyce Shanahan returned, she carried a saddle cut in half, lengthwise. "I got this for five dollars," she bragged and set it on the floor next to Joe's foot. "They wanted ten, but I dickered them down."

"*I hate that garage sale shit,*" Sam mimicked, then added a shrill "*Braa—ck*" for good measure.

Joyce's gaze moved from her son to the bird on the back of her couch. "He'd better not make a mess on my davenport."

Joe couldn't promise a thing. He pointed to the saddle. "What am I supposed to do with it? Find half a horse?"

"You hang it on the wall." The telephone rang, and she added over her shoulder as she headed toward the kitchen, "It's got some little loops on the one side."

"Better nail it to the wall studs, son," his father advised. "Or that thing's liable to pull down your drywall."

Joe stared at the saddle with its one stirrup. The space beneath his bed was about to get real crowded. His mother's laughter erupted from the other room, startling Sam. He flapped his wings, showing the red feathers beneath his tail, then he flew to the television and perched on top of a wooden birdhouse with a fake nest and plastic eggs glued at the bottom. He tilted his gray head to one side, raised his beak, and did a carbon imitation of the ringing telephone.

"Sam, don't do it," Joe warned a fraction of a second before the bird mimicked Joyce's laugh so perfectly that it was downright spooky.

"That bird of yours is going to end up in a bag of Shake 'n Bake," his father predicted.

"Don't I know it." He just hoped Sam wouldn't take it into his head to tear apart that little wooden house with his beak.

The front door opened with a loud bang, and Joe's seven-year-old nephew Todd ran into the house, followed by thirteen-year-old Christy and ten-year-old Sara, Joe's nieces.

"Hi, Uncle Joe," his nieces chimed at the same time.

"Hey, girls."

"Did you bring Sam?" Christy wanted to know.

Joe nodded to the television. "He's getting a little nervous. Don't yell around him and make sudden moves. And don't teach him any more bad words."

"We won't, Uncle Joe," Sara promised, her eyes a little too wide, a little too innocent.

"What's that?" Todd asked, pointing to the saddle.

"It's half a saddle."

"Why?"

Exactly. "Do you want it?"

"Cool!"

Joe's sister Tanya entered the house next and shut the door behind her. "Hi, Daddy," she said, then turned her attention to her brother. "Hi Joey. I see Mom gave you the saddle. Can you believe she got it for five bucks?"

Obviously Tanya had been infected with the garage sale sickness too.

"Who farted? Braa—ck."

"Hey you guys," Joe admonished the two girls, who were falling on the floor in a fit of laughter.

"What's so funny?" his mother asked as she walked into the room, but before anyone could answer, the telephone rang again. "For pity's sake." She shook her head and moved to the kitchen once more, only to return a few short moments later still shaking her head. "They hung up before I could answer."

Joe slanted a skeptical gaze at his bird, and his suspicions were confirmed when Sam cocked his head to one side and the telephone just happened to ring again.

"Pity's sake." His mother spun toward the kitchen.

"My dad ate a bug," Todd told Joe, drawing his attention to him. "We roasted hot dogs and he ate a bug."

"Yeah, Ben took him camping because he thinks the girls and I are turning him into a sissy," Joe's sister elaborated as she sat on the sofa next to him. "He said he needed to get Todd away and do man stuff."

Joe understood perfectly. He'd been raised with four older sisters, who'd dressed him up in their clothes and made him wear lipstick. At the age of eight, they'd convinced him he'd been born a hermaphrodite named Josephine. He hadn't even known what a hermaphrodite was until he'd turned twelve and could look it up in the dictionary. After that, for several weeks, he'd lived in fear of growing big breasts like his oldest sister, Penny. Luckily, his father had caught him checking out his body for weird changes, and he'd assured Joe that he wasn't a hermaphrodite. Then he'd taken him camping and fishing and hadn't made him bathe for a week.

His sisters stuck together like Bondini and never forgot a damn thing. Growing up, they'd loved to harass him, and they'd been just plain hell on his psyche. But if he ever suspected that for one second the men in his sisters' lives weren't treating them right, he'd gladly beat the shit out of them.

"And I guess a bug landed on Todd's hot dog so he cried and wouldn't eat it," Tanya continued. "Which is completely understandable, and I don't blame him one bit, but Ben grabbed the bug and ate it, trying to be macho. He said, 'If I can eat the damn bug, you can eat the damn hot dog.'"

Sounded reasonable. "Did you eat the hot dog?" Joe asked his nephew.

Todd nodded, and his smile showed his missing front teeth. "Then I ate a bug too. A black one."

Joe looked into his nephew's freckled face, and they shared a conspiratorial smile. The "I can pee standing up" guy-club smile. A smile girls could never understand.

"They hung up again," Joyce announced to the room.

"You need to get Caller ID," Tanya advised. "We've got it, and I always check to see who's calling before I answer."

"I just might do that," his mother said as she lowered herself into an old tole-painted rocker, but just as her butt hit the seat, the ringing started again. "This is getting old," she sighed and rose. "Someone is playing on the phone."

"Use last call return. I'll show you." Tanya

stood and followed her mother into the kit-chen.

The girls dissolved into a new fit of laughter, and Todd covered his mouth with his hand.

"Yep," Dewey said without taking his eyes off the Duke, "that bird is flirting with disaster all right."

Joe wove his fingers behind his head, crossed his ankles, and relaxed for the first time since the theft of Mr. Hillard's Monet. The Shanahans were a large, rowdy bunch, and sitting on his mother's couch surrounded by the commotion felt like coming home. It also reminded him of his own empty house across town.

Up until about a year ago, he hadn't worried all that much about finding a wife and starting a family. He'd always thought he had time, but getting shot tended to put one's life in perspec-tive. It reminded a man of what was really im-portant in life. A family of his own.

True, he did have Sam, and living with Sam was like living with a naughty, but very enter-taining, two-year-old. But he couldn't build campfires and roast weenies with Sam. He couldn't eat bugs. Most of the other cops his age had children, and as he'd lain around his house recuperating, with nothing but time on his hands, he'd begun to wonder what it would be like to sit on the sidelines at a Little League game and watch his kids run around the bases. Seeing his own children in his head was the easy part. Picturing a wife was a bit more difficult.

He didn't think he was too picky, but he knew what he wanted and what he didn't want. He didn't want a woman who freaked out about little things like monthly anniversaries and who didn't like Sam. He knew from experience that he didn't want a vegetarian who was overly concerned about fat grams and the size of her minuscule thighs.

He wanted to come home from work and have someone waiting for him. He wanted to walk in the door without dinner in his hand. He wanted a down-to-earth girl, someone who had both feet planted firmly on the ground. And of course, he wanted someone who liked sex the way he liked it. Hot, definitely hot. Sometimes down and out dirty, sometimes not, but always uninhibited. He wanted a woman who wasn't afraid to touch him or afraid to let him touch her. He wanted to look at her and feel lust twist low in his gut. He wanted to look at her and know she felt the same thing for him.

He'd always figured he'd know the right woman when he met her. He didn't really know how he'd know, he just would. He'd feel it smack him between the eyes like a knock-out punch or a bolt of lightning, and that would be it. He'd know.

Tanya walked back into the room with a frown wrinkling her brow. "That last call return number belonged to mom's friend Bernese.

Why would Bernese make a prank phone call?"

Joe shrugged and decided to throw his sister off the track of the real culprit. "Maybe she's bored. When I was a rookie, an old lady called in about once a month to report that someone kept breaking into her house, attempting to steal her priceless afghans."

"And they weren't?"

"Hell no. You should've seen those things— all bright green and orange and purple. Damn near made you go blind just looking at 'em. Anyway, she'd always have Nilla Wafers and root beer waiting for us. Sometimes old people get real lonely and do weird things just to have someone to talk to."

Tanya's brown eyes stared into his, and her frown deepened. "That's what's going to happen to you if you don't find someone to take care of you."

The women in his family had always nagged him about his love life, but ever since he'd been shot, his mother and sisters had stepped up their efforts to see him happily wed. They equated marriage with happiness. They wanted him to settle down into their version of a nice cozy life, and while he understood their concern, they drove him crazy with it. He didn't dare let them know he'd actually been giving it some serious thought. If he did, they'd be all over him like magpies on roadkill.

"I know a really nice woman who—"

"No," Joe interrupted, not even willing to

consider one of his sister's friends. He could just imagine having every little detail reported back to his family. He was thirty-five, but his sisters still treated him as if he were five. As if he couldn't find his own ass if they didn't tell him it was at the bottom of his spine.

"Why?"

"I don't like nice women."

"That's what's wrong with you. You're more interested in the size of hooters than personality."

"There's nothing wrong with me. And it's not the size of hooters, it's the shape that counts."

Tanya snorted, and he didn't remember ever hearing a sound like that coming out of a woman before.

"What?" he asked.

"You're going to be a very lonely old man."

"I have Sam to keep me company, and he'll probably outlive me."

"A bird doesn't count, Joey. Do you have a girlfriend these days? Someone you might consider bringing around to meet your family? Someone you might consider marrying?"

"No."

"Why not?"

"I haven't found the right woman."

"If men on death row find women to marry, how hard can it be?"

Four

THE SMALL HISTORICAL DISTRICT OF Hyde Park lay nestled at the bottom of the Boise foothills. In the seventies, the district had suffered from neglect brought on by an exodus to the suburbs and the popularity of strip malls. But in recent years, its businesses had been given a face-lift and a fresh coat of paint, and they had benefited from the resurgence of life back into the city.

Three blocks long, Hyde Park was surrounded on all sides by one of the oldest residential neighborhoods in town. The residents themselves were a diverse mix of bohemia and affluence. Rich, poor, young, and those as old and humped as the cracked sidewalks. Struggling artists and prosperous yuppies lived side by side. Run-down purple houses with orange sunbursts around the windows sat beside restored Victorians, complete with pocked carriage blocks next to the curb.

The businesses were as eclectic as the residents. The shoe repair shop had operated in the district since before anyone could remember, and down the block, a guy could still get his hair cut for seven bucks. A person could grab a taco, pizza, espresso, or a pair of edible undies at the Naughty or Nice lingerie boutique. You could pull into the local 7-11 and buy a Slurpie and a National Enquirer after you filled your car with gas, or walk half a block and shop for books, bicycles, or snowshoes. Hyde Park had it all. Gabrielle Breedlove and Anomaly fit in perfectly.

The morning sun poured over the district and in through Anomaly's front windows, washing the room with light. The large windows were crammed with a display of Oriental porcelain plates and washbowls. A two-foot goldfish with its great fantail cast irregular shadows on the Berber carpet.

Gabrielle stood in her darkened store, squeezing several drops of patchouli oil into a delicate cobalt vaporizer. For almost a year now, she'd been experimenting with different essential oils. The whole process was a continuous cycle of trying, failing, and trying again.

Studying chemical properties, mixing the oils into the little bottles, using her burners and blending bowls, it all made her feel a bit like a mad scientist. Creating wonderful aromas appealed to her artistic side. Her belief was that certain aromas could potentially heal the mind, spirit, and body, either through their chemical properties or by triggering warm, pleasant memories that calmed the soul. Just last week she'd successfully created her own unique blend. She'd packaged it in beautiful rose-colored bottles, then, as part of her marketing ploy, she'd filled the store with the gentle fragrance of citrus and voluptuous flowers. She'd sold out the first day. She hoped to do as well at the Coeur Festival.

Today's blend wasn't unique but was reputed to have calming effects. She screwed the dropper lid back onto the brown patchouli bottle and replaced it in the wooden box containing her other oils. She reached for the sage oil and carefully added two drops. Both oils were supposed to help reduce stress, promote relaxation, and relieve nervous exhaustion. This morning, with an undercover cop due in her store in twenty minutes, Gabrielle needed all three.

The back door to Anomaly opened and closed, and dread settled in the pit of her soul. She glanced over her shoulder toward the rear of the store. "Good morning, Kevin," she called out to her business partner. Her hands shook as she replaced the bottle of sage. It was only nine-thirty in the morning, her nerves were already shot, and she was exhausted. She'd been up all night trying to convince herself that she could lie to Kevin. That by allowing Detective Shanahan to work undercover in her store, she was really helping to clear Kevin's name. But she had several big problems: She was a notoriously bad liar, and she didn't honestly think she could pretend to like the detective, let alone imagine herself as his girlfriend.

She hated lying. She hated creating bad karma. But really, what was one more lie when she was about to create karmic retribution of seismic proportions?

"Hey there," Kevin called from the hallway and flipped on the light switches. "What are you cooking today?"

"Patchouli and sage."

"Is it going to smell like a Grateful Dead concert in here?"

"Probably. I made it for my mother." Besides aiding in relaxation, the scent reminded her of pleasant memories, like the summer she and her mother had chased the Grateful Dead throughout the country. Gabrielle had been ten and had loved camping in their Volkswagen bus, eating tofu and tie-dyeing everything she owned. Her mother had called it their summer of awakening. Gabrielle didn't know about *their* awakening, but it had been the first time her mother had claimed psychic powers. Before that, they'd been Methodists.

"How's your mother and aunt doing on vacation? Have you heard from them?"

Gabrielle closed the lid to the wooden box and looked across the room at Kevin, who stood in the doorway of the office they shared. "Not for a few days."

"When she gets back, will she and your aunt stay at their house in town for a while, or go spend time up north with your grandfather?"

She suspected Kevin's interest in her mother and aunt had less to do with genuine curiosity and more to do with the fact that they made him nervous. Not only were Claire and Yolanda Breedlove sisters by marriage but they were also best friends and lived together. And sometimes they read each other's minds, which could be spooky if you weren't used to them. "I'm not sure. I suspect they'll land here in Boise to pick up Beezer, then drive up to check on my grandfather."

"Beezer?"

"My mother's cat," Gabrielle answered, guilt knotting her stomach as she gazed into her friend's familiar blue eyes. He'd just turned thirty but looked about twenty-two. He stood a few inches shorter than Gabrielle, and his blond hair was bleached by the sun. He was a bookkeeper by profession and an antique dealer at heart. He handled the business side of Anomaly, freeing Gabrielle to express her creativity. He wasn't a criminal, and she didn't believe for one second that he would use their store as a front to sell stolen property. She opened her mouth to voice the lie she'd practiced at the police station, but the words got stuck in her throat.

"I'll be in the office working this morning," he said, then disappeared through the doorway.

Gabrielle reached for a lighter and lit a tea candle in the little vaporizer. Again, she tried to tell herself she was actually helping Kevin even though he wouldn't know it. She wasn't *really* sacrificing him to Detective Shanahan.

She still couldn't make herself believe it, but it didn't matter. The detective was due in her store in less than twenty minutes, and she had to make Kevin believe she'd hired him to do odd jobs over the next few days. She stuck the lighter into the pocket of her gauze skirt and walked past the front counter, cluttered with impulse items, to the office. She glanced at Kevin's blond head bent over some papers on his desk, and she took a deep breath. "I hired someone to move those shelves from the side of the store to the back wall," she said, forcing the lie past her lips. "Remember we talked about it before?"

Kevin looked up, and a frown creased his brow. "I remember we decided to wait until next year."

No, he'd decided that for them. "I don't think it can wait that long, so I've hired someone. Mara can help him," she said, referring to the young college student who worked part time in the afternoons. "Joe will be here in a few minutes." Forcing her guilty gaze to remain on Kevin was one of the hardest things she'd ever done.

Silence filled the room for several excruciating moments as he frowned at her. "This Joe's a member of your family, isn't he?"

Just the thought of Detective Shanahan swimming in the same gene pool disturbed her almost as much as posing as his girlfriend. "No." Gabrielle straightened a stack of invoices. "I assure you Joe isn't family." She pretended an interest in the paper before her. Then she choked out the most difficult lie of all. "He's my boyfriend."

His frown disappeared, and he just looked puzzled. "I didn't even know you had a boyfriend. Why haven't you ever mentioned him before?"

"I didn't want to talk about it until I was sure of my feelings," she said, piling one lie on top of another. "I didn't want to create bad juju."

"Oh. Well, how long have you known him?"

"Not long." That much was the truth, she supposed.

"How did you meet him?"

She thought of Joe's hands on her hips, thighs, and between her breasts. Of his groin pressed into hers, and heat rose up her neck to her cheeks. "Jogging in the park," she said, knowing she sounded as guilty as she felt.

"I don't think we can afford it this month. We have to pay for that shipment of Baccarat. Next month would be better for us."

Next month might be better for them, but not the Boise P.D. "It has to be done this week. I'll pay for it myself. You can't object to that."

Kevin sat back and crossed his arms over his

chest. "You want it done pretty badly. Why now? What's up?"

"Nothing," was the best answer she could think up.

"What aren't you telling me?"

Gabrielle looked into Kevin's speculative blue eyes and not for the first time she thought about just coming clean. Then the two of them could secretly work together to clear Kevin's name. She thought of the confidential informant's agreement she'd signed. The consequences of breaking that agreement were very serious, but damn the consequences. Her first loyalty was to Kevin, and he deserved her honesty. He was her business partner, and more importantly, her friend.

"You look all flushed and bothered."

"Hot flash."

"You're not old enough for a hot flash. There's got to be more to this than you're letting on. This isn't like you. Are you in love with your handyman?"

Gabrielle barely contained a horrified gasp. "No."

"Must be lust."

"No!"

A knock shook the back door. "There's your boyfriend," Kevin said.

She could tell by the look on his face that he really did believe she had the hots for her *handyman*. Sometimes Kevin thought he knew everything, when he was mostly clueless. But what she knew of men told her that was generally the case with all of them. She set the invoices on her desk and walked from the room. The thought of posing as Joe's girlfriend was disturbing. She moved through the back storage area, which doubled as a small kitchen. She opened the heavy wood door.

And there he stood in worn Levi's, white T-shirt, and black aura. He'd had his dark hair trimmed, and a pair of aviator sunglasses covered his eyes. His features were unreadable.

"You've come on time," she spoke to her reflection in his glasses.

One dark brow lifted. "I always do." He reached for her arm with one hand and shut the door behind her with the other. "Is Carter here?"

A thin slice of air separated the front of her peasant blouse from his chest, and her head was enveloped with the scent of sandlewood and cedar and something so intriguing that she wished she could name so she could bottle it.

"Yes," she said and removed his grasp from her bare arm. She slid past him and down the alley to the far side of the Dumpster. She could still feel the impression of his fingers on her skin.

He moved with her. "What have you told him?" he asked in a low-pitched voice.

"What I was told to tell him." Her own voice was barely above a whisper when she continued, "I told him I hired my boyfriend to move some shelves."

"And he believed you?"

Talking to her own reflection unnerved her, and she lowered her gaze from his sunglasses to the dip of his top lip. "Of course. He knows I never lie."

"Uh-huh. Anything I should know before you introduce me to your business partner?"

"Well, kind of."

His lips compressed slightly. "What?"

She really didn't want to admit that Kevin thought she was in love with him, so she prevaricated just a little bit. "He thinks you're madly in love with me."

"Now why would he think that?"

"Because I told him you were," she said, and wondered when lying had become so fun. "So you better be extra nice."

His lips remained in a flat line. He wasn't amused.

"Maybe you should bring me roses tomorrow."

"Yeah, and maybe you should start holding your breath."

Joe scribbled down a fake address and Social Security number on a W2 form and soaked up his surroundings, noticing everything without looking at anything. He hadn't worked undercover for almost a year, but working under-

cover was like riding a bike. He hadn't
forgotten how to con a con.

He listened to the soft tap of Gabrielle's retreating sandals as she walked from the room,
and the annoying click-click-clicking of Kevin
Carter's pen as his thumb pumped the end of
his Montblanc. When Joe had first walked in,
he'd noticed two tall file cabinets, two narrow
floor-to-ceiling windows on Gabrielle's side of
the room, and a stack of assorted junk on her
desk. On Kevin's desk sat a computer, wire in
basket, and a payroll book. Everything on
Kevin's side of the room looked like it had been
strategically measured, then placed with a
ruler. A real uptight control freak.

When he finished with the W2, Joe handed it
to the man sitting directly across the desk. "I
don't usually fill one of these out," he told
Kevin. "I usually get paid in cash, and the government never has to know."

Kevin glanced over the form. "We do everything nice and legal around here," he said without looking up.

Joe leaned back in his chair and crossed his
arms over his chest. What a lying little shit. It
had taken him about two seconds to determine
that Kevin Carter was guilty as hell. He'd arrested too many felons not to know the signs.

Kevin lived way beyond his means, even for
the got-to-have-it-now nineties. He drove a Por-
sche and wore designer everything, from his
shirts to his Italian loafers. Two Nagel prints

hung on the wall behind his desk, and he wrote with a two-hundred-dollar pen. In addition to Anomaly and his appraisal business, he had several enterprises around town. He lived in a chunk of the foothills where a man's value was judged on the view of the city through his living room window. Last year he'd reported a combined income of fifty thousand to the IRS. Not hardly enough to sustain his lifestyle.

If there was one common thread that pointed to criminal behavior, it was excess. Sooner or later all crooks get cocky enough, doped up enough, or in debt enough to ignore moderation.

Kevin Carter was a living poster boy for criminal excess, and he might as well be walking around with a neon sign pointed at his head. Like the many others before him, he was foolish enough to flaunt his excess and cocky enough to believe he wouldn't get caught. But this time he was in over his head and had to be feeling the pressure. Fencing antique candlesticks and gravy boats wasn't quite the same as fencing a Monet.

Kevin set the form aside, then looked up at Joe. "How long have you known Gabrielle?"

Now, Gabrielle Breedlove was a different story. At this point, it didn't matter if she was guilty or as innocent as she claimed, but he would like to know what made her tick. She was much harder to peg than Kevin, and Joe didn't know what to make of her—other than the fact that she was nuttier than a jar of Skippy. "Long enough."

"Then you probably know she's too trusting. She'll do just about anything to help the people she cares about."

Joe wondered if that help extended to helping those she cared about fence stolen property. "Yep, she's a real sweetheart."

"Yes she is, and I'd hate to see anyone take advantage of her. I'm a pretty good judge of character, and I can tell you're the kind of guy who works just enough to get by. Probably not a lot more."

Joe tilted his head to the side and smiled at the little man with the big complex. The last thing he wanted was to alienate Kevin. Just the opposite was true. He needed to get the guy to trust him, convince him they were buddies. "Oh yeah? You can tell all that after knowing me for five minutes?"

"Well, let's face it, there can't be a lot of money in being a handyman. And if your business was doing well, Gabrielle wouldn't have fabricated a job for you here." Kevin wheeled his chair backward and stood. "None of her other boyfriends have needed jobs. That philosophy professor she dated last year could have used a personality, but at least he had money."

Joe watched Kevin walk to a tall file cabinet and open a drawer. He kept quiet and let Kevin do all the talking.

"Right now she thinks she's in love with

you," he continued as he filed the W2. "And chicks don't think about money when they've got it bad for your body."

Joe stood and crossed his arms over his chest. That wasn't exactly what he'd been told by the lady herself. So much for her claim of never lying.

"I was a little surprised when you walked in here this morning. You're not the kind of guy she usually dates."

"What kind is that?"

"She usually goes for the squirrely New Age type. The kind of guys who sit around meditating and discussing crap like the cosmic consciousness of man." The drawer slid shut, and he leaned a shoulder into it. "You don't look like the kind of guy who likes to meditate."

Now there was a relief.

"What were you two talking about in the alley?"

He wondered if Kevin had listened at the back door, but he supposed if he had they wouldn't be having this conversation. Joe let a smile slowly curve the corners of his mouth. "Who said we were talking?"

Kevin smiled back, one of those I'm-in-the-guys-club-too smiles, and Joe left the office.

The first thing that Joe noticed when he walked to the front of the store was the smell. It smelled like a head shop, and he wondered if his confidential informant took frequent trips on the ganja train. It would explain a lot.

Joe's gaze roamed the room, and he took in the odd assortment of old and new. In one corner, fancy pens, letter openers, and boxes of stationery sat on a pigeonhole desk. He glanced at the center counter and a display of antique jewelry in a glass case next to the cash register. He took a mental note of everything before his attention was drawn to the ladder placed by the front window and the woman standing at the top.

Bright sunshine lit her profile, filtered through her long auburn hair, and turned her yellow gauzy shirt and skirt transparent. His gaze slid down her face and chin to her slim shoulders and full breasts. Yesterday, he'd been mad as hell, and his thigh had ached, but he hadn't been dead. He'd been very aware of her soft body pressed tight against him. Of her breasts as he'd checked for concealed and a few minutes later as they'd walked to his car, the cold rain drenching her T-shirt, chilling her flesh and hardening her nipples.

His eyes moved to her waist and the flair of her hips. It didn't look like she was wearing anything beneath her skirt but a pair of bikini panties. Probably white or beige. After tailing her for the past week, he'd developed an appreciation for her nicely rounded behind and long legs. He didn't care what her driver's license said, she was close to six feet tall and had the legs to prove it. The kind of legs that just naturally hooked around a man's waist.

"Do you need some help?" he asked as he moved toward her, raising his gaze up the lush feminine curves of her body to her face.

"That would be great," she said, pulling her mass of hair over one shoulder and looking down at him over the other. She selected a big blue-and-white plate from a stand in the window. "I have a customer who will be here sometime this morning to pick this up."

Joe took the plate from her, then stepped back as she climbed down the ladder.

"Did Kevin believe you're my handyman?" she asked barely above a whisper.

"More than just your handyman." He waited until she stood before him. "He thinks you want me for my body." He watched her run her fingers through her hair, tangling all those soft curls like she'd just got out of bed. She'd done the same thing yesterday at the police station. He hated to admit it, but it was sexy as hell.

"You're kidding."

He took several steps toward her and whispered in her ear. "He thinks I'm your own personal boy toy." Her silky hair smelled like roses.

"I hope you set him straight."

"Now, why would I do that?" He leaned back and smiled into her horrified face.

"I don't know what I ever did to deserve this," she said as she took the plate and walked around him. "I'm sure I've never done anything bad enough to deserve this kind of rotten karma."

Joe's smile died, and a chill bit the back of his neck. He'd forgotten. He'd seen her standing on that ladder, with sunlight spilling over every soft curve, and for a few minutes he'd forgotten she was crazy.

Gabrielle Breedlove looked normal, but she wasn't. She believed in karma and auras and judging a person's character by the stars. She probably believed she could channel Elvis, too. She was a kook, and he supposed he should thank her for reminding him that he wasn't in her store to stare at her behind. Thanks to her, his career as a detective was on the line, and he had to come through with a big bust. No doubt about it. He removed his gaze from her back and glanced about the shop. "Where are the shelves you want moved?"

Gabrielle set the plate on the counter next to the cash register. "There," she said, pointing to the metal-and-glass shelving system bolted to the wall across the room. "I want those moved to the back wall."

Yesterday, when she'd said *shelves*, he'd assumed she'd meant display cabinets. With the mounting and patching involved, this job would take him several days. If he painted, he could stretch it into two, maybe three, days of searching for anything to nail Kevin Carter. And he would nail him. He didn't doubt it for a minute.

Joe moved across the room to the glass shelves, glad the job would take a while. Unlike the portrayal of police work on television, cases weren't solved in an hour. It took days and weeks, sometimes months, to gather enough evidence for an arrest. There was a lot of waiting involved. Waiting for someone to make a move, mess up, or get ratted out.

Joe let his gaze skim across colored glass and porcelain, silver and pewter picture frames. Several woven baskets sat on an old trunk beside the shelves, and he reached for a small cloth satchel and held it to his nose. He was more interested in what might be inside the trunk than what was on it. Not that he really expected to find Mr. Hillard's paintings so easily. It was true that he'd sometimes found stashes of drugs and stolen goods in obvious places, but he figured he wouldn't be that lucky with this case.

"That's just potpourri."

Joe glanced over his shoulder at Gabrielle and tossed the small satchel back into the basket. "I'd already figured that out, but thanks anyway."

"I thought you might confuse it for some kind of mind-altering drug."

He looked into her green eyes and thought he detected a glint of humor, but he wasn't sure. It could just as easily be a spark of dementia. His gaze moved past her to the empty room. Carter was still in the office. Hopefully, busy setting himself up. "I was a narcotics agent for eight years. I think I know the difference. Do you?"

"I don't think I should answer that question on the grounds that it might incriminate me." An amused smile lifted the corners of her red lips. She obviously thought she was a riot. "But I will say that if I ever did use drugs, and keep in mind that I'm not confessing anything, it was a long time ago for religious reasons."

He had a feeling he was going to be real sorry, but he asked anyway. "Religious reasons?"

"To seek truth and enlightenment," she elaborated. "To break the boundaries of the mind in search of higher knowledge and spiritual fulfillment."

Yep, he was sorry.

"To explore the cosmic connection between good and evil. Life and death."

"To seek new life, new civilizations. To boldly go where no man has gone before," he added, keeping his tone bland. "You and Captain Kirk seem to have a lot in common."

A frown flattened her smile.

"What's in this trunk?" he asked.

"Christmas lights."

"When was the last time you checked?"

"Christmas."

Movement behind Gabrielle drew Joe's attention to the front counter, and he watched Kevin walk to the cash register and pop it open. "I have a few business errands to run this morning, Gabrielle," Kevin said as he filled the drawer with money. "I should be back by three."

Gabrielle spun around and looked at her business partner. Tension choked the air, but no one besides her seemed to notice. It clogged her throat, but for the first time since she'd been arrested, relief lifted her spirits a little, too. There was an end to this madness in sight. The sooner Kevin left, the sooner the detective could search, and the sooner he would find nothing. The sooner he would leave her store and her life. "Oh, okay. Take all the time you need. If you get really busy, you don't have to come back at all."

Kevin shifted his gaze from Gabrielle to the man standing directly behind her. "I'll be back."

As soon as Kevin was gone, Gabrielle glanced over her shoulder. "Do your thing, Detective," she said, then moved to the front counter and began wrapping the blue plate in tissue paper. Out of the corner of her eye, she watched him pull a small black notebook out of the back pocket of his Levi's. He flipped it open and slowly walked through her store, thumbing past one page and pausing to scribble on another.

"When does Mara Paglino come to work?" he asked without looking up.

"One-thirty."

He checked the marking on the bottom of a

Wedgwood butter dish, then flipped the note-book closed again. "If Kevin comes back early, keep him out here with you," he said as he walked to the office and shut the door behind him.

"How?" she asked the empty store. If Kevin came back early, she didn't know how—short of tackling him—to keep him from discovering the detective rifling through his desk. But it really wouldn't matter if Kevin came back early and caught Joe red-handed. Kevin would *know*. He was so over-the-top neat that he always just *knew* if someone had touched his things.

During the next two hours, Gabrielle's nerves coiled tighter and tighter. Every tick of the clock pushed her closer to a complete breakdown. She tried to lose herself in daily routine, she failed. She was much too aware of the detective searching for incriminating evidence behind the closed door of her office.

Several times she walked toward the office door with the intention of sticking her head inside and seeing exactly what he was doing, but she always lost her nerve. Every little sound made her jump, and a knot formed in her throat and stomach, preventing her from eating the broccoli soup she'd brought for her lunch. By the time Joe finally emerged from the office at one o'clock, Gabrielle was so tense that she felt like screaming. Instead, she took deep breaths and silently chanted the soothing seven-syllable mantra she'd composed eighteen years ago to cope with the death of her father.

"Okay." Joe interrupted her attempt to find her quiet center. "I'll see you tomorrow morning."

He must not have found anything incriminating. But Gabrielle wasn't surprised; there wasn't anything to find. She followed him to the back room. "You're leaving?"

He looked into her eyes, and one corner of his mouth lifted. "Don't tell me you're going to miss me?"

"Of course not, but what about the shelves? What am I supposed to tell Kevin?"

"Tell him I'll start tomorrow." He took his sunglasses from the pocket of his T-shirt. "I need to put a wiretap on your business phone. So come in a little early in the morning. It won't take me but a few minutes."

"You're going to bug my telephone? Don't you need a court order or something?"

"No. I just need your permission, which you're going to give me."

"No, I'm not."

His dark brows lowered and his eyes turned hard. "Why the hell not? I thought you said you didn't have anything to do with the theft of Hillard's Monet."

"I didn't."

"Then don't act like you have something to hide."

"I'm not. It's a horrible invasion of privacy."

He rocked back on his heels and looked at her through narrowed eyes. "Only if you're guilty. Giving your permission could help prove you and Kevin are innocent as babes."

"But you don't believe that, do you?"

"No," he answered without hesitation.

It took a great deal of effort not to tell him exactly where he could shove his wiretap. He was so sure of himself. So absolutely certain, but so mistaken. A wiretap would gain him nothing, and there was only one way to prove him wrong. "Fine," she said. "Do whatever you want. Put up a video camera. Wheel out the polygraph. Bring out the thumbscrews."

"The tap will be sufficient for now." He opened the back door and shoved his sunglasses on the bridge of his straight nose. "I save my thumbscrews for kinky informants who get off on that sort of thing." The sensual lines of his lips curved into the kind of provocative smile that could make a woman almost forgive him for handcuffing her and hauling her to jail. "Are you interested?"

Gabrielle looked down at her feet, away from the mesmerizing effect of that smile, horrified that he could affect her at all. "No, thank you."

He hooked a finger beneath her chin and lifted her gaze back to his. His seductive voice brushed across her flesh. "I can be real gentle."

She looked into his sunglasses and couldn't tell if he was joking or if he was serious. If he was trying to seduce her or if it was just her imagination. "I'll pass."

"Chicken." He dropped his hand and took a step backward. "You let me know if you change your mind."

For a few moments after he left, she stared at the closed door. A funny little flutter tickled her stomach, and she tried to tell herself it was because she hadn't eaten. But she didn't really believe it. With the detective gone, she should have felt better, but she didn't. He'd be back tomorrow with his wiretap, eavesdropping on conversations.

By the time Gabrielle left for the day, she felt as if her brain had swelled and her head was about to explode. She didn't know for certain, but she thought she just might be developing a stress fracture at the base of her skull.

The drive home, which normally took Gabrielle ten minutes, was accomplished in five. She darted her blue Toyota pickup in and out of traffic and was never so glad to pull into the one-car garage in the back of her house.

The brick house she'd bought a year ago was small and crammed with bits and pieces of her life. In a bay window facing the street, an enormous black cat stretched amongst peach-colored cushions, too fat and lazy to summon a proper greeting. The sun's rays poured through the multiple panes of glass, spreading cubes of light across the hardwood floor and floral rugs.

The sectional couch and chairs were upholstered in pastel green and peach, while lush plants flourished about the oblong room. A watercolor portrait of a black kitten poised on a wing-backed chair hung over a polished brick fireplace.

When Gabrielle had first laid eyes on the house, she'd fallen in love with it. It, like the previous owners, was old and crafted with the kind of character that could only originate through vintage. The small dining room was fitted with built-in cabinets and led to a kitchen with long cupboards reaching from the floor to the ceiling. She had two bedrooms, one of which she used as her studio.

The pipes groaned. The hardwood floors were cold, and water dripped in the bathroom sink. The toilet ran continually unless she jiggled the handle, and the windows in her bedroom were painted shut. Still, she loved her home both despite its faults and because of them.

Shucking her clothes as she went, Gabrielle headed for her studio. She hurried through the dining room and kitchen, past the little bowls and bottles of essential sunscreen and other oils she'd prepared. By the time she reached the studio door, all she wore was a pair of white bikini panties.

A paint-splattered shirt hung on an easel in the center of the room. Once she'd buttoned it halfway up her chest, she began collecting her supplies.

She knew of only one way to release the demon rage that surrounded her and blackened her aura. She was long past meditation and aromatherapy, and there was only one way to express her anger and inner torment. Only one way to get it out of her system.

She didn't bother to prepare the canvas or sketch an outline first. She didn't bother to thin the heavy oil paint or attempt to lighten the dark colors. She didn't even have a clear idea of what she intended to paint. She just painted. She didn't take the time to carefully calculate each brush stroke, nor did she care that she was making a mess on the drop cloth.

She just painted.

Several hours later, she wasn't surprised to see that the demon in her painting bore a striking resemblance to Joe Shanahan or that the poor little lamb, bound with silver handcuffs, had silky red hair on its head instead of wool.

She took a step back to critically eye the painting. Gabrielle knew she wasn't a great artist. She painted for the love of it, but even she knew this work wasn't her best. The oils had been applied too heavily, and the halo surrounding the lamb's head looked more like a marshmallow. The quality wasn't nearly as good as the other portraits and paintings stacked against the white walls of her studio. And as she'd done with the others, she'd left the painting of hands and feet for another time.

She felt lighter of heart, and a smile lifted her cheeks. "I like it," she announced to the empty room, then stabbed her brush into some black paint and added a gruesome set of wings to the demon.

Five

THE HAIRS ON THE BACK OF GABRIELLE'S neck stood up as she watched Detective Shanahan place a transmitter into the telephone receiver. Then he reached for a screwdriver and put everything back into place.

"Is that it?" she whispered.

An open toolbox lay at his feet, and he dropped the screwdriver inside. "Why are you whispering?"

She cleared her throat and said, "Are you finished, Detective?"

He glanced across his shoulder at her and set the phone back in its cradle. "Call me Joe. I'm your lover, remember?"

She'd spent the night before trying to forget. "Boyfriend."

"Same thing."

Gabrielle tried not to roll her eyes. Tried and failed. "So tell me," she paused and blew out her breath, "Joe. Are you married?"

He turned to face her and rested his weight on one foot. "No."

"Some lucky girl's hunk of burnin' love?"

He crossed his arms over his gray T-shirt. "At the moment, no."

"Recent breakup?"

"Yes."

"How long were you together?"

His gaze lowered to her turquoise nylon shirt with the big green-and-yellow butterflies on each breast. "Why do you care?"

"Just trying to make pleasant conversation."

He slid his gaze up to her face once more. "Two months."

"Really? What took her so long to come to her senses?"

His eyes narrowed, and he leaned toward her. "Are you crazy? Is that your problem? Your butt's in a sling, and I'm the one who can get it out for you. Instead of irritating the hell out of me, you should be trying to get on my good side."

It was barely past nine in the morning, and Gabrielle had already had enough of Detective Joe Shanahan to last her nine years. She'd had enough of him calling her crazy and having him mock her personal beliefs. She was tired of him pushing her around, forcing her to play informant, and putting a bug in her phone. She stared at him, debating whether to provoke him further. Usually she tried to be a nice person, but she didn't feel very nice this morning. She placed her hands on her hips and decided to risk his anger. "You don't have a good side."

His gaze moved slowly over her face, then slid past her. When he looked back, his dark eyes bored into hers, but his voice was low and sexy when he spoke. "That isn't how you felt last night."

Last night? "What are you talking about?"

"Getting naked in my bed, rolling in the sheets, you screaming my name and praising God in the same breath."

Gabrielle's hands fell to her sides. "Huh?"

Before she could even comprehend what he was doing, he placed his palms on the sides of her face and pulled her to him. "Kiss me, baby," he said, his breath whispering across her cheek. "Give me your tongue. "

Kiss me, baby? Stunned beyond speech, Gabrielle could do no more than stand there like a mannequin. The scent of his sandlewood soap assailed her, as he lowered his mouth and pressed it against hers. He placed soft kisses at the corners of her lips, and held her face in his warm hands as his fingers tangled in the hair above her ears. His brown eyes filled her vision, hard and intense, a direct contradiction to his hot, sensual mouth. The tip of his tongue touched the seam of her lips, and her breath caught in her throat. She felt a jolt clear in the soles of her feet, a warm tingling that curled her toes and settled in the pit of her stomach. The kiss was tender, almost sweet, and she fought to keep her eyes open, fought to remind herself that the lips brushing hers, as if he really were her lover, belonged to a hard-nosed cop with a black aura. But at that moment, his aura didn't feel black. It felt red, the sultry hot red of passion, his passion, surrounding them both and urging her to surrender to his persuasive touch.

She lost the fight. Her eyes slid closed and her lips parted. He coaxed her mouth open, and his tongue touched hers, hot and slick and enticing a response. She pressed her mouth against his, deepening the kiss, and gave herself to the sensations surging through her. He smelled good. He tasted better. She leaned into him, but he dropped his hands from her face and ended the kiss.

"He's gone," he said, barely above a whisper.

"Hmm . . ." Cool air brushed her moist lips, and she opened her eyes. "What?"

"Kevin."

She blinked several times before her mind began to clear. She glanced behind her, but the room was empty except for the two of them. From the front of the store, she heard the cash drawer slide open.

"He was standing in the doorway."

"Oh." She turned back to him but couldn't look him in the eyes. "Yeah, that's what I figured," she muttered and wondered when lying had become so easy for her. But she knew the answer—the minute Detective Shanahan had tackled her in Julia Davis Park. She walked around him to her desk and sat down before her knees gave way.

She felt dazed and a little disoriented, like after the time she'd tried to meditate hanging upside down and had ended up falling out of her gravity boots. "I'm meeting with the Silver Winds rep today, so I won't be here from noon until probably two. You'll be on your own."

He shrugged. "I can handle it."

"Fantastic!" she said with just a little too much enthusiasm. She reached for the first catalog on top of a stack and opened it to the middle. She had no idea what she was looking at; her mind was too busy replaying the last few humiliating moments. He'd kissed her to shut her up in front of Kevin, and she'd melted like butter beneath his lips. Her hands shook, and she pulled them into her lap.

"Gabrielle."

"Yes?"

"Look at me."

She forced her gaze to his and wasn't surprised to find a scowl on his dark brooding face.

"You're not all bent out of shape over that kiss, are you?" he asked low enough that his voice wouldn't be heard outside the room.

She shook her head and pushed one side of her hair behind her ear. "I knew why you were doing it."

"How? Your back was to him." He bent to

pick up the toolbox and drill, then looked at her once again. "Oh, yeah, I forgot. You're psychic."

"No, I'm not."

"Now, there's a relief."

"But my mother is."

His scowl deepened, then he turned toward the door and muttered something under his breath that sounded like "Sweet baby Jesus save me."

As he walked from the room, her gaze traveled from the short comma curls touching the back of his neck, past his wide shoulders, and down the back of the soft gray T-shirt he'd tucked inside the waistband of his Levi's. A wallet bulged the right pocket of his jeans, and the heels of his work boots thudded across the linoleum.

Gabrielle placed her elbows on her desk and rested her face in her hands. She wasn't a huge believer of chakras, but she absolutely believed in a harmonious relationship of body, mind, and spirit. And right now all three were in total chaos. Her mind was appalled at her physical reaction to the detective, and her spirit was just plain confused by the dichotomic division.

"I guess it's safe to come in here now."

Gabrielle dropped her hands and looked at Kevin as he entered the room. "Sorry," she said.

"Why? You didn't know I'd be coming into work early." He set a briefcase on his desk and added unwittingly to her guilt. "Joe's a studly guy, I understand."

Not only had she betrayed her friendship with Kevin but now he had also unwittingly made everything so much worse by excusing her behavior with the man who'd bugged the telephone hoping to discover something incriminating. Kevin, of course, didn't know about the bug, and she couldn't warn him.

"Oh, geez," she sighed and once again rested her cheek in her hand. By the time the police eliminated her and Kevin from their list of suspects, she feared she was going to be as crazy as the detective already accused her of being.

"What's the matter?" Kevin asked as he walked around his desk and reached for the telephone.

"You can't use that right now," she said, stopping him, saving him from the bug.

He pulled his hand back. "Do you need to use it first?"

What was she doing? He wasn't guilty. The police would hear nothing but Kevin's business calls, which were about as exciting as watching paint dry. His calls were so boring that it would serve them right. But . . . Kevin did have several girlfriends, and sometimes when Gabrielle walked into the office, he'd turn his back and cover the receiver with his hand as if she'd caught him discussing intimate details of his love life. "No, I don't need to use it right now, but just don't . . ." She paused, wondering how to save him without sounding too vague or getting too specific. How could she save him without telling him that the police were eavesdropping on his calls? "Just don't get too personal," she began again. "If you have something really private to say to a girlfriend, maybe you should wait until you get home."

He looked at her the way Joe looked at her—as if she were demented. "What did you think I was going to do? Make an obscene phone call?"

"No, but I don't think you should talk about private things with your girlfriends. I mean, this is a business."

"Me?" He folded his arms across the front of his suit jacket, and his blue eyes narrowed. "What about you? A few minutes ago, your face was glued to your handyman."

He was angry now, but someday soon he would thank her. "I'm having lunch with the Silver Winds rep this afternoon," she said, purposely changing the subject. "I'll be gone about two hours."

Kevin sat and booted up his computer, but he didn't say anything. He didn't talk to her while she checked shipping receipts, or when—in an effort to appease him—she tidied her side of the room.

The three hours until her lunch appointment seemed to take forever. She filled the porcelain vaporizer with lavender and sage, made some sales, and always kept a covert eye on the detective dismantling the shelves on the wall to her right.

She watched to make sure he didn't plant any more bugs or pull a revolver out of his boot and shoot someone. She watched the strain of his biceps beneath his T-shirt as he removed heavy glass shelving, and she watched his broad, muscular shoulders as he carried it to the back room. He'd slung his tool belt low on his hips like a gunfighter, and his hand slid smoothly into the front pouch, depositing wood screws.

Even when Gabrielle wasn't watching him, she knew when he walked from the room and when he entered it again. She could feel him like the invisible pull of a black hole. When she wasn't helping customers, she busied herself with the never-ending chore of dusting, and she avoided talking to him as much as possible, answering only his direct questions.

By ten o'clock, tension tightened the base of her skull, and at eleven-thirty, she developed a tic in the outside corner of her right eye. Finally, at a quarter to twelve, she grabbed her small leather backpack and walked out of the stress-filled shop into the bright sunshine, feeling like she'd just been granted parole after a ten-year stint.

She met the Silver Winds representative at a restaurant in the heart of downtown, and they sat outside on the balcony and discussed dainty silver necklaces and earrings. A slight breeze fluttered the green umbrellas overhead as traffic passed on the street below. She ordered her favorite chicken stir-fry and a glass of iced tea and waited for the morning's tension to leave her skull.

The tic in her eye went away, but she couldn't seem to completely relax. No matter how she tried, she couldn't find her center or reharmonize her spirit. No matter how she fought it, her mind returned to Joe Shanahan, and the many ways the detective might trick an erroneous confession from Kevin while she was away. She didn't believe there was a subtle bone in Detective Joseph Shanahan's big muscular body, and she half expected to return and find poor Kevin cuffed to a chair.

What greeted her when she reentered her shop two hours later was about the last thing she expected. Laughter. Kevin's laughter mixed with Mara's as they both stood next to a ladder, grinning up at Joe Shanahan as if they were all great buddies.

Her business partner was laughing it up with the cop determined to put him in prison. And Gabrielle knew Kevin would hate prison more than most men. He'd hate the clothes and the haircuts and not having a cellphone.

Her gaze moved from poor Kevin's smiling face to the eight new mounting standards that ran from floor to ceiling on the back wall. Joe stood at the top of the ladder with a drill in one hand, a level in the other, and a tape measure attached to the back of his tool belt.

She hadn't really expected him to know enough about carpentry to do the job right, but the metal shelving system looked straight to her, so he apparently knew more than she'd thought. Mara knelt next to the wall and held the bottom of the last standard. The expression in her big brown eyes was a little too awestruck as she gazed up at the detective. Mara was inexperienced and, Gabrielle supposed, susceptible to the musky pheromones Joe exuded.

The three of them hadn't noticed Gabrielle, or the customer looking at a display of porcelain vases.

"It's not that easy," Kevin said to the detective above him. "You have to have an informed eye and natural instincts to make money dealing in antiques."

Conversation stopped as Joe drilled two screws into the top of the metal standard. "Well, I know next to squat about antiques," he confessed as he climbed down from the ladder. "My mother is a garage sale fanatic, and all that stuff looks the same to me." He knelt beside Mara and drilled two remaining screws. "Thanks for the help," he said before standing once again.

"No problem. What else can I do for you?" Mara asked, looking as if she wanted to take a bite out of crime.

"I'm about finished." He braced his feet and drilled several more screws.

"Some people find antiques at garage sales," Kevin said when it was quiet once more. "But serious dealers usually only go to estate sales and auctions. That's how I met Gabrielle. We were both bidding on the same watercolor. It was a pastoral scene by a local artist."

"I don't know much about art either," Joe confessed and rested his forearm on a ladder rung, the drill still gripped in his hand like a .45 magnum. "If I wanted to buy a painting, I'd have to ask somebody who knows about that sort of thing."

"You'd be real smart to do that, too. Most people don't know what's really valuable and can't tell if their art is legitimate. You'd be surprised at how many fakes hang in prestigious galleries. There was a break-in at . . ."

"It was mourning art," Gabrielle interrupted before Kevin could incriminate himself further. "We were bidding on mourning pictures."

Kevin shook his head as she walked toward him. "I don't think so. Mourning pictures give me the creeps."

Joe looked at her over his shoulder. His gaze met hers as he said slowly, "Morning as in sunrise?" He wasn't fooled. He knew what she was doing.

"No." She didn't really care what he knew. "Mourning as in pictures made from the hair of the dearly departed. They were popular in the seventeen and eighteen hundreds, and there is still a small market for hair art. Not everyone has an aversion to pictures made with great-great-great-grandmother's hair. Some of it is quite beautiful."

"Sounds morbid to me." Joe turned and used the orange cord to lower the drill to the floor.

Mara's nose wrinkled. "I agree with Joe. Morbid and disgusting."

Gabrielle loved hair art. She'd always found it fascinating, and no matter how irrational, Mara's opinion felt like a defection. "You need to help the customer looking at vases," she told her employee, the tone in her voice much harsher than she intended. Confusion furrowed Mara's brow as she walked across the store. The tic in Gabrielle's eye came back, and she pressed her fingers to it. Her life was falling apart, and the reason stood in front of her in tight jeans and a T-shirt, looking like one of those construction workers in a Diet Coke commercial.

"Are you feeling okay?" Kevin asked, his obvious concern making her feel worse.

"No, my head aches a little and my stomach feels queasy."

Joe reached across the short distance that separated them and pushed her hair behind her ear. He touched her as if he had the right, as if he cared about her. But of course he didn't. It was all an act to deceive Kevin.

"What did you eat for lunch?" he asked.

"Lunch didn't make me sick." She stared into his brown eyes and answered truthfully, "It started this morning." The funny little flutter in the pit of her stomach had started with a kiss. A kiss from an emotionally barren cop who disliked her as much as she disliked him. He patted her cheek with his warm palm as if to tell her to toughen up.

"It? Ah, cramps," Kevin deduced as if her behavior suddenly made perfect sense to him. "I thought you concocted an herbal remedy for those mood swings."

The corners of Joe's lips curved into an amused smile, and he lowered his hand and hooked his thumbs in his tool belt.

It was true. She'd created an essential oil that seemed to help her friend Francis with her PMS. But Gabrielle didn't need it. She didn't have PMS and she was always extremely nice to everyone—damnit. "I don't have mood swings." She crossed her arms under her breasts and tried not to glare. "I'm perfectly pleasant all the time. Ask anyone!"

The two men looked at her as if they were afraid to say another word. Kevin had clearly turned traitor on her. He'd defected to the enemy camp—his enemy.

"Maybe you should take the rest of the day off," Kevin suggested, but she couldn't. She had to stay and save him from Joe and from himself. "I used to have a girlfriend who laid around with a heating pad and ate chocolate. She said it was the only thing that seemed to help with those cramps and mood swings."

"I'm not having cramps or mood swings!" Weren't men supposed to hate talking about this sort of thing? Wasn't it supposed to freak them out? But neither man looked embarrassed; in fact, Joe looked as if he was trying not to laugh.

"Maybe you should take some Midol," Joe added through his smile, even though he knew perfectly well that what ailed her couldn't be cured with Midol.

Kevin nodded. Gabrielle's headache moved to her temples, and she no longer cared to save Kevin from Joe Shanahan or from prison. If he ended up as some iron-pumping convict's special buddy, her conscience was clear. Gabrielle raised her hands to the sides of her head as if to keep it from splitting.

"I've never seen her look this mad," Kevin said as if she weren't standing right in front of him.

Joe tilted his head to one side and pretended to study her. "I had a girlfriend who reminded me of a praying mantis once a month. If you said the wrong thing, she'd bite your head off. The rest of the time she was real sweet, though."

Gabrielle curled her nonviolent hands into fists and dropped them to her sides. She wanted to punch someone. Someone solid with dark hair and eyes. He was forcing her to have evil thoughts. Forcing her to create bad karma. "Which girlfriend was that? The one who dumped you after a whole two months?"

"She didn't dump me. I broke up with her." Joe reached for Gabrielle and wrapped his arm around her waist. He hauled her up against his side and caressed her skin through the thin nylon of her shirt. "God, I love it when you're jealous," he whispered in a low, sensual voice just above her ear. "You get all squinty-eyed and sexy."

His breath warmed her scalp, and if she turned her head just a little, his lips would brush her cheek. The wonderful smell of his skin enveloped her head, and she wondered how such an evil man could smell so heavenly. "You look normal," she said, "but you are really a demon from hell." She stuck her elbow in his ribs. Hard. The air whooshed from his lungs and she stepped out of his embrace.

"Guess this means I won't be getting any tonight," Joe groaned as he grabbed his side.

Kevin the defector laughed, as if the detective was a comedian.

"I'm going home," she said and walked from the room without looking back. She'd tried. If Kevin incriminated himself in her absence, her conscience was clear.

Kevin heard the back door slam shut, then he turned his gaze to Gabrielle's boyfriend. "She's really mad at you."

"She'll get over it. She just hates it when I mention old girlfriends." Joe shifted his weight to one foot and crossed his arms over his chest. "She told me that you and she dated once or twice."

Kevin looked for signs of jealousy but didn't

see any. He'd seen the possessive way Joe touched Gabrielle, and he'd witnessed them kissing that morning. For as long as he'd known her, she'd gone for tall, skinny men. This guy was different. This guy was all bulky muscles and brute strength. She must be in love. "We went out a few times, but we make better friends," he assured Joe. Actually, he'd been a lot more interested in her than she'd been in him. "You don't have anything to worry about."

"I'm not worried. I just wondered."

Kevin had always admired confidence, and Joe had it in spades. If the man had had a good income besides his good looks, Kevin probably would have hated him on sight. But he was such a loser that Kevin didn't feel at all inadequate. "I think you are probably going to be good for Gabrielle," he said.

"How's that?"

Because he wanted her distracted for the next few days, and Joe seemed to occupy her completely. "Because neither of you expect too much," he answered and turned toward his office. He shook his head as he entered the room and sat at his desk. Gabrielle's boyfriend was a low-expectation loser who was perfectly happy to scrape by.

Not Kevin. He hadn't been born rich like Gabrielle, or good-looking like Joe. Instead, he'd been born number six in a Mormon family of eleven children. With so many kids packed into one small farmhouse, it had been easy to get overooked. Except for slight variation in hair color and obvious differences in gender, the Carter kids all looked alike.

Except for once a year on birthdays, there'd been no special attention given to each individual child. They'd been dealt with as a whole. A clan. Most of his brothers and sisters had loved growing up in such a large family. They'd felt a bond, a special closeness with the other siblings. Not Kevin. He'd just felt invisible. He'd hated that.

All of his life, he'd worked hard. Before school, after school, and all summer long. Nothing had been given to him except hand-me-down clothes and a new pair of shoes every fall. He still worked hard, but now he enjoyed himself a hell of a lot more. And if there were things he wanted but couldn't obtain the money for through legal enterprise, there were other ways. There were always other ways.

Money was power. Absolutely. Without it a man was worse than nothing. He was invisible.

Six

 FLOATING ON A CLEAR BLOW-UP RAFT IN the middle of her backyard kiddie pool, Gabrielle finally found the inner peace she'd sought all day. Shortly after she'd returned from her shop that afternoon, she'd filled the pool and pulled on her silver bikini. The pool was ten feet across and three feet deep and had orange and blue jungle animals circling the outside. Wildflowers, rose petals, and lemon slices drifted on the surface of the water, soothing away her nervous tension with the scent of flowers and citrus. Clearing her head completely of Joe was impossible, of course, but she did succeed in absorbing enough positive energy from the universe to push him to the back of her mind.

Today was the first opportunity she'd had to test her sunscreen, and she'd rubbed her exposed skin with the blended oils of sesame, wheat germ, and lavender. The lavender had been a last-minute inspiration, a sort of hedge bet. Lavender didn't have screening properties, but it did have healing characteristics, in case she did burn. And also, the perfumed scent covered the smell of seeds so she wouldn't attract the unwanted attention of hungry birds in search of a feeder.

Periodically, she lifted an edge of her bathing suit and checked her tan. Throughout the afternoon, her skin bronzed nicely without a hint of pink.

At five-thirty, her friend Francis Hall-Valento-Mazzoni, now just Hall once again, stopped by to present Gabrielle with a red lace thong and matching bra. Francis owned Naughty or Nice, the lingerie shop half a block from Anomaly, and she often dropped by with her latest inventory of crotchless underwear or sheer nightgowns. Gabrielle didn't have the heart to tell her friend that she wasn't into racy undies. Consequently, most of the gifts ended up in a box in Gabrielle's closet. Francis was blond and blue-eyed, thirty-one, and twice divorced. She'd been in more relationships than she cared to remember, and believed most problems between men and women could be solved with a pair of licorice panties.

"How's that skin toner I made for you working out?" Gabrielle directed the question toward her friend, who sat in a wicker chair beneath the porch awning.

"Better than the oatmeal mask or PMS oil."

Gabrielle skimmed her fingers across the top

of the water, disturbing the rose petals and wildflowers. She wondered if her treatments or Francis's impatience were at fault. Francis was always looking for the quick fix. The easiest answer, never bothering to search her own soul and find inner peace and happiness within. As a result, her life was always in crisis. She was a magnet for loser men and had more issues than a magazine rack. Francis also had qualities Gabrielle admired. She was funny and bright, went after what she wanted, and had a pure heart.

"I haven't talked to you for awhile. Not since last week when you thought some big guy with dark hair was following you."

For the first time in over an hour, Gabrielle thought of Detective Joe Shanahan. She thought of his intrusion in her life and the bad karma she'd accumulated thanks to him. He was domineering and rude and filled with so much testosterone that a five o'clock shadow darkened his cheeks at four-fifteen. And when he kissed, his aura turned the deepest red of any man she'd ever known.

She thought of telling Francis about the morning she'd pulled a derringer on an undercover cop and ended up as his confidential informant. But this was too huge a secret to tell.

Gabrielle shaded her eyes with her hand and looked over at her friend. She'd never been any good at keeping secrets. "If I tell you something, you have to promise not to tell," she began, then proceeded to squeal like a jailhouse rat. She hit the high points, but purposely left out the disturbing details, like the fact that he had the hard, rippling muscles of an underwear model and kissed like a man who could seduce even the most frigid woman out of her support hose. "Joe Shanahan is overbearing and rude, and I'm stuck with him until Kevin's cleared of this whole ridiculous nonsense," she finished, feeling purged. For once, Gabrielle's problems were bigger than her friend's.

Francis was silent for a moment, then murmured, "Hmm." She pushed a pair of rose-colored sunglasses up the bridge of her nose. "So, what does this guy look like?"

Gabrielle turned her face to the sun. She closed her eyes and saw Joe's face, his intense eyes and spiky lashes, the sensual lines of his mouth, and the perfect symmetry of his wide forehead, straight nose, and strong chin. His thick brown hair tended to curl about his ears and the back of his neck, softening his powerful, masculine features. He smelled wonderful. "Nothing special."

"That's too bad. If I were forced to work with a cop, I'd want one of those beefcake-calendar boys."

Which, Gabrielle supposed, pretty much described Joe.

"I'd make him carry heavy boxes and get all sweaty," Francis continued with the fantasy.

"And I'd watch his buns of steel when he bent over."

Gabrielle frowned. "Well, I look at a man's soul. His appearance is unimportant."

"You know what? I've heard you say that before, and if it's true, then why didn't you sleep with your old boyfriend Harold Maddox?"

Francis had a point, but no way was Gabrielle going to admit looks were as important as the essence of a man's soul. They weren't. A mentally developed enlightened man was so much sexier than a cave dweller. Problem was, that physical attraction thing sometimes got in the way. "I had my reasons."

"Yeah, like he was boring and had a scraggly ponytail and everyone mistook him for your dad."

"He wasn't *that* old."

"Whatever you say."

Gabrielle could make a few comments about Francis's choice of men and husbands but chose not to.

"I'm not all that surprised Kevin is a suspect," Francis said. "He can be a weasel."

Gabrielle looked across at her friend and frowned. Francis and Kevin had dated for a short time, and now the two of them had a sort of love-hate relationship. Gabrielle had never asked why or what had happened; she didn't want to know. "You're only saying that because you don't like him."

"Maybe, but promise me you'll keep your

eyes open anyway. You put too much blind trust in your friends." Francis stood and straightened her sundress.

Gabrielle didn't think she gave blind trust, but she believed the trust she gave was the trust she received. If she didn't give it freely, she wouldn't get it back. "Are you leaving?"

"Yeah, I got a date with a plumber. Should prove interesting. He's got a great body, but he doesn't say much. If he isn't too boring, I'll let him take me home and show me his monkey wrench."

Gabrielle purposely didn't comment on that last remark. "Could you hit play on my tape recorder?" she asked and pointed to the old cassette player sitting on a wicker table.

"I don't know how you can listen to this crap."

"You should try it. You might find the meaning of life."

"Yeah well, I'd rather listen to Aerosmith. Steven Tyler gives my life meaning."

"Dream On."

"Ha ha," Francis said, and the slamming of the back screen door signaled her departure. Gabrielle checked her tan line for signs of burning, then closed her eyes and contemplated her connection in the universe. She sought answers. Answers to the questions she didn't understand. Like why fate had determined Joe should enter her life with the force of a cosmic tornado.

*　　*　　*

Joe tossed his cigarette into a rhododendron bush, then raised his hand to the heavy wooden door. Just as he knocked, it opened, and a woman with short blond hair and glossy pink lips stared at him from behind a pair of rose-colored sunglasses. Even though he'd watched this address for weeks, he stepped back and looked at the bright red street numbers tacked to the side of the house. "I'm looking for Gabrielle Breedlove," he said.

"You must be Joe."

Surprised, his gaze returned to the woman before him.

Behind the lenses of her sunglasses, her blue eyes slid down his chest. "She told me you're her boyfriend, but she obviously left out a lot." She raised her gaze to his face and smiled. "I wonder why she left out the good stuff?"

Joe wondered exactly what his informant had said about him. He had a few other questions he wanted to ask her as well, but that wasn't the only reason he needed to see her. He'd never worked with anyone as uptight and hostile as Gabrielle, and he feared she might flip on him completely and blow his cover. He needed her calm and cooperative. No more scenes. No more placing herself between him and his new buddy, Kevin. "Where is Gabrielle?"

"In the pool in the backyard." She stepped outside and shut the door behind her. "Come on. I'll show you." She escorted him to the side of the house and pointed toward a tall fence covered in climbing roses. An arch with an open gate divided the fence in two sections.

"Through there." The woman pointed, then turned to leave.

Joe walked under the arch and took two full steps before stopping in his tracks. The backyard was filled with a profusion of color and fragrant flowers. And Gabrielle Breedlove floating in a kiddie wading pool. His gaze took her in all at once, but his attention was drawn to the belly ring he'd felt while frisking her a few days before. He'd never been partial to women with body piercings, but . . . damn. That little ring of silver made his mouth dry.

Her hand brushed the top of the water, and she rubbed her wet fingers over her abdomen. Several droplets drifted across her stomach and her sides. One clear drop caught a ray of sunlight as it slid slowly down her belly and disappeared into her navel. His insides got all itchy and hot, and desire pulled in his groin. He stood with his feet rooted to the lawn, growing hard and heavy, powerless to control the unwelcome thoughts that assaulted him. Thoughts of walking into that pool, wrapping his arms around her waist and sucking that droplet of water from her navel, then dipping his tongue inside and licking her warm flesh. He tried to remind himself that she was crazy, nutty, cuckoo, but after nine hours, he still remembered the soft texture of her lips pressed against his.

That kiss had been part of his job, to shut her up before she blew his cover. His body had responded, of course, and he hadn't been surprised by his reaction to the taste of her warm mouth and the closeness of her breasts, but he'd made a big mistake with her. He'd slipped his tongue in her mouth, and now he knew she tasted a little like peppermint and a lot like passion. He knew the soft tangle of her hair around his fingers and knew she smelled like exotic flowers. She hadn't pushed him away or resisted, and her response had reached down and grabbed him by the curlies. He'd gone from semi to hard in about two seconds. He'd barely managed to stay in control. Barely managed to keep his hands from sliding down and filling his palms with her breasts. He was a cop, but he was also a man.

Standing in her backyard with his gaze slipping to the little triangle of silver material covering her crotch and his thoughts sliding to what lay beneath had nothing to do with being a cop and everything to do with being a man. His gaze moved to the little mole on the inside of her right thigh, down her long legs to her purple toenails, then back up past that silver belly ring to her bikini top. A wide seam ran across her nipples, and the tight top pushed up two mounds of perfect, tan breasts. The ground beneath his feet shifted, seeming to change and fall out from underneath him, sucking him down. She was his informant. She was nuts. She was also extremely fine, and he wanted nothing more than to peel away that bikini like a tinfoil snack pack and dive face first into her cleavage.

His gaze moved to the hollow of her throat, past her chin, to her full mouth. He watched her lips move and, for the first time since he'd set foot in the backyard, he became aware of a tranquil male voice saying something about a cave. "This is your cave," the man droned as if he'd popped Seconal. "This is your place. A place where you can truly find yourself, where you come to find your center. Take a deep breath . . . bring your awareness into your abdomen . . .

"Let it go and repeat after me . . . I am at peace . . . Ohm-Nah-Mah-Shee-Vah-Yahh . . . Hmm."

The ground beneath his feet shifted back, becoming solid once more. Suddenly, everything was all right again in Joe Shanahan's world. Stable. He was okay. She was still crazy, and nothing had changed. He felt an overwhelming urge to laugh, like he'd just cheated death. "I should have known you'd listen to Yanni," he said loud enough to be heard over the tape.

Gabrielle's eyes flew open, and she sat up. The clear raft tipped, and Joe watched her legs and arms flail as she tumbled into the water. When she came back up, pink and red rose petals were stuck to her hair. She sat on the bottom of the pool while lemon slices and wildflowers floated about her.

"What are you doing here?" she sputtered.

"We need to talk," he answered through a smile he tried, and failed, to suppress.

"I don't have anything to say to you."

"Then you can listen." He moved toward the tape player by the back door. "First we need to get rid of Yanni."

"I don't listen to Yanni. That's meditation with raja yoga."

"Uh-huh." He hit the off button and turned to face her.

Water slid down her body as she stood, and a sprig of purple flowers stuck out of the top of her bikini. "This is so typical." She pulled her hair over one shoulder and squeezed the water out of it. "I just find my peaceful center and then you barge into my yard and ruin my balance."

Joe didn't figure she'd ever had more than a passing acquaintance with anything resembling balance. He picked up a white bath towel hanging across a wicker chair and walked to the edge of the pool. But it didn't matter if she had a mental imbalance. He was stuck posing as her boyfriend, but for the past two days, she'd behaved as if he were as welcome as a plague. Kevin might not be suspicious now, but Joe couldn't keep passing off her hostile behavior as nothing more than jealousy and menstrual cramps. "Maybe we can work on it," he said and handed her the towel.

Her hands stilled, and she stared at him, distrust narrowing her green eyes. "Work on what?" She took the towel and stepped out of the pool.

"How we deal with each other. I know you think I'm your enemy, but I'm not." Although he didn't trust his informant out of his sight, he needed her to trust him. He was responsible for her safety, and part of his job was to protect her—physically.

He couldn't protect her if she ran to Kevin if things got ugly. He didn't really think Kevin would hurt Gabrielle, but if there was one thing he'd come to anticipate, it was the unexpected. That way he was never caught with his pants down around his ankles. "You need to let me do my job. The sooner I get what I need, the sooner I'll be out of your life. We need to come to some sort of an agreement."

She patted her face and neck with the towel and plucked the purple flowers from her bikini. "You mean a compromise?"

Not hardly. He'd meant she needed to stop acting so neurotic and start behaving like she was hot for him. No more calling him a demon from hell. "Sure."

She studied him and tossed the sprig of flowers back into the pool. "How?"

"Well first, you need to calm down and stop acting like the swat team is about to bust through the front window of your store."

"And second?"

"Neither of us may like it, but you're supposed to be my girlfriend. Quit acting like I'm
a serial killer."

As she patted the tops of her breasts with the
towel, he purposely kept his eyes pinned to her
face. No way was he going to lower his gaze
and get sucked into fantasy land again.

"And if I do?" she asked. "What are you going to do for me?"

"Make sure you aren't implicated—"

"Uh-uh." She shook her head and wrapped
the towel around her waist. "That threat doesn't
scare me anymore, since I don't believe Kevin
is guilty."

Joe shifted his weight to one foot and crossed
his arms over his chest. He knew the drill. This
was the part where informants tried to shake
him down for money, or wanted all their unpaid parking tickets to disappear quicker than
a dime bag in rehab, or maybe get a badge of
their very own. "What do you want?"

"I want you to keep an open mind. Don't just
assume Kevin's guilty."

The unpaid parking tickets would have been
easier. There wasn't a doubt in Joe's mind that
Kevin Carter was as guilty as sin, but part of
being an undercover cop was having a God-
given talent to pass off boldfaced lies without a
flicker of remorse. "Sure. I'll keep an open
mind."

"Really?"

He relaxed the corners of his mouth and slanted her his I'm-your-buddy smile. "Absolutely."

She stared into his eyes as if she were trying to read the back of his brain. "Your nose is growing, Officer Shanahan."

His smile turned genuine. She was crazy, not stupid. He'd had enough experience to know the difference, and given a choice, he'd prefer crazy over stupid any day. He raised his hands, palms up. "I can try," he said and lowered his arms to his sides. "How's that?"

She sighed and tied a knot in the towel over her left hip. "I guess if that's the best you can do, it will have to be good enough." She turned toward the house, then looked back at him over her shoulder. "Have you eaten dinner yet?"

"No." He'd figured he'd stop at the grocery store on the way home and pick up some chicken for him and some carrots for Sam.

"I'm going to make dinner. You can stay if you want." Her tone was less than enthusiastic.

"Are you inviting me to have dinner with you? Like a real girlfriend?"

"I'm hungry and you haven't eaten." She shrugged and headed toward the back door. "Let's just leave it at that."

His gaze followed the waves in her wet hair and the droplets of water dripping from the ends and sliding down her spine. "Can you cook?"

"I'm a wonderful cook."

As he walked behind her, his eyes lowered to the sway of her hips, her rounded bottom he'd come to appreciate in the past week, and the brush of the towel across the backs of her knees. Dinner prepared by a wonderful cook sounded great. And of course, it gave him the opportunity both to ask her a few questions about her relationship with Kevin and to get her to relax around him. "What's for dinner?"

"Stroganoff, French bread, and salad." She climbed several steps to the screen door and opened it.

Joe followed close behind and reached over her head, grabbing the top of the wood frame and holding the door open.

She paused, and if he hadn't been paying attention, he would have knocked her flat. His chest lightly grazed her bare back. She turned, and her shoulder brushed his chest through the thin cotton of his T-shirt. "Are you a vegetarian?" she asked.

"God forbid. Are you?"

Her wide green eyes stared into his, and a distressed little furrow creased her brow. Then she did something weird—although he guessed he shouldn't be surprised by anything she did. She breathed really deep through her nose as if she smelled something. Joe couldn't smell anything beyond the floral scent clinging to her skin. Then she shook her head slightly as if to clear her mind and continued into the house as

if nothing had happened. Joe followed and resisted a sudden urge to sniff his armpits.

"I have tried veganism," she informed him as
they moved through a small back room with a
washer and dryer and into a kitchen painted
bright yellow. "It's a lot healthier lifestyle. But
unfortunately I'm lapsed."

"You're a lapsed vegetarian?" He'd never
heard of such a thing, but he wasn't real surprised.

"Yes, I've tried to resist my carnivorous
urges, but I'm weak. I have control issues."

Control usually wasn't an issue for him—
until now.

"I love most things that are bad for my ar-
teries. Sometimes I'm halfway to McDonald's
before I realize it."

A stained glass window above the breakfast
nook threw patches of color about the room and
on the rows of little glass bottles lined up on
the small wooden table. The room smelled like
Anomaly, like rose oil and patchouli, but nothing else, and he grew suspicious of her claim to
be a wonderful cook. No Crock-Pot filled with
bubbling stroganoff sat on the counter. No scent
of baked bread. His suspicions were confirmed
when she opened the refrigerator and pulled
out a container of sauce, a package of fresh
pasta, and a loaf of French bread.

"I thought you were a wonderful cook."

"I am." She shut the refrigerator and set
everything next to the stove. "Would you do

me a favor and open the cabinet by your left leg and pull out two saucepans?"

When he leaned down and opened the door, a colander fell out on his foot. Her cabinets were messier than his.

"Oh, good. We'll need that too."

He grabbed the pots and colander and straightened. Gabrielle stood with her back pressed against the refrigerator door, a hunk of French bread in one hand. He watched her gaze slide up the front of his jeans to his chest. She slowly chewed, then swallowed. The tip of her tongue licked a crumb from the corner of her mouth, and she finally looked up at him. "Want some?"

His gaze searched her face for a hint that she wasn't asking about bread, but he saw nothing provocative in her clear green eyes. If she'd been any other woman besides his CI, he would have loved to show her exactly what he wanted—starting with her mouth and slowly working his way to the little mole on her inner thigh. He'd downright love to fill his hands with her big, creamy breasts straining against that bikini top. But she wasn't any other woman, and he had to behave like a Boy Scout. "No, thanks."

"Okay. I'm going to change my clothes. While I'm gone, put the stroganoff sauce in the small pan, then fill the larger pan with water. When the water starts to boil, add the pasta. Cook it for five minutes." She pushed away from the refrigerator, and as she walked past him, she paused for a second and breathed deeply through her nose. Just like before, a crease furrowed her brow, and she shook her head. "Anyway, I should be back by then."

Joe watched her breeze from the room, tearing off a bite of bread, and he wondered exactly how it had happened that he'd been invited to dinner by a woman in a bikini who claimed to be a wonderful cook but left him to cook the meal while she changed. And what was up with that smelling thing? She'd done it twice now, and he was starting to get a little paranoid.

Gabrielle popped her head back into the kitchen. "You aren't going to search for that Monet while I'm out of the room, are you?"

"No, I'll wait until you get back."

"Great," she said through a smile, then was gone again.

Joe moved to the sink and filled the larger pot with water. A fat black cat rubbed against his legs and wound its tail around his calf. Joe didn't really like cats, figuring they were pretty useless. Not like dogs that could be trained to sniff out dope or birds that could be trained to talk and hang upside down by one foot. He nudged the cat away with the toe of his workboot and turned to the stove.

His gaze strayed to the doorway, and he wondered how long before she returned. It wasn't that he had any scruples about searching through drawers while she was out of the room, he just had two very good reasons why he chose not to. First, he didn't believe he'd find anything. If Gabrielle was involved in the theft of Mr. Hillard's painting, he doubted she would have invited him into her house. She was much too high-strung to shoot the breeze over stroganoff if she had a Monet rolled up in her closet. And second, he needed her trust, and that would never happen if she caught him ransacking her house. He needed to show her he wasn't such a bad guy, which he didn't think would be too terribly difficult. He wasn't the type of man who bragged about conquests over a few beers, but women generally liked him. He knew he was a good lover. He always made sure the women in his bed had as much fun as he did, and despite what Meg Ryan said, he'd be able to tell if a woman was faking. He didn't roll off and start snoring afterward, and he didn't collapse and crush a woman beneath his weight.

He dumped the stroganoff into the saucepan on the stove and turned the burners on medium. Although he wasn't one of those sensitive, pansy-assed weenies who cried in front of women, he was pretty sure women thought he was nice.

Something sat on his foot, and he looked down at the cat perched on his boot. "Get lost, furball," he said and nudged the cat just enough to send it sliding across the linoleum.

*   *   *

Gabrielle hooked the lace bra between her breasts, then pulled a short blue T-shirt over her head. Even though Joe said he wouldn't search her kitchen, she didn't really believe him. She didn't trust him out of her sight. Heck, she didn't trust him with her eyes glued right on him. But he was right, she had to find a calm way to deal with him in her shop and in her life. She had a business to run, and she couldn't do it if she had to watch his every move or leave early.

She stepped into a pair of faded jeans and buttoned them just below her navel. Besides her business concerns, she knew her health was at risk. She didn't know how much longer she could walk around with stress headaches and unattractive facial tics before she developed serious health-related issues, like a hormonal imbalance and an overactive pituitary gland.

Gabrielle grabbed a brush off her dresser and pulled it through her damp hair. She sat on the lace spread covering her four-poster bed and tried to remind herself that everyone entered her life for a reason. If she opened her mind, she would find the higher purpose for Joe's existence. A picture of his behind as he'd bent over to retrieve pots from her cabinet entered her head, and she scowled at her reflection in a cheval mirror across the room. The way he filled out his jeans had absolutely nothing to do with spiritual meaning.

Tossing the brush beside her, she wove her hair into a loose braid, then tied a blue ribbon around the bottom. Joe was a dark, brooding cop who'd wreaked havoc on her nerves, turned her life upside down, and caused disharmony. An imbalance of body and spirit. A war for supremacy. Anarchy. She certainly didn't see a higher purpose in all of that.

But he did smell nice.

When she entered the kitchen several minutes later, Joe stood in front of the sink pouring noodles into a colander. A cloud of steam enveloped his head while her mother's cat traversed a figure eight between his feet, wrapping her tail around his calves and meowing loudly.

"Beezer!" She scooped up the cat and held her against her breasts. "You better leave the detective alone or he'll slam you to the ground and arrest you. I know from experience."

"I never slammed you to the ground," Joe said as the steam cleared. "If anyone was slammed, it was me."

"Oh, yeah." She smiled at the memory of him lying on the ground with his lashes stuck together. "I got the jump on you."

He looked across his shoulder at her and shook the colander. A slight smile curved a corner of his mouth, and the humidity curled the hair about his temple. "But who ended up on top, Miss Bad Ass?" His gaze slipped over her from the braid in her hair to her bare feet, then back up again. "Pasta's done."

"Go ahead and dump it in with the stroganoff."

"What are you going to do?"

"Feed Beezer or she'll never leave you alone. She knows you're making dinner, and she's food obsessed." Gabrielle walked to a cabinet by the back door and retrieved a package of Tender Vittles. "After I feed her, I'll make the salad," she said as she ripped off the top. She dumped the food in a porcelain saucer, and once Beezer began to eat, she opened the refrigerator and pulled out a bag of chopped-up salad.

"That figures."

Gabrielle looked over at Joe, who stood in front of the stove stirring the pasta into the sauce with a wooden spoon. The shadow of his beard darkened his tan cheeks and emphasized the sensual lines of his mouth. "What?"

"That your lettuce is precut. You know, this is the first time I've ever been invited to dinner, then been asked to cook it myself."

She hadn't really thought of him as a guest, more like unavoidable company. "How odd."

"Yeah. Odd." He pointed the spoon at the breakfast nook in the corner of the room. "What is all that?"

"Essential oils for the Coeur Festival," she explained as she dumped lettuce into two bowls. "I make my own aromatherapies and healing oils. Today is the first free day I've had to test a sunscreen oil I made out of sesame, wheat germ, and lavender. That's what I was doing in the pool."

"Does it work?"

She pulled down the neck of her T-shirt and studied the stark white bikini line against her tan chest. "I didn't burn." She glanced at him, but he wasn't looking at her face or her tan line. He stared at her bare stomach; his gaze so hot and intent heat flushed her skin. "What kind of dressing do you like on your salad?" she managed.

Then he shrugged one shoulder and focused his attention on the pot of stroganoff, making her wonder if she'd imagined the way he'd looked at her. "Ranch."

"Oh . . ." She turned to the refrigerator to hide her confusion. "Well I only have Italian and fat-free Italian."

"Why did you ask like I had a choice?"

"You do." If he could pretend that nothing had passed between them, so could she, but she had a feeling he was a better actor. "You can have Italian or fat-free Italian."

"Italian."

"Great." She dressed the salad, then carried the bowls into the dining room and set them on the cluttered table. She didn't have dinner company often and had to shove her catalogs and oil recipes into the built-in china hutch. Once the table was clear, she placed a short beeswax candle in the center of the pedestal table and lit it. She brought out her linen place mats and matching napkins, a pair of silver napkin rings, and the antique silver flatware she'd inherited from her grandmother. She grabbed two Ville-roy & Boch plates painted with red poppies and told herself she wasn't trying to impress the detective. She wanted to use her "good stuff" because she hardly ever got the chance. There was no other reason.

With her finest china in her hands she walked back into the kitchen. He stood where she'd left him, his back to her. She paused in the doorway, her eyes taking in his dark hair and the back of his neck, his broad shoulders and back. She let her gaze move to the back pockets of his Levi's and down his long legs. She couldn't remember the last time she'd had a good-looking guy to dinner. Her last two boyfriends didn't count because they hadn't been all that great in the looks department. Harold had been brilliant, and she'd loved listening to him talk about spiritual enlightenment. He hadn't been preachy or too far out, but Francis had been right, Harold had been too old for her.

Before Harold, she'd dated Rick Hattaway, a nice, average-looking man who made Zen alarm clocks for a living. Neither man had made her pulse race or her stomach flutter, or made her skin flush from the heat of his gaze. Her attraction to both Harold and Rick hadn't been sexual, and neither relationship had progressed beyond kissing.

It had been years since she'd judged a man by his looks and not the quality of his soul. It had been before her conservationist conversion, when she'd hated washing dishes so much she'd only used paper plates. The guys she'd dated in those days probably wouldn't have even noticed the difference between Wedgwood and Chinet. At that time in her life she'd considered herself a serious artist, and she'd chosen men for purely aesthetic reasons. None of them had been enlightened, some hadn't been very smart, but really, intellect hadn't been the point. Muscles. Muscles and tight buns and stamina had been the point.

Gabrielle's gaze moved up Joe's spine, and she begrudgingly admitted that she'd missed looking across a dinner table at a handsome, hormone-enriched he-man. Joe certainly didn't seem concerned with his own enlightenment, but he did seem more intelligent than the average muscle neck. Then he raised his arm, bent his head, and sniffed his pit.

Gabrielle looked at the plates in her hands. She should have used paper.

Seven

GABRIELLE WAS SURPRISED AT HIS TABLE manners. Surprised he didn't chew with his mouth open, scratch himself, or belch like a frat boy with a sixer of Old Milwaukee. He'd actually placed his napkin on his lap and was entertaining her with outrageous stories about his parrot, Sam. If she didn't know better, she might think he was trying to charm her or that perhaps he had a decent soul buried somewhere deep within that solid body.

"Sam has a weight problem," he told her in between bites of stroganoff. "He loves pizza and Cheetos."

"You feed your bird pizza and Cheetos?"

"Not so much anymore. I had to build him a gym. Now I make him work out when I do."

Gabrielle didn't know whether to believe him or not. "How do you make a bird work out? Won't he just fly away?"

"I trick him into thinking he's having fun." Joe broke off a piece of bread and ate it. "I put

the gym next to my weight bench," he continued after he'd swallowed. "And as long as I
stay in the room with him, he'll climb his lad-
ders and chains."

Gabrielle took a bite of her own bread and
watched him over the top of the beeswax candle. Muted light from the dining room windows poured through the sheer curtains,
bathing the room and Detective Joe Shanahan
in soft light. His strong, masculine features appeared relaxed and subdued. Gabrielle figured
it had to be a trick of the light, because despite
his present charm, she knew from very recent
experience that there was nothing subdued
about the man across from her. Nothing soft,
but she supposed that a man who loved his bird
couldn't be totally without redeeming qualities.
"How long have you had Sam?"

"Not quite a year now, but it seems like I've
always had him. My sister Debby bought him
for me."

"You have a sister?"

"I have four."

"Wow." Growing up, Gabrielle had always
wanted a sister or brother. "Are you the oldest?"

"Youngest."

"The baby," she said, although she couldn't
envision Joe as anything other than a grown
man. He had too much testosterone for her to
think of him as a nice little boy with shiny

cheeks. "I bet growing up with four big sisters was fun."

"Mostly it was hell." He twirled a bite of pasta onto his fork.

"Why?"

He shoved the noodles into his mouth and watched her as he chewed. He didn't look like he would answer, but then he swallowed and confessed, "They made me wear their clothes and pretend I was the fifth sister."

She tried not to laugh, but her bottom lip trembled.

"It's not funny. They wouldn't even let me pretend to be the dog. Tanya always got to be the dog."

She did laugh this time and even thought about reaching out to pat his hand and telling him he would be okay, but she didn't. "Sounds like your sister made up for it. She bought you a bird for your birthday."

"Debby gave me Sam when I was laid up at home for a while. She thought a bird would keep me company until I was back on my feet and would be less trouble than a puppy." He smiled now. "She was wrong about that."

"Why were you laid up at home?"

His smile fell, and he shrugged his big shoulders. "I was shot in a drug bust that went wrong from the very beginning."

"You were shot?" Gabrielle felt her brows raise up her forehead. "Where?"

"In my right thigh," he said and abruptly

changed the subject. "I met your friend when I knocked on your door earlier."

Gabrielle would have loved to know the details of the shooting, but he obviously wanted the subject dropped. "Francis?"

"She didn't give me her name, but she did say you told her I was your boyfriend. What else did you tell her?" he asked before he stuck the last bite of pasta in his mouth.

"That's about it," Gabrielle prevaricated as she reached for her iced tea. "She knew I thought a stalker was following me, so she asked me about it today. I told her we're dating now."

He swallowed slowly, and his gaze studied her across the slight distance that separated them. "You told her you're dating the guy you thought was stalking you?"

Gabrielle took a drink and nodded. "Mmm-hmm."

"And she didn't think that was weird?"

Gabrielle shook her head and set her tea back down. "Francis has relationship issues. She knows that sometimes a woman has to take a chance. And being pursued by a man can be very romantic."

"By a stalker?"

"Yeah well, in life you have to kiss a few toads."

"Have you kissed a lot of toads?"

She speared salad with her fork and pointedly directed her attention to his lips. "Just one," she said and shoved the lettuce in her mouth.

He reached for his own glass, and his quiet laughter filled the room. They both knew she hadn't responded as if he were a toad. "Besides kissing toads, tell me more about yourself." A bead of condensation slid down the glass, then dripped onto his T-shirt, making a tiny wet circle on his right pectoral.

"Are you interrogating me?"

"Absolutely not."

"Don't you have a file on me somewhere filled with information, like how many cavities or speeding tickets I've had?"

His eyes met hers over the top of the glass, and he watched her as he took a long drink. Then he set the glass back down and told her, "I didn't check your dental record, but you got a ticket last May for doing thirty-five in a twenty. When you were nineteen you wrapped your Volkswagen around a telephone pole and were lucky enough to walk away with minor bruises and three stitches in the top of your head."

She wasn't surprised he knew her driving record, but it was a little disconcerting that he knew things about her life when she knew next to nothing about him. "Fascinating stuff. What else do you know?"

"I know you get your name from your grandfather."

Not another big surprise. "We're one of those

families that name children after their grand-
parents. My grandmothers were Eunuch Beryl
Paugh and Thelma Dorita Cox Breedlove. I consider myself lucky." She shrugged. "What
else?"

"I know that you attended two universities
but didn't receive a degree from either."

Obviously he didn't know anything of sub-
stance. He knew nothing about *her*. "I didn't go
to get a degree," she began as she placed her
near empty salad bowl on her plate and pushed
them aside. She hadn't eaten much of her stroganoff, but with Joe sitting across the table, she
suddenly wasn't very hungry. "I went to learn
about things that interested me. When I'd
learned what I wanted, I moved on to what interested me next." She placed her arm on the
table and rested her cheek in her hand. "Anyone can get a degree or a certificate in something. Big deal. A piece of paper from a
university somewhere doesn't define a person.
It won't tell you who I am."

He took the linen napkin from his lap and set
it next to his glass. "So, why don't you tell me
who you are. Tell me something I don't already
know."

She supposed he wanted her to divulge incriminating evidence, but she didn't know anything. Anything at all, so she told him
something she was positive he would never
guess about her. "Well, I've been reading what
Freud had to say about compulsions and fe-

tishes. According to him, I have an oral fixa-
tion."

A smile tugged one corner of his mouth, and
he lowered his gaze to her lips. "Really?"

"Don't get too excited," she laughed. "Freud
was the brilliant mind behind penis envy,
which is absurd. Only a man would think up
something so stupid. I've never met a woman
who wanted a penis."

As he stared at her from across the table, the
other corner of his mouth slid upward into a
grin. "I've known a few who wanted mine."

Despite her liberal views on sex, Gabrielle felt
her cheeks warm. "I didn't mean it that way."

Joe laughed and tilted his chair back on two
legs. "Why don't you tell me how you met
Kevin."

Gabrielle figured Kevin had already told Joe
everything, and she wondered if he was asking
to catch her in a lie. She didn't have anything
to lie about. "Like Kevin probably told you, we
first met at an estate auction a few years before
we opened Anomaly. He'd just moved here
from Portland and was working for an antique
dealer downtown, and I was working for a
dealer with stores in Pocatello, Twin Falls, and
Boise. After that first time, I ran into him quite
a bit." She paused and brushed a bread crumb
from the table. "Then I got fired from my job,
and he called me up and asked me if I wanted
to go into business with him."

"Just out of the blue?"

"He'd heard I'd gotten fired over the purchase of more hair art. The owner of the store didn't have an open mind about it. Even after I reimbursed him for the cost, he fired me anyway."

"So Kevin calls you up, and you two decided to open a business." He folded his arms across his chest and rocked the chair a little. "Just like that?"

"No. He wanted to strictly sell antiques, but I was a little burned out on antiques, so we compromised and settled on a curio shop. I came up with sixty percent of the starting costs."

"How?"

Gabrielle hated to talk about money. "I'm sure you know I have a modest trust fund." And she'd invested more than half of it into Anomaly. Usually, when people learned her last name, they assumed she had a bottomless bank account, but that wasn't the case. If her store failed, she would be almost broke. But the thought of losing her financial investment didn't bother her nearly as much as the thought of losing the time and energy and the emotional attachment she had to her store. Most people measured success by monetary gains. Not Gabrielle. Sure she wanted to pay the bills, but to her success was measured by happiness. She considered herself very successful.

"What about Kevin?"

While success meant happiness to Gabrielle,

she knew it didn't to Kevin. To him, success was tangible. Something he could hold or drive or wear. Which made him unenlightened, but didn't make him a criminal. It also made him a good partner. "He got a bank loan for the other forty percent."

"Did you bother to do any investigating at all before you started this business?"

"Of course. I'm not a fool. Location is the most important factor to the success of a small business. Hyde Park has a steady stream of—"

"Wait." He held up one hand and stopped her. "That isn't what I meant. I was asking if you'd ever thought to investigate Kevin's background before you invested so much of your own money?"

"I didn't do a criminal check or anything, but I spoke with his previous employers. They all said great things about him." This next part she knew he would never understand, but she told him anyway—quickly. "And I meditated about it for a while before I gave him my answer."

His hands fell to his sides, and a scowl wrinkled his forehead. "You meditated? Didn't you think going into business with a man you hardly knew required more than *meditation*?"

"No."

"Why the hell not?"

"It was karma."

With a loud thud, the chair legs hit the floor. "Come again?"

"My karma was rewarding me. I was unhappy and out of a job, and Kevin presented me with the opportunity to be my own boss."

He didn't speak for several prolonged moments. "Are you telling me," he began, again, "that Kevin's business offer was a reward for some good deed you'd performed in a past life?"

"No, I don't believe in reincarnation." Her belief in karma confused some people, and she didn't really expect Detective Shanahan to understand. "Going into business with Kevin was my reward for something I'd done in this life. I believe the good or bad you do affects you now, not after you've died. When you die, you move to a whole different plane of consciousness. The enlightenment, or knowledge, you attain while in this life determines to which plane your soul ascends."

"Are you talking about heaven or Hell Bop?"

She'd expected a derogatory question from him and wasn't surprised. "I'm sure you call it heaven."

"What do you call it?"

"I don't call it anything, usually. It could be heaven. Hell. Nirvana. Whatever. I only know it's the place my soul will go when I die."

"Do you believe in God?"

She was used to that question. "Yes, but probably not in the way you do. I believe God would rather I sat in a field of daisies and fill my senses with the awesome beauty He's created while I contemplate inner peace. He'd rather I actually live the Ten Commandments than sit in a stuffy church and listen to some *guy* tell me *how* to live them. I think there is a big difference between being religious and being spiritual. Maybe you can be both, I don't know. I only know that a lot of people wear religion like a name tag, and they reduce it to bumper stickers. But spirituality is different. It comes from the heart and soul." She expected him to laugh or look at her as if she'd sprouted horns and hooves. He finally surprised her.

"You might be right about that," he said as he rose to his feet. He placed his salad bowl on his plate, gathered his silverware, and walked into the kitchen.

Gabrielle followed and watched him rinse his plate in the sink. She never would have guessed him for the kind of guy who cleaned up after himself. Maybe because he just seemed so macho. Like one of those guys who crushed beer cans on his forehead.

"Tell me something," he said as he turned off the faucet. "Was my arresting you in Julia Davis Park karma?"

She folded her arms beneath her breasts and leaned a hip into the counter beside him. "Nope, I've never done anything bad enough to deserve you."

"Maybe," he said, his voice low and seductive as he looked at her across his shoulder, "I'm your reward for good behavior."

She ignored the shivers running up her spine

as if she were attracted to emotionally barren cops with bad attitudes. Which she wasn't. "Get real. You're about as enlightened as a toadstool," she said and pointed to the pots on the stove. "Aren't you going to do all the dishes?"

"Not a chance. I did all the cooking."

She'd sliced the bread and dressed the salad. He hadn't done *all* the cooking. This was a new century—men like Joe had to step out of the cave and do their share, but she chose not to enlighten him on the subject. "I suppose I'll see you bright and early in the morning then."

"Yep." He shoved a hand into the front pocket of his Levi's and pulled out a set of keys. "But Friday I have to testify in court, so I probably won't be in until after noon sometime."

"I'll be at the Coeur Festival Friday and Saturday."

"That's right. I'll stop by your booth and check up on you."

She'd been looking forward to a break from Joe and the stress he created. "No need."

He glanced up from the keys in his hand and cocked his head to the side. "I'll come by anyway, just so you don't start missing me."

"Joe, I'll miss you about as much as a canker sore."

He chuckled, then turned to the back door. "You better watch out, I hear lying creates bad karma."

*   *   *

Joe's red Bronco rolled into the furthest slot in the parking lot at Albertson's. The four-wheel drive was less than two months old, and he didn't want some kid dinging his doors. It was half past eight, and the setting sun hung just above the mountain peaks surrounding the valley.

There wasn't much activity in the grocery store as Joe rushed inside and grabbed a bag of Sam's favorite baby carrots.

"Hey, is that you, Joe Shanahan?"

Joe looked up from the carrots to a woman loading cabbages into a cart. She was short, petite, and had thick brown hair pulled up into a glossy ponytail on top of her head. She wore very little cosmetics, and she had the kind of pretty face that looked like it had been cleaned to a shine. Her big blue eyes staring at him looked vaguely familiar, and he wondered if he'd ever arrested her.

"It's me. Ann Cameron. We grew up in the same neighborhood. I used to live down the street from your parents. You used to date my older sister, Sherry."

Which, he supposed, was why she looked familiar. In the tenth grade he'd done some pretty heavy groping with Sherry in the backseat of his parents' Chevy Biscayne. She'd been the first girl to let him touch her breasts—under the bra. Naked palm to bare breast. A real milestone for any guy. "Sure, I remember. How are you doing, Ann?"

"I'm good." She tossed a few more cabbages into her cart, then reached for a bag of carrots. "How's your mom and dad?"

"Pretty much the same as always," he answered, eyeing the mound of vegetables in her cart. "Do you have a large family to feed, or do you raise rabbits?"

She laughed and shook her head. "Neither. I'm not married and don't have kids. I own a deli on Eighth, and I ran out of produce today and can't get my next delivery of fresh vegetables until tomorrow afternoon. Too late for my lunch crowd."

"A deli? You must be a good cook, then?"

"I'm a wonderful cook."

He'd heard that same claim about two hours ago from a woman in a silver bikini who'd then disappeared into her bedroom and left him to cook dinner. Then she'd added insult to injury by picking at the meal *he'd* prepared.

"You should come by and let me make you a sandwich, or you can try my pasta. I make a mean shrimp scampi with tender angel-hair. All from scratch, of course. We can catch up on old times."

Joe looked at her clear blue eyes and the dimples denting her cheeks as she smiled up at him. Normal. No signs of craziness, but a guy could never tell at first glance. "Do you believe in karma, auras, and do you listen to Yanni?"

Her smile fell and she gazed at him as if he were nuts. Joe laughed, tossed the bag into the air, and caught it. "Yeah, I'll come by. Where on Eighth?"

Gabrielle considered herself a compulsive cleaner. When the compulsion hit, she cleaned. Unfortunately, the compulsion to clean her closets and cupboards only hit once a year and lasted just a few hours. If she was out of the house when it hit, her closets would have to wait another full year.

She squeezed lemon-scented soap into the sink and filled it with warm water. Maybe after she washed the stroganoff pot, she'd try to work up enough enthusiasm to straighten the cupboards so her colander wouldn't fall out on another guest's foot like it had on Joe's.

Just as she snapped on a pair of yellow rubber gloves, the telephone rang. She picked up on the third ring, and her mother's voice filled her ear.

"How's Beezer?" Claire Breedlove began without a greeting.

Gabrielle glanced over her shoulder at the big ball of fur passed out on the rug by the back door. "Prostrate with joy."

"Good, did she behave herself?"

"Mostly she ate and slept," Gabrielle answered. "Where are you? Here in town?"

"Yolanda and I are with your grandfather. We'll drive to Boise in the morning."

Gabrielle wedged the telephone receiver between her ear and shoulder and asked, "How was Cancún?"

"Oh it was fine, but I have to tell you about what happened. Your aunt and I had to cut the trip short because I've been plagued with a persistent foreboding. I knew a horrible tragedy would befall someone in the neighborhood up here. I felt your grandfather would be involved, so I flew home to warn everyone."

Gabrielle turned her attention to the plates in the sink. Her life was already in cosmic upheaval, and she really wasn't in the mood to travel the Twilight Zone with her mother. "What happened?" she asked, although she knew her mother would tell her anyway.

"Three days ago, while your aunt Yolanda and I were in Mexico, your grandfather ran over Mrs. Youngerman's poodle."

She almost dropped the receiver and had to grab it with a soapy hand. "Oh, no! Not little Murray?"

"Yes, I'm afraid so. Smashed him flatter than a crepe. Sent his soul to poodle paradise, poor thing. I'm not altogether sure it was an accident and neither is Mrs. Youngerman. You know how your grandfather felt about Murray."

Yes, Gabrielle knew how her grandfather felt about the neighbor's dog. Little Murray had not only been a nonstop barker, but he'd been a habitual leg-humper, too. Gabrielle didn't like to think her grandfather would go so far as to purposely run the dog over, but at the same time, Murray had directed his ardent attention to her grandfather's calf on more than one occasion, and she couldn't rule out the possibility.

"That's not all. This afternoon, Yolanda and I paid a condolence visit, and while I was sitting in Mrs. Youngerman's front room, trying to calm her, I felt the space behind my forehead clear. I'm telling you, Gabrielle, it was the strongest clairvoyant vision I've ever had. The vision was so clear to me. I could see the dark curls of hair brushing his ears. He's a tall man . . ."

"Tall, dark, and handsome, huh?" Once again she cradled the telephone between her shoulder and ear, then set to work on the dinner plates.

"Oh, yes. I can't tell you how excited I was."

"Yeah, I'll bet," Gabrielle murmured. She ran the plates under water, then set them in the dish drainer.

"But he isn't for me."

"Bummer. Is he Aunt Yolanda's?"

"He's *your* fate. You're to have a passionate romance with the man in my vision."

"I don't want a romance, Mother," Gabrielle sighed and dropped the salad bowls and tea glasses into the sink. "My life just can't take the excitement right now." She wondered how many mothers predicted passionate lovers for their daughters. Probably not many, she guessed.

"You know you can't wish fate away, Gabrielle," the voice on the other end scolded.

"You can fight it if you choose, but the outcome will always remain the same. I know you don't believe in fate as strongly as I do, and I would never tell you that you're wrong. I've always encouraged you to seek your own spiritual feast, to choose your own path to enlightenment. When you were born . . ."

Gabrielle rolled her eyes. Claire Breedlove had never imposed, dictated, or dominated her daughter. She'd introduced her to the world and insisted Gabrielle choose her own path. For the most part, living with a mother who believed in free love and freedom had been great, but there had been those years in the late seventies and early eighties when Gabrielle had envied children who took nice normal vacations to Disneyland instead of dowsing for Indian relics in Arizona or communing with nature at a clothing optional beach in northern California.

". . . when I was thirty, I was gifted with second sight," Claire continued with her favorite story. "I remember it as if it happened yesterday. As you know, it was during our summer of spiritual awakening, shortly after your father died. I didn't just wake up one morning and choose my psychic ability. I was chosen."

"I know, Mom," she answered as she rinsed the bowls and glasses and set them in the drainer.

"Then you know what I'm telling you isn't something I've made up. I saw him, Gabrielle, and you *will* have a passionate encounter with this man."

"A few months ago that might have been welcome news, but not today," Gabrielle sighed. "I don't think I have the energy for passion."

"I don't think you have a choice. He had a very stubborn look about him. Forceful. He was actually rather frightening. Such intense, dark eyes and such a sensual look about his mouth."

A chill ran up Gabrielle's spine to the base of her neck, and slowly she lowered a pot into the dishwater.

"As I said, I thought he was mine, and I was absolutely thrilled. I mean, it's not every day fate hands a woman my age a young man in tight jeans and a tool belt."

Gabrielle stared at the white bubbles, her throat suddenly dry. "He could be yours."

"No. He looked right through me and whispered your name. There was such unmistakable desire in his voice, I thought I just might faint for the first time in my life."

Gabrielle knew the feeling. She felt faint herself.

"Mrs. Youngerman became so concerned she momentarily forgot all about poor Murray. I'm telling you, dear, I saw your fate. You've been blessed with a passionate lover. He's a marvelous gift."

"But I don't want him. Take him back!"

"I can't take him back, and by the look on his

face, I have a feeling that what you want isn't going to matter."

Ridiculous. Her mother was only right about one thing, Gabrielle didn't believe in fate. If she didn't *choose* to have a passionate affair with a man wearing a tool belt, then she just would *not*.

By the time Gabrielle hung up the telephone, she was numb and a little shaken. Over the years, she'd come to think of her mother's psychic predictions in terms of Pin the Tail on the Donkey. Sometimes her visions were off the wall and headed in the wrong direction, sometimes they were reasonably close, and every now and then she pinned them so accurately it was spooky.

Gabrielle turned back to the sink and reminded herself that her mother had also foretold the reunion of Sonny and Cher, Donald and Ivana, and Bob Dylan and Joan Baez. Obviously, when it came to amorous psychic predictions, Claire didn't have a clue.

This time her mother was off the wall and spinning out of control. Gabrielle didn't want a passionate dark-haired lover. She didn't want to think of Joe Shanahan as anything other than a hard-nosed cop.

But that night she dreamed of him for the first time. She dreamed he came into her bedroom, looking at her through heavy dark eyes, sensuality curving a corner of his mouth, and wearing nothing but his deep red aura. When she woke the next morning, she didn't know whether she'd just had the most erotic dream of her life or experienced her worst nightmare.

Eight

NO DOUBT ABOUT IT. THE DREAM HAD been a nightmare.

The second Joe set foot in Anomaly the next morning, wearing a pair of jeans worn soft in all the right places and a Cactus Bar T-shirt, Gabrielle's whole body flushed. She'd purposely worn her green-and-black lace crinkle dress to work because it was comfortable and cool, but the moment her eyes locked with his, her body temperature shot up and she'd had to go into the bathroom and press cold paper towels to her cheeks. She couldn't even look at him without remembering the way he'd touched her and the things he'd whispered to her in her dream. Things he wanted to do and where he wanted to start.

She tried to keep herself busy and her mind off Joe, but Thursdays were typically slow, and today was no exception. She squeezed drops of orange and rose oil into the defuser and lit the tea candle beneath. Once the store began to fill with the blend of citrus and floral scents, she took apart a display of cut crystal nymphs and butterflies. She dusted and rearranged, and out of the corner of her eye watched him spackle the holes left in the far wall by the shelving system he'd moved the day before. Her gaze moved up his spine to the back of his head, and she remembered the way she'd imagined his hair would feel between her fingers. It had seemed so real, but of course it had only happened in her mind, and she felt silly letting it knock her off balance and letting it affect her in the light of day.

As if he could feel her eyes on him, Joe looked over his shoulder and caught her scrutiny. His watchful gaze stared back, and she quickly turned her attention to a frolicking nymph, but not before her cheeks burned.

As usual, Kevin stayed in the office with the door closed for most of the morning, talking to suppliers or wholesalers or taking care of his other business interests. Thursdays were Mara's day off, so more than likely, Gabrielle knew she would find herself alone with Joe until closing. She took deep controlling breaths and tried not to think of the hours stretching before her. Empty hours. Alone. With Joe.

Over the top of the crystal display case, she watched him dip his putty knife into the tub of spackle and wondered what type of woman attracted the interest of a man like Joe. Beautiful athletic women with hard bodies, or soft women who baked bread and worried about dust bunnies? She was neither.

By ten o'clock, her nerves had calmed to a manageable level. The holes where filled, and she had to think up another job for Joe. They decided on shelves in the back storage room. Nothing complicated. Just three-quarter-inch plywood held in place with heavy L joints.

Since there weren't any customers to worry about, she showed Joe the storage room, which was hardly bigger than the bathroom and had a single sixty-watt bulb hanging from the ceiling. If a customer entered the front of the store, a bell would ring in the back and let her know.

The two of them slid packing boxes and Styrofoam peanuts to one side of the small room. Joe strapped his tool belt low on his hips and handed her one end of the metal tape measure. She knelt down and held it to the corner of the wall.

"Can I ask you a personal question, Joe?"

He knelt on one knee and found the opposite corner with his end of the measure, then he glanced over at her. His gaze never reached her face. It slid up her arm to her breasts and stayed there. Gabrielle looked down at the front of her dress where the bodice fell forward, giving Joe an abundant view of her white cleavage and black lace bra. She placed her free hand on the bodice and straightened.

Without a hint of shame, Joe finally raised his gaze to her face. "You can ask, doesn't mean I'll answer you, though," he said, then wrote something in pencil on the wall.

Gabrielle had caught men staring at her in the past, but at least they'd had the sense to look embarrassed. Not Joe. "Have you ever been married?"

"Nope. I was close once."

"You were engaged?"

"No, but I came close to thinking about it."

She didn't believe *close to thinking about it* counted. "What happened?"

"I got a good look at her mother and ran like hell." He looked over at her again and smiled like he was really funny. "You can let go now," he said, and the measuring tape zipped across the wall, flipped up, and snapped his thumb. "Shit!"

"Oops."

"You did that on purpose."

"You're mistaken. I'm a pacifist, but I did come close to thinking about it." She stood, leaned one shoulder into the wall, and crossed her arms beneath her breasts. "I bet you're one of those really picky guys who wants his wife to cook like Betty Crocker and look like a supermodel."

"She doesn't have to look like a supermodel, just reasonably attractive. And no really long fingernails. Women with those really long fingernails scare me." Again, he smiled at her, this time slow and sexy. "Nothing scarier than seeing those long daggers anywhere near the jewels."

She didn't ask if he was speaking from experience. She really didn't want to know. "But I'm right about the Betty Crocker part, aren't I?"

He shrugged and slid the metal tape up the wall to the ceiling. "It's important to me. I don't like to cook." He paused to read the measurement and wrote it next to the first. "I don't like to shop or clean house or do laundry. The things women don't mind doing."

"Are you serious?" He looked so normal, yet at some point in his life, he'd been mentally stunted. "What makes you think women don't mind doing laundry and cleaning a house? It may surprise you to know that we aren't born with a biological predisposition to wash socks and scrub toilets."

The tape measure slid smoothly back into the metal case, and he hooked it to his belt. "Maybe. All I know is that women don't seem to mind cleaning and laundry as much as men do. Just like men don't mind changing the oil in the car, and women will drive ten miles out of the way to go to a Jiffy Lube."

Of course women went to Jiffy Lube. What kind of weirdo changed his own oil? She shook her head. "I predict you'll be single for a while yet."

"What, are you my psychic friend?"

"No, I don't need to be psychic to know that no woman wants to be your maid for life. Un-

less there is something in it for her," she
amended, thinking of a desperate homeless
woman.

"There is something in it for her." With two
long strides he closed the distance between
them. "Me."

"I was thinking something good."

"I'm good. Real good," he said low enough
so he wouldn't be overheard outside the room.
"Do you want me to show you how good?"

"No." She straightened away from the wall,
and he stood so close she could see the black
rims of his irises.

Joe raised his hand and pushed one side of
her hair behind her ear; his thumb brushed her
cheek. "Your turn."

She shook her head, afraid that if he decided
to show her how good, she wouldn't try all that
hard to stop him. "No, really. I'll take your
word for it."

His quiet laughter filled the small room. "I
meant it's your turn to answer a question."

"Oh," she said and didn't know why she
should feel so disappointed.

"Why is a girl like you still single?"

She wondered what he meant and tried to
summon a bit of indignation, but her response
came out more breathy than offended. "Like
me?"

He slid his thumb across her jaw to her chin,
then brushed her bottom lip. "With your wild
just-got-laid hair, and those big green eyes, you

can make a man forget everything."

The heat of his words settled in the pit of her stomach and weakened her knees. "Like what?"

"Like why it isn't a good idea if I kiss you," he said and slowly lowered his mouth to hers. "All over." His hand caressed her hip, and he pulled her close. The leather pockets of his tool belt pressed into her abdomen. "Like why I'm really here, and why we can't spend the day like we would if you really were my girlfriend." His lips brushed across hers and she opened to him, unable to resist the pull of desire curling her toes. The tip of his tongue touched her own, then he drew it inside his warm mouth. He took his time kissing her, drawing out the pleasure with the slow, lingering caress of his lips and tongue. Even as he pushed her back against the wall, entwined their fingers, and pinned her hands by the side of her head, her moist lips clung to his and his tongue gently plunged inside, then retreated.

Teasing even as he soothed her with his mouth. Her position against the wall arched her back and thrust her breasts into his hard chest. Her nipples drew tight, and when he deepened the kiss, Gabrielle got all squishy inside. Hot liquid pooled low in her abdomen and dragged a moan from deep within her chest. She heard it but barely recognized it as coming from her.

Then she heard something like Joe clearing his throat, but standing within the hypnotic influence of his deep red aura, she wondered how he could clear his throat when his tongue was in her mouth.

"When you get done with the handyman, Gabe, I need you to look over those invoices for that damaged shipment of sushi plates."

Joe pulled back and looked as dazed as she felt. She realized he hadn't spoken at all, and she turned her head just in time to see Kevin walk from the back room toward the front of the store. The bell signaling a customer rang, and if Kevin had a doubt in his mind that Joe was really her boyfriend, he wouldn't now.

Joe stepped back and ran his fingers through the sides of his hair. He let out a breath, and his hands dropped to his sides, his gaze still a bit glazed and bewildered as if he'd been hit over the head by some unseen force. "Maybe you shouldn't wear stuff like that to work."

With desire still rushing through her veins, Gabrielle rocked back on her heels and cast a puzzled glimpse downward at her dress. The hem reached her calves, and the loose bodice showed very little. "This? What's wrong with this?"

He shifted his weight to one foot and crossed his arm over his chest. "It's too sexy."

Astonishment kept her silent for a moment, but when she looked into his eyes and realized he was serious, she burst into laughter. She couldn't help it.

"What's so funny?"

"By no stretch of the imagination would any-one ever consider this dress sexy."

He shook his head. "Maybe it's that black lace bra you're wearing."

"If you hadn't been staring down my dress, you wouldn't know about my bra."

"And if you hadn't been showing me, I wouldn't have been looking."

"Showing you?" Anger cooled any lingering desire, and she no longer thought there was anything amusing about the situation. "Are you saying that the sight of a black bra makes you lose control?"

"Normally no." He looked her up and down. "What's in that stuff you were burning earlier?"

"Orange and rose oil."

"Nothing else?"

"No. Why?"

"Anything mind altering in all those weird little bottles you carry around with you? Spells or voodoo or something?"

"You think that you kissed me because of some sort of voodoo oil?"

"Makes sense."

It was beyond ridiculous. She leaned forward and poked his chest with her index finger. "Were you dropped on your head as a child?" She poked him again. "Is that your problem?"

He unfolded his arms and grasped her hand in his hot palm. "I thought you were a pacifist."

"I am, but you've just pushed me past my . . ." Gabrielle paused and listened to the voices coming from the front. They moved toward the back room, and she didn't need to see them to know who'd walked into the store.

"Gabe is back here with her boyfriend," Kevin said.

"Boyfriend? Gabrielle didn't mention a boyfriend when I spoke to her last night."

Gabrielle tugged her hand from Joe's grasp, took a step back, and quickly studied him from head to toe. He stood before her looking exactly as her mother had described. Stubborn and determined and sensual. The jeans and tool belt were like a neon sign. "Quick," she whispered, "give me that tool belt."

"What?"

"Just do it." Without the tool belt, maybe her mother wouldn't confuse Joe for the man in her vision. "Hurry."

His hands lowered to the front of his jeans, and he unbuckled the wide leather belt. Slowly, he handed it over and asked, "Anything else?"

Gabrielle snatched it from him and tossed it behind a box in the corner. It hit the wall hard, and she spun around in time to see her mother, Aunt Yolanda, and Kevin walk into the back. She stepped out of the storage room and pinned a smile on her face. "Hi," she said as if nothing was out of the ordinary. As if she hadn't been making out with a dark, passionate lover.

Joe watched Gabrielle's straight shoulders as she moved from the small room. He quickly turned his back to the doorway and took a moment to rearrange himself. He didn't care what she said, there had to be some sort of mind-altering aphrodisiac in that stuff she burned all the time. It was the only explanation for why he'd completely lost his mind.

When he stepped from the storage room, he didn't recognize the women with Kevin, but the taller of the two bore a striking resemblance to Gabrielle. She wore her long auburn hair parted in the middle and pulled back on the sides, held in place with thin strips of beaded leather.

"Joe," Gabrielle said, looking across her shoulder at him, "this is my mother, Claire, and my aunt, Yolanda."

Joe offered his hand to Gabrielle's mother and found it clenched in a tight grasp. "It's nice to meet you," he said as he gazed into blue eyes drilling him as if she could see through his forehead.

"I've met you before," she informed him.

No way. Joe would have remembered meeting this woman. There was a strange intensity about her that he wouldn't have forgotten. "I think you may have me confused with someone else. I don't believe we've met."

"Oh, you didn't meet me," she added as if that cleared up the mystery.

"Mother, please."

Claire turned his hand over and stared at his palm. "Just as I suspected. Look at this line, Yolanda."

Gabrielle's aunt stepped close and bent her

blond head over Joe's palm. "Very stubborn." She raised her soft brown gaze to him, then looked sadly at Gabrielle and shook her head. "Are you sure about this man, dear?"

Gabrielle groaned, and Joe tried to pull his hand from Claire's grasp. He had to tug twice before she finally released him.

"When were you born, Joe?" Claire asked.

He didn't want to answer. He didn't believe in all that zodiac crap, but as she stared at him with that spooky gaze, the hair on the back of his neck stood up, and he opened his mouth and admitted, "May first."

Now it was Claire's turn to look at her daughter and shake her head. "And a Taurus to boot." Then she directed her attention to Yolanda. "Very earthy. Loves good food and good love. Taureans are the zodiac's sensualists."

"True hedonists. Great endurance, and relentless when focusing on a certain goal or task," Yolanda added to the list. "He's very possessive of his mate and protective of offspring."

Kevin laughed, and Gabrielle's lips pursed. If the two women hadn't been discussing him as if he were potential stud service, Joe might have laughed too. Gabrielle obviously didn't see any humor in the situation, but she couldn't exactly inform her mother and aunt that he wasn't her boyfriend. Not with Kevin standing so near. Joe couldn't do much to help her out, but he might have tried to change the subject if she hadn't opened her mouth and insulted him.

"Joe is *not* the dark, passionate lover that you think he is," she said. "Just take my word on this."

Joe was fairly certain he was a passionate guy. He was fairly certain he was a good lover, too. He'd never had any complaints. She just might as well have come right on out and accused him of being a lousy lay. He slid his arm around her waist and kissed her temple. "Careful or you'll give me performance anxiety," he said, then he chuckled as if even the thought of performing badly was ridiculous. "Gabrielle's a little mad at me for suggesting that cleaning house and cooking is women's work."

"And you're still breathing?" Kevin asked. "I suggested she be in charge of cleaning the bathroom here at work because she's a girl, and I thought she would deck me."

"Naw, she's a pacifist," Joe assured Kevin. "Aren't you, sweet cheeks?"

The look she turned on him was anything but nonviolent. "I'm always willing to make exceptions for you."

He squeezed her tight against him and said, "That's what a man likes to hear from his woman." Then before she could utter a word and accuse him again of being a demon from hell, he pressed his mouth to hers, trapping her anger with his kiss. Her eyes widened, then narrowed, and she raised her hands to his shoulders. Before she could shove him away, he let her go, and her attempt to push him looked more like a grasp to keep him close. He smiled, and, for a few brief seconds, he thought her resentment might overcome her belief in nonviolence. But being the true pacifist she professed, she took a deep breath and slowly let it out. Then she turned her attention to her mother and aunt and ignored him completely.

"Did you come to take me to lunch?" she asked.

"It's only ten-thirty."

"Brunch then," she amended. "I want to hear all about your vacation."

"We need to pick up Beezer," Claire said, then looked at Joe. "Of course you're invited. Yolanda and I need to check your life energy."

"We should test him with your new aurameter," Yolanda added. "I think it's more accurate than—"

"I'm sure Joe would rather stay here and work," Gabrielle interrupted. "He loves his job. Don't you?"

Aurameter? Jesus H. The nut didn't fall far from the family tree. "That's right. But thank you, Claire. Maybe another time."

"Count on it. Fate has given you someone very special, and I am here to make sure you take care of her gentle spirit," she said, her gaze so directed the hair on the back of his neck stood up again. She opened her mouth to say more, but Gabrielle took her arm and walked with her toward the front of the store.

"You know I don't believe in fate," Joe heard

Gabrielle saying. "Joe is not my fate."

Kevin shook his head and let out a low whistle once the door shut behind all three women. "You barely dodged that bullet, my friend. Gabe's mother and aunt are real nice ladies, but sometimes when they get to talking, I expect to see their heads spinning like Linda Blair in *The Exorcist.*"

"That bad, huh?"

"Yeah, I think they channel Elvis, too. Magnify Gabrielle by about a thousand, and you get her relatives."

For once he didn't think Kevin was lying. He turned to the fenceman and slapped him on the back as if they were old buddies. "She might have weird relatives, but she has great legs," he said. Time to get to work. Time to remember he wasn't there to pin his confidential informant against the wall and feel her soft body pressed to his, making him so hard that he forgot everything but her breasts poking his chest and the sweet taste of her mouth. Time to befriend Kevin, then nail him for the theft of Mr. Hillard's Monet.

The next morning Detective Joe Shanahan walked into Fourth District Court, raised his right hand, and swore to tell the truth, in *The State v. Ron and Don Kaufusi.* The Kaufusi boys were three-time losers facing a long stint in prison if found guilty of a string of residential burglaries. The case had been one of the first

assigned to Joe shortly after he'd been transferred to property crimes.

He took his seat in the witness box and
calmly straightened his tie. He answered questions from the prosecutor and the boys' public
defender, and if Joe hadn't already had a prej-
udice against defense attorneys, he might have
actually felt sorry for the lawyer assigned this
case. It was a real slam dunk.

Seated behind the defense table, the Kaufusis
looked like sumo wrestlers, but Joe knew from
past experience that the brothers had balls of
steel and were as loyal as Old Yeller. They'd
conducted a real gutsy operation for several
months before being arrested exiting a home on
Harrison Boulevard. Every few weeks, the boys
would park a stolen U-Haul next to the back
door of a particular home they'd cased. They'd
load the truck with valuables like precious
coins, stamp collections, and antiques. In one
instance, the neighbors across the street had
watched, believing the brothers were professional movers.

When Don had been searched, the arresting
officer had found a Wonder Bar in the pocket
of his twill work pants. The tool's distinctive
marks had matched a dozen others left in
wooden door and window casements throughout the city. The prosecutor's office had gathered enough direct and circumstantial evidence
to put the brothers away for a long time, and
yet they'd refused to name their fence in

exchange for leniency. Some might believe their unwillingness to cooperate had something to do with honor among thieves, but Joe didn't think so. He figured it probably had more to do with good business. The relationship between thief and fence was symbiotic. One parasite fed off the other parasite to survive. The brothers were betting on a short prison stay and already planning their return to business. It didn't pay to alienate a good fence.

Joe testified for two hours, and when he was through, he felt like raising his fists over his head like a prize fighter. The odds were in his favor, and the good guys were going to win this round. In a world where the bad guys were winning with more and more frequency, it was good to take a few of them off the streets for a while. Two down and two thousand more to go.

He walked from the courtroom with a slight smile on his face and shoved his sunglasses onto the bridge of his nose. He moved from the recycled courtroom air and out into the sunlight. An endless blue sky and cotton-ball clouds hung over his head as he drove to his house off Hill Road. The ranch-style home had been built in the fifties, and in the five years he'd lived there, he'd replaced the carpeting and vinyl throughout. Now all he had to do was rip out the olive green tub in one of the bathrooms, and he figured he was done for awhile. He liked the creak of the floors and the worn bricks in the raised hearth. Mostly, he liked the lived-in character of his house.

The minute Joe walked in the front door, Sam flapped his wings and whistled like a cat-calling construction worker.

"You need a girlfriend," he told his bird as he let him out of his cage. He walked into the bedroom to change his clothes, and Sam followed.

"You, behave," the bird screeched from his perch on Joe's chest of drawers.

Joe shrugged out of his suit, and his mind turned to the who-what-where-when-and-whys of the Hillard case. He wasn't any closer to an arrest, but yesterday hadn't been a complete bust. He'd learned the why. He'd learned what motivated Kevin Carter. He'd learned how much Kevin had resented being from a large family. And even more, how much he'd resented the hell out of growing up poor.

"You behave."

"You need to take your own advice, buddy." Joe tucked a blue T-shirt into the waistband of his Levi's and glanced up at Sam. "I'm not the one who bites wood or pulls out my feathers when I get mad," he said, then pulled on a New York Rangers baseball cap to cover his hair. He never knew when he would run into someone he'd arrested in the past, especially at something as weird as the Coeur Festival.

It was close to one o'clock when he left his house, and he made one quick stop on the way to the park. He stopped at Ann's Eighth Street Deli. Ann stood behind the counter; a warm smile lit her face as she looked up and saw him. "Hi, Joe. I was hoping you'd come in."

The way she looked at him, he couldn't help but return her smile. "I told you I would." He liked the spark of interest shining in her eyes. A nice *normal* spark. The kind a woman showed a man she wanted to know better.

He ordered a ham and salami on white bread, and since he didn't know what a lapsed vegetarian would eat, he ordered Gabrielle a turkey on whole wheat—lots of sprouts.

"When I called my sister, Sherry, last night and told her that I'd run into you, she said she thought you were a cop. Is that right?" she asked as she sliced the bread and placed a heap of meat on each slice.

"I'm a property crimes detective."

"I'm not surprised. Sherry said you used to like to frisk her in the ninth grade."

"I thought it was the tenth."

"Nope." She wrapped the sandwiches and placed them in a paper sack. "Do you want any salad or chips?"

Joe stepped back and looked into the long display case filled with different kinds of salads and desserts. "What's good?"

"It's all good. I just made it this morning. How about some cheesecake?"

"I don't know." He slid a twenty from his

wallet and handed it to her. "I'm pretty particular about my cheesecake."

"I'll tell you what," she said and opened the cash register. "I'll give you a few slices, and if you like it, you come back tomorrow and buy me a cup of coffee on my break."

"When's your break?"

Her smile once again lit her eyes, and dimples creased her cheeks. "Ten-thirty," she answered and handed him his change.

He had to work at ten. "Make it nine."

"Okay." She opened the glass case and cut two slices of cheesecake and wrapped them in waxed paper. "It's a date."

He wouldn't go that far. But she was nice and could obviously cook. She certainly didn't look at him as if the only thing saving him from a good sock in the gut was her belief in nonviolence. He watched her place the cake and two plastic forks on top of the sandwiches, then she handed him the sack.

"See you in the morning, Joe."

Maybe Ann was just what he needed.

Nine

 THIRTY STRIPED CANOPIES LINED A SEC-
tion of Julia Davis Park near the band
shell. A knot of impromptu musicians sat cross-
legged beneath a towering oak, beating their
steady fingers against the tight skin of bongos.
They were joined by several pan flutists and a
small group of nomadic bus dwellers coaxing
haunting strains from handmade instruments.
Barefoot dancers swayed, their gauze skirts and
long braids swirling to the hypnotic pulse,
while white bread America watched from the
sidelines looking a bit perplexed.

At the Coeur Festival, you could buy healing
crystals and books on the art of seeing. Get your
palm read, your life charted, and past lives in-
terpreted. The food booths offered such organic
delights as vegetarian tacos, veggie stir-fry, chili
con veggie, and bean loaf with peanut sauce.

Gabrielle's booth sat between Mother Soul,
the spiritual healer, and Organic Dan, master
herbalist. The festival was a blend of New Age

spirituality and commerce, and Gabrielle had dressed for the occasion in a white sleeveless peasant blouse, embroidered with gold sunburst and unicorns and tied beneath her breasts. The matching skirt rode low on her hips and buttoned up the front. She'd left it unbuttoned from her knees to her ankles, and she'd slipped her feet into a pair of handmade leather sandals. She'd left her hair down, and the thin gold hoops in her ears matched the ring in her navel. Her outfit reminded her a little of the short time she'd taken up belly dancing.

Her essential oils and aromatherapies were selling even better than she'd hoped. So far, her biggest sellers were her medicinal oils, with her massage oils coming in a close second. Directly across from Gabrielle's booth was a woman who did mendi, and next to her, Doug Tano, the colon hydrotherapist.

Unfortunately for Gabrielle, Doug wasn't in his booth. He was in hers, regaling her with the benefits of colonic hydrotherapy. Gabrielle prided herself on her open mind. She was enlightened. She understood and accepted other people's beliefs in different metaphysical plains. She supported unorthodox healing arts and therapies, but geez, discussing *waste material* was beyond her range of comfort and bordered the realm of gross.

"You should come in and get cleansed," he told her as she straightened small bottles of beauty and bath oils.

"I just don't see that I would have the time."
Nor could she ever see herself making the time.
As a job, she'd rank colon cleaning in the same
ballpark as being a mortician. One of those jobs
she supposed someone had to do but thanked
her lucky karma that it wasn't her.

"You can't put off something so important,"
he said, kind of reminding her of a mortician,
too. His voice was a bit too tranquil, his fingernails a little too polished, and his skin a lot too
pale. "I'm telling you, you feel so much lighter
once all those toxins are expelled."

She was going to take his word for it. "Oh,
yeah?" was all she managed, then pretended
great interest in her aromatherapies. "I think
someone is at your booth," she said, so desperate to get rid of him she lied on purpose.

"No, they're just walking by."

Out of the corner of her eye, a brown paper
sack was plopped down next to her crystal va-
porizers. "I made lunch," spoke a deep voice
she'd never thought she'd actually be glad to
hear. "Are you hungry?"

She let her gaze travel up Joe's plain white T-
shirt, past the hollow of his tan throat, to the
deep furrow of his top lip. The shadow of a red-
and-blue baseball cap covered the top half of
his face, accentuating the carnal lines of his
mouth. After her conversation with Doug, she
was surprised she was hungry. "Starved," she
answered and turned to the man standing beside her. "Joe, this is Doug Tano. Doug has the

booth over there." She pointed across the walk-way and couldn't help but notice the obvious difference in the two men. Doug was a calm soul in touch with his spiritual nature. Joe ra-diated raw, masculine energy and was about as calming as a nuclear blast.

Joe glanced over his shoulder, then turned his attention to Doug. "Colonic hydrotherapy? Is that you?"

"Yes. My practice is off Sixth. I aid in weight loss, detoxification of the body, improving di-gestion, and increasing energy levels. Hydro-therapy has a very calming effect on the body."

"Uh-huh. Don't you have to get a hose shoved up your butt?"

"Well, ahh . . . ahh," Doug stammered. "*Shoved* is an awfully strong word. We do place a very soft, malleable tube—"

"I'm going to have to stop you there, buddy," Joe interrupted and held up one hand. "I'm about to eat lunch, and I really do want to enjoy my ham and salami."

Disapproval pinched Doug's features. "Have you ever seen what processed meat does to your colon?"

"Nope," Joe answered as he dug around in the sack. "I figure the only way I'm ever going to see the inside of my colon is to shove my head up my ass. And you know what, Doug? That's just never going to happen."

Gabrielle felt her jaw drop a little. He was so rude . . . even for Joe . . . yet so effective. Doug turned and practically ran from her booth to get away from him. And although she hated to admit it, she was grateful and even a bit envious.

"Jesus, I didn't think he was ever going to leave."

"Thank you, I guess," she uttered. "He wouldn't stop talking about my colon, and I couldn't get rid of him."

"That's because he wants to see your naked tush." Joe grabbed her hand and slapped a sandwich wrapped in waxed paper into her palm. "Can't say that I blame him."

He walked past her to the back of the booth and sat in one of the two director's chairs she'd brought from home. She wasn't sure, but she thought he'd just given her a compliment.

"Is Mara going to help you out today?" he asked.

"She'll be here in just a little bit." Gabrielle looked at the sandwich in her hand. "What's this?"

"Turkey on whole wheat."

She sat in the seat next to him and glanced about. "I guess you didn't know," she said just above a whisper, "but the Coeur Festival is vegetarian."

"I thought you were lapsed."

"I am." She opened the waxed paper and gazed at a huge mound of turkey and sprouts shoved between two pieces of soft bread. Her stomach growled and her mouth watered, and she felt guilty and conspicuous, like a heretic at a born-again revival.

Joe knocked her arm with his elbow. "Go ahead. I won't tell anybody," he said as if he were Satan offering her original sin.

Gabrielle closed her eyes and sank her teeth into the sandwich. Since Joe had been uncharacteristically nice and brought her lunch, it would be impolite not to eat. She'd left her house that morning without eating breakfast, and she really was starving. So far, she just hadn't been able to work up an appetite for chili con veggie. She sighed, and her lips curved into a blissful smile.

"Hungry?"

She opened her eyes. "Mmm-hmm."

He stared at her from beneath the bill of his cap, watching her as he slowly chewed, then swallowed. "There's some cheesecake if you want it."

"You bought me cheesecake?" She was surprised and more than a little touched by his thoughtfulness.

He shrugged. "Yeah, sure. Why not?"

"Because I didn't think you liked me."

His gaze lowered to her mouth. "You're okay." He took a big bite of his sandwich, then turned his attention to the crowded park. Gabrielle grabbed two bottles of water from a small cooler next to her chair and handed one to Joe. He took it from her, and they ate in companionable silence. She was surprised she didn't feel a need to fill up the quiet with conversation. She felt comfortable sitting beside Joe, eating her turkey, not talking, and that surprised her even more.

She kicked off her sandals and crossed her legs, settling back to watch the crowd flowing past her booth. It was a real mix of everything from Benetton preppies to Birkenstock New Agers, from polyester-loving retirees, to Woodstock wanna-bes born the same year as disco fever. And for the first time since Joe had tackled her in the park not far from where they sat now, she wondered what he saw when he looked at her. Some of the other vendors were extremely bizarre looking, and she wondered if he saw her that way, too. Like Mother Soul, with her tangle of dreadlocks, nose ring, and bright robes meditating on her prayer rug. And she wondered why she should care what he thought.

Gabrielle was full halfway through the huge sandwich, so she wrapped the other half back up, then set it on top of a block of ice in her cooler. "I didn't think I'd see you today," she said, finally breaking the silence. "I thought you'd be at my store, keeping your eyes on Kevin."

"I'll go there in just a bit." He polished off the last of his sandwich and washed it down with half his water. "Kevin isn't going anywhere, but even if he does, I'll know about it."

The police were following Kevin. She didn't

think they'd told her that, but she supposed she wasn't surprised. She picked at the label on her bottle and watched him out of the corner of her eye. "What are you going to do today? Finish the shelves in the storage room?" By closing time the day before, he'd cut the shelves and screwed the brackets to the wall. All he had to do was put the shelves in place. That wouldn't take long.

"I'm going to paint them first, but I should be finished by the end of the day. I need something to do tomorrow."

"What about a countertop in the back room? Kevin mentioned that he wouldn't mind seeing it replaced, and a job like that ought to last through Monday."

"Hopefully, Kevin will make his move this weekend, and I won't be there Monday."

Gabrielle's fingers stilled. "Maybe we shouldn't talk about this. You still think Kevin is guilty, and I don't."

"I'd rather not talk about Kevin right now anyway." He raised the water and squirted a stream into his mouth. When he was finished he sucked a bead of water off his lower lip and said, "I have a few important questions I want to ask you."

She should have suspected he'd been nice to her because he wanted something. "What?"

"Where did you get that Barbara Eden, I Dream of Jeannie, outfit?"

She glanced downward at her little blouse

and bare middle. "That's one of your important questions?"

"No, I was just curious."

Since his gaze was directed at her stomach, she couldn't tell what he was thinking. "You don't like it?"

"I didn't say that." He looked into her face, his cop's eyes carefully blank, and she still couldn't tell what he thought. "After you left the store yesterday," he continued, "what did you tell your mother and aunt about me?"

"I told them the truth." She crossed her arms beneath her breasts and watched him show his displeasure the usual way. He scowled at her.

"You told them about me being an under-cover cop?"

"Yep, but they won't say anything to any-one," she assured him. "They promised, and be-sides, they believe fate brought us together. They don't mess with fate." She'd tried to tell Claire that Joe wasn't the dark passionate lover of her psychic vision, that he was really just a bad-tempered detective. But the more she'd ex-plained, the more her mother had become convinced that fate had indeed played a role in Gabrielle's love life. After all, Claire had rea-soned, getting tailed, tackled, and forced to play girlfriend to a macho undercover police officer like Joe just wasn't a normal event, not even in the universal course of cosmic coincidence. "Anything else you want to know?" she asked.

"Yeah. How did you know I was following

you last week? And don't give me a bunch of crap about feeling my vibes."

"I don't feel *vibes*. What if I told you it was your black aura?" she asked, although truthfully, she hadn't noticed his aura until after he'd arrested her.

From within the shadow of his cap, his eyes narrowed, and Gabrielle decided to let him off the hook. "It was easy. You smoke. I don't know of any joggers who have a nice healthy cigarette before they set off on a run. Wheat grass, yes. A Marlboro, no."

"I'll be damned."

"The first time I noticed you, you were standing under a tree, smoke surrounding your head like a mushroom cloud."

Joe crossed his arms over his chest, and his mouth settled into a grim line. "Do me a favor, will you? If anyone asks how you detected your surveillance, stick to that black aura thing."

"Why? Don't you want the other cops to know a cigarette blew your cover?"

"Not if I can help it."

She tilted her head to one side and gave him a smile she hoped made him nervous. "Okay, I'll help you out, but you owe me."

"What do you want?"

"I don't know yet. I'll think about it and get back to you."

"My other informants always knew what they wanted."

"What did they want?"

"Usually something illegal." His eyes stared into hers as he said, "Like for me to make their criminal record disappear or look the other way while they smoked a doobie."

"You'd do that?"

"No, but you can ask. It would give me a reason to frisk you." Now it was his turn to smile. And he did. A lazy turn of his lips that made her stomach flutter. He lowered his gaze to her mouth, then let it slide right on down the front of her blouse. "Maybe even force me to strip-search you."

The breath caught in her lungs. "You wouldn't do that."

"Of course I would." His gaze slipped down the row of buttons, lingered on her navel, then lowered to her skirt and the split riding up her left thigh. "I took a solemn oath. I've a sworn duty to protect and serve and strip-search. It's my job."

The flutter in her stomach turned hot. She'd never been a good flirt, but she couldn't help asking, "And are you good at your job?"

"Very."

"You sound pretty confident."

"Let's just say I stay at it until business is taken care of."

She could feel herself melt, and it had nothing to do with the temperature outside the booth. "What business?"

He leaned toward her and said in a low voice that poured across her skin and raised her temperature a few more degrees, "Whatever blows your hair back, honey."

She quickly stood and smoothed the crinkles in her skirt. "I have to . . ." She pointed to the front of her booth, confused. Her body was at war with her mind and spirit. Her physical desire was fighting for dominance over reason. Anarchy. "I'll just—" She moved to a table of massage oil and straightened a neat little row of blue bottles. She didn't want anarchy. One emotion ruling the others wasn't good. No, it was bad. Real bad. She didn't want to feel her skin tingle, her stomach flutter, and her breath catch. Not now. Not in the middle of the park. Not with *him*.

Several college-aged girls approached the table and asked Gabrielle questions about her oils. She answered and explained and tried to pretend she didn't feel Joe's presence as strongly as if he were touching her. She sold two bottles of jasmine and felt, rather than saw, him come to stand behind her.

"Do you want me to leave your cheesecake?"

She shook her head.

"I'll put it in the refrigerator at your shop."

She thought he would leave then, but he didn't. Instead, he slid one hand around her waist to her bare stomach and pulled her back against his chest. Gabrielle froze.

He turned his face into her hair and spoke next to her ear. "See that guy in the red tank top and green shorts?"

She glanced across the walkway to Mother Soul's booth. The man in question looked like a lot of the other men at the festival. Clean. Normal. "Yes."

"That's Ray Klotz. He has a pawn shop off Main. I arrested him last year for receiving and selling stolen VCRs." He spread his fingers wide over her abdomen, and his thumb brushed the knot in her blouse just below her breasts. "Ray and I go back a long way, and it might be better if he doesn't see me with you."

She tried to think past the brush of his fingers on her bare flesh but found it difficult. "Why? Do you think he knows Kevin?"

"Probably."

She turned, and without her shoes, the top of her head fit just beneath the bill of his cap. His arms slid to her back and held her so close that his nose touched hers and her breasts brushed his chest. "Are you sure he'd remember you?"

His free hand slipped up her arm to just past her elbow. "When I worked narcotics, I popped him on a drug charge. I had to shove my fingers down his throat and make him puke up the cocaine-filled condoms he'd swallowed," he said, his fingers brushing up and down her spine.

"Oh," she whispered. "That's disgusting."

"It was evidence," he spoke just above her mouth. "Couldn't let a guy get away with my evidence."

Standing so close to him, smelling his skin,

the rich timbre of his voice filling her head, he sounded so reasonable. Like making a guy throw up was normal. Like his hot palm on her bare skin had no effect on him. "Is he gone?"

"No."

She stared into his eyes and asked, "What are you going to do?"

Instead of answering, he took a few steps backward into the shadow of the booth, pulling her with him. He raised his gaze to her hair. "What am I going to do about what?"

"About Ray."

"He'll move on." He looked into her eyes, and his fingers stroked the small of her back. "If I kiss you, are you going to take it personal?"

"Yes. Won't you?"

"No." He shook his head, and his lips brushed across hers. "It's part of my job."

She held herself still to keep from melting into the warm, solid wall of his chest. "Kissing me is your job?"

"Yes."

"Like strip searches?"

"Uh-huh."

"Won't that draw Ray's attention to you?"

"Depends," he said against her mouth. "Are you going to moan?"

"No." His heart beat heavy against her breasts, and she placed her hands on his shoulders and felt the hard muscles beneath her palms. Her spiritual balance teetered in favor of falling headfirst into the desire robbing her of self-control and making her weak. "Are you going to moan?"

"I just might." He softly kissed her mouth, then said, "You taste good, Gabrielle Breedlove."

She had to remind herself that the man holding her within his strong embrace was as enlightened as a pet rock. He wasn't her soul's mate. He wasn't even close. But he tasted good.

His mouth opened over hers, and he slipped his tongue inside. She didn't moan, but she wanted to. Her fingers curled into T-shirt and flesh, and she held on to him. He tilted his head to one side and delved deeper into her mouth. His palm slid to her side, and he stroked her bare ribs and sunk his thumb into her navel. And just as she was about to sink into the kiss and stay there awhile, he pulled back and dropped his hands to his sides.

"Ah shit," he whispered next to her left ear.

"Joey, is that you?"

"What are you doing, Joey?" a female voice asked from somewhere behind Gabrielle.

"Looks like he's making out with a girl."

"Who?"

"I didn't know he had a girlfriend. Did you, Ma?"

"No. He never said anything to me."

Joe whispered next to Gabrielle's ear. "Just go along with whatever I say, and maybe we'll survive without them picking out china and making our wedding plans."

Gabrielle turned and looked into five pairs of brown eyes staring back at her with obvious interest. The women were surrounded by a group of smiling, giggling children, and she didn't know whether to laugh or hide.

"Who's your girlfriend, Joey?"

She glanced across her shoulder at the man by her side. *Joey?* Deep grooves bracketed his mouth, while a sort of weird déjà vu feeling raised the hair on the back of her arms. Only this time he wasn't meeting *her* family. She was meeting his. If Gabrielle believed in fate, she might have thought her mother was right, that this was just too big to be cosmic coincidence. No, she didn't believe in fate, but she couldn't think of any other explanation for the freaky turns in her life since she'd met Joe.

After several prolonged seconds, Joe took a long-suffering breath and made the introductions. "Gabrielle," he began, "this is my mother, Joyce." He pointed to an older woman wearing a T-shirt with Betty Boop's head stuck on Rambo's body. Across Betty's headband were written the words Rambo Boop. "These are my sisters, Penny, Tammy, Tanya, and Debby."

"I'm here too, Uncle Joey."

"Me, too."

"And these are most of my nieces and nephews," he said, checking them off with his index finger. "Eric, Tiffany, Sara, Jeremy, Little Pete, and Christy. There are four more someplace."

"They're either at the mall or playing basket-ball at the church," one of the sisters explained.

Gabrielle looked at Joe, then back at his family. There were more? The group before her was overwhelming enough. "How many are there of you all?"

"I have five children," Joyce answered. "And ten grandchildren. Of course that will change when Joey marries and gives me a few more." She took a small step back and looked at the table filled with small bottles. "What are these?"

"Gabrielle makes some sort of oils," he answered.

"I make essential oils and aromatherapies," she corrected. "I sell them in my shop."

"Where's your shop?"

"You wouldn't be able to find it," Joe answered before she could open her mouth, as if he feared what she might say.

One of the sisters picked up a bottle of ginger and cedarwood. "Are these aphrodisiacs?"

Gabrielle smiled. It was time she helped Detective Shanahan's karma pay him a visit. "A few of my massage oils have the chemical characterstics of aphrodisiacs. The one you have in your hand drives Joe *wild*." She wrapped her arm around his waist and snuggled close. She was definitely going to enjoy watching him squirm for a change. "Isn't that right . . . sweet cheeks?"

His gaze narrowed, and her smile brightened.

The sister set the bottle back down and winked at Joe. "How long have you two known each other?"

"A few days," he said, giving the back of her hair a slight tug, which she supposed was meant to remind her to let him do the talking.

The sisters glanced at each other. "It looked like more than a few days to me. That was a serious kiss. Did it look like a serious kiss to you?"

All the sisters nodded to each other. "It looked like he was trying to eat her whole. I'd say that was a kiss a man gives after three weeks. Definitely more than a few days."

Gabrielle laid her head against Joe's and confided, "Well, we may have known each other in a previous life."

The women in his family just stared.

"She's kidding you," he assured them.

"Oh."

"When you were over at the house the other day," his mother began, "you didn't mention a girlfriend. You never said anything."

"Gabrielle is just a friend," Joe informed his family. He gave her hair another slight tug. "Isn't that right?"

She leaned back, purposely gave him a blank look, then said, "Oh! Oh, yeah. That's right."

His brows lowered, and he warned the women in front of him, "Don't get ideas."

"Ideas about what?" one of the sisters asked, her eyes wide and innocent.

"About me getting married anytime soon."

"You're thirty-five."

"At least he likes girls. We used to worry that he was going to turn out gay."

"He used to put on Mom's red heels and pretend he was Dorothy from *The Wizard of Oz*."

"Remember when he skipped into the wall and had to have stitches in his forehead."

"That was hysterical."

"Jesus, I was five," he gritted through his teeth. "And you girls made me dress up like Dorothy."

"He loved it."

"Girls, you're embarrassing your brother," Joyce admonished.

Gabrielle removed her arm from around Joe's waist and hung her wrist over his shoulder. Beneath his tan skin, his cheeks were suspiciously red, and she tried not to laugh. "And now that you're no longer a cross-dresser in red heels, you're a good catch?"

"And now that he isn't getting shot at anymore," a sister added.

"He's a great guy."

"Loves children."

"And pets."

"He's really good to his bird."

"He's pretty handy with tools."

As if so much praise could not go unpunished, one sister turned to the others and shook her head. "No he's not. Remember when he took apart my Paula Pitter Pat to see what made her walk?"

"That's right. He never could get that one leg back on. She'd just fall on her side and wiggle."

"Yeah, Paula couldn't pitter-pat after that."

"Well," a sister said above the rest, reminding them all they were supposed to be selling Joe's better qualifications, "he does his own wash."

"That's right, and he doesn't turn his socks pink anymore."

"He makes decent money."

"And he—"

"I have all my teeth," Joe interrupted, grinding out the words. "I don't have hair on my back, and I can still get a hard-on."

"Joseph Andrew Shanahan," his mother gasped and covered the ears of the closest child.

"Don't you women have someone else to bother?" he asked.

"We better go. We've made him cranky." As if the sisters didn't want to jinx a good thing, they quickly herded their children and said their good-byes practically on top of each other.

"It was nice to meet all of you," Gabrielle told them just before they moved deeper into the park.

"Have Joe bring you to dinner sometime next week," Joyce got in before she too walked away.

"What was that about?" he asked. "Were you getting even with me for yesterday?"

She dropped her hand from his shoulder and

rocked back on her heels. "Oh, just a little bit."

"How does it feel?"

"I hate to admit it, but it feels really good, Joe. In fact, I never thought revenge could actually feel this good."

"Well, enjoy it while it lasts." Now it was his turn to smile. "Paybacks are a bitch."

Ten

JOE WATCHED HIS SISTERS AND MOTHER quickly disappear into the crowd, and his brows drew together. They'd let him off easy. Usually, when he got "cranky" they went in for the kill. He didn't know why they hadn't dragged out any more tired remember-when stories, but he suspected it had to do with the woman by his side. His family obviously believed Gabrielle really was his girlfriend, no matter what he'd said about it, and they'd fallen over each other to make him seem like a real good catch in her eyes. Which surprised him, when he considered that just one look at Gabrielle should have been enough to convince his family that she wasn't his type of woman.

He glanced at her, at her beautiful face, her wild hair, and smooth bare stomach that made him want to fall to his knees and press his open mouth to her flat belly. She'd wrapped her gorgeous body up in an outfit he could easily shred with his hands, and he wondered if she'd done it on purpose just to drive him crazy.

"You have a nice family."

"They weren't being nice." He shook his head. "They were just tricking you into thinking they're nice in case you're their future sister-in-law."

"Me?"

"Don't be too flattered. They'd be happy with just about any woman. Why do you think they said all that stuff about me loving children and pets?"

"Oh!" Gabrielle made her big green eyes go all wide with surprise. "Was that you? Except for the cranky part, I didn't know who they were talking about."

He grabbed the paper sack he'd brought from the deli. "Be nice or I'll tell Doug you want your colon cleansed."

Soft laughter spilled from her lips, catching him by surprise. He'd never heard her genuine laughter before, and the feminine sound was all sweet and breathy and so pleasant it curved the corners of his lips into an unexpected smile. "See you tomorrow morning."

"I'll be here."

Joe turned and wove his way through the festival to the lot where he'd parked his car. If he weren't careful, he might end up liking her more than was wise. He would see her as something other than a means to an end, and he couldn't afford for her to become anything more than his confidential informant. He couldn't afford to see her as a desirable woman, as someone he wouldn't mind stripping naked and searching with his tongue. He couldn't afford to mess up this case any more than he had already.

His gaze scanned the crowd, subconsciously looking for the dopers. The crank users, the puffy-eyed pot smokers, and the jumpy, swivel-headed heroin addicts. All of them thinking they were maintaining, controlling their buzz, when the buzz was so obviously controlling them. He hadn't worked narcotics for almost a year, and there were times, especially when he was in a crowd, when he still viewed the world through a narc's eyes. It was what he'd been trained to do, and he wondered how long that training would stay with him. He knew homicide cops who'd been retired for ten years and still looked at everyone as either potential murderers or victims.

The beige Chevy Caprice was parked on a side street next to the Boise public library. He slid behind the wheel of the unmarked police car and waited for a minivan to pass before he pulled out into traffic. He thought of Gabrielle's smile, the taste of her mouth, and the texture of her skin beneath his hands. He thought of the smooth thigh he'd glimpsed between the part in her dress. The heavy ache of desire pulled at his groin, and he tried not to think of her at all. Even if she weren't a kook, she was trouble. The kind that would get him busted back to a patrol cop working graveyard. That kind of trouble he didn't need; he'd barely survived the last internal affairs investigation. He didn't ever want to go through that again. Not for his job. Not for anything.

It had been less than a year, but he knew he would never forget the Department of Justice inquest and interviews and why he'd been forced to answer their questions. He'd never forget chasing Robby Martin down a black alley, the blast of orange fire from Robby's Luger and his own returning shots. For the rest of his life, he knew he would never forget lying in an alley, the cool grip of his empty Colt .45 in his hand. The night air ripped apart by screaming sirens and the whirl of red, white, and blue bouncing off trees and the sides of houses. The warmth of his blood seeping through the hole in his thigh, and Robby Martin's unmoving body twenty feet away. His white Nike running shoes vivid in the darkness. He'd never forget his disjointed thoughts tick-tick-ticking in his head as he'd shouted at the boy who couldn't hear.

It wasn't until much later, as he'd lain in the hospital, with his mother and sisters weeping on his neck, his father watching him from the end of the bed, his leg immobilized by a metal brace that looked like something a kid would build with an Erector set, that the evening slowed and played over and over in his head. He'd second-guessed every move he'd made.

Maybe he shouldn't have chased Robby down that alley. Maybe he should have let him go. He'd known where the kid lived, maybe he should have waited for backup and driven to his house.

Maybe, but it was his job to chase the bad guys. The community wanted drugs off their streets—right?

Well, maybe.

If Robby's name had been Roberto Rodriguez, chances were no one but the boy's family would have cared. Might not have even been the top story on the television news, but he'd looked like a someday senator. An all-American boy. An all-American *Caucasian* boy with straight white teeth and an angelic grin. The morning after the shooting, the *Idaho Statesman* had printed Robby's picture on the front page. His hair shining like a surfer dude, and his big blue eyes staring out at readers over their morning coffee.

And those readers looked at that face, and they began to wonder if it had been necessary for the undercover cop to shoot to kill. Never mind that Robby had run from the police, that he'd drawn first, and that he had a history of drug abuse. In a city struggling with growing pains, a city that had a blatant tendency to blame all its problems on the influx of foreigners and out-of-staters, a nineteen-year-old homegrown dope dealer, born at the hospital downtown, didn't sit real comfortably with the citizens' views of themselves and their city.

And they questioned their police force. They wondered if the city needed a citizen review board to evaluate the police department's deadly force policy, and they wondered if they had a renegade undercover cop, running around killing their young men.

The chief of police had appeared on the local news and reminded everyone of Robby's record. Toxicology had found significant traces of methamphetamine and marijuana in his blood. The Department of Justice and Internal Affairs had cleared Joe of any wrongdoing and had determined that deadly force had been necessary. But every time Robby's picture was flashed across the screen or appeared in the papers, the people still wondered.

Joe had been required to see the police psychologist, but he'd said very little. What was there to say, really? He'd killed a kid, not even a man yet. He'd taken a life. He'd been justified in what he'd been forced to do. He knew with absolute certainty that he'd be dead if Robby had been a better shot. He hadn't had a choice.

That's what he'd told himself. That's what he'd *had* to believe.

After two months of sitting on his ass at home and four more months of intense physical therapy, Joe had been cleared to return to work. But not to the narcotics division. He'd been quietly transferred to property crimes. That's what they'd called it, a transfer. But it had sure as hell felt like a demotion to him, like he'd been punished for doing his job.

He pulled the Caprice into a parking spot half a block away from Anomaly and retrieved a can of paint and a sack filled with brushes and a roller and pan from the trunk. Although he'd been transferred, he'd never considered what had happened in that alley with Robby a mistake. Sad and unfortunate, and something he tried not to think about—something he refused to talk about—but not his mistake.

Not like Gabrielle Breedlove. Now *that* had been his fuck up. He'd underestimated her, but really, who would have thought she'd come up with such a lamebrained plan as to lure him into the park with nothing more than an antique derringer and a can of hair spray?

Joe walked into the back of the store and set the paint and sack of supplies on a counter next to the sink. Mara Paglino stood at the other end of the counter unpacking freight the store had received the day before. The shipment didn't appear to include antiques. "What do ya have there?"

"Gabrielle ordered some Baccarat crystal." Her big brown eyes stared at him a little too intensely. She'd curled her thick black hair, and her lips shined a glossy red. Since the moment he'd met her, he'd been aware that she might have a small crush on him. She followed him around and offered to bring him things. He was a little flattered but mostly unnerved. She was only a year or two older than Tiffany, his niece, and Joe wasn't interested in girls. He liked women. Fully developed women who didn't have to be shown what to do with their mouths and hands. Women who knew how to move their bodies to create just the right friction. "Do you want to help me?" she asked.

He took a paintbrush out of the sack. "I thought you were supposed to be at the park helping Gabrielle."

"I was going to, but Kevin told me I had to unpack this crystal and get it out of the way in case you wanted to measure the countertop to-day."

His carpentry skills didn't extend to replacing countertops. "I won't get to that until next week." Hopefully, he wouldn't have to worry about it next week. "Is Kevin in his office?"

"He hasn't come back from lunch yet."

"Who's out front?"

"No one, but I'll hear the bell if a customer comes in."

Joe grabbed a brush and the paint can and walked into the small storage room. This was the part of undercover police work that drove him just south of sane—the waiting around for a suspect to make a move. Still, he supposed working inside the shop was better than sitting outside in an unmarked car and getting fat on Yankee Dogs. Better, but not by much.

He covered the floor with a drop cloth and leaned the boards he'd cut for shelves the day before against the wall. Mara followed him like a puppy and chatted nonstop about the immature college guys she'd dated. She left once when the bell rang, but she reappeared shortly to assure him she was in the market for a mature, *older* man.

By the time Kevin returned, Joe had just finished painting the two shelves and was preparing to paint the walls of the small room. Kevin took one look at Mara and sent her to help Gabrielle, leaving the two of them alone.

"I think she has a crush on you," Kevin said as Mara cast one last look over her shoulder and walked out the door.

"Yeah, maybe." Joe placed one hand on the back of his own shoulder and raised his arm above his head. As much as he hated to admit it, his muscles ached like a bitch. He kept his body in good shape. There was only one other explanation. He was getting old.

"Is Gabrielle paying you enough to put up with sore muscles?" Kevin was dressed in designer everything and held a sack from a party outlet store in one hand and a bag from the women's underwear shop down the street in the other.

"She pays me enough." He dropped his arms to his sides. "Money isn't all that important to me."

"Then you've never been poor. I have, my friend, and it sucks. It affects your whole life."

"How do you figure?"

"People judge you on the brand of your shirt and the condition of your shoes. Money is everything. Without it people think you're trash. And women, forget it. Women won't have anything to do with you. Period."

Joe sat on the edge of a trunk and crossed his arms over his chest. "Depends on what kind of women you're trying to impress."

"Strictly high maintenance. Women who know the difference between a Toyota and a Mercedes."

"Ahh." Joe tilted his head back and looked at the man before him. "Those women cost serious cash. Do you have that kind of money?"

"Yeah, and if I don't, I know how to get it. I know how to get the things I need."

Bingo. "How's that?"

Kevin just smiled and shook his head. "You wouldn't believe me if I told you."

"Try me," Joe pressed.

"Afraid I can't."

"Do you invest in the stock market?"

"I invest in me, Kevin Carter, and that's all I'm going to say."

Joe knew when to back off. "What's in the sack?" he asked and pointed to Kevin's hand.

"I'm giving a birthday party for my girl-friend, China."

"No shit? Is China her real name or her stage name?"

"Neither," Kevin chuckled. "She just likes it better than her real name, Sandy. I mentioned

the party to Gabe this morning when I stopped
by her booth. She said the two of you had made
other plans."

Joe thought he'd made himself real clear
when he'd told Gabrielle she had to stop getting
in the way of his investigation. Obviously, he
was going to have to talk to her again. "I think
we can make it to your party for a little while."

"Are you sure? She seemed pretty set on
spending the evening at home."

Normally, Joe wasn't the sort of guy to sit on
a bar stool and talk about women, his or anyone
else's. But this was different, this was his job,
and he knew how to play. He leaned forward
slightly as if he were about to share a secret.
"Well, just between you and me, Gabrielle is a
nymphomaniac."

"Really, I always thought she was a prude."

"She's the closet kind." He leaned back and
grinned like he and Kevin were of the same
hound brotherhood. "But I think I can hold her
off for a few hours. What time is your party?"

"Eight," Kevin answered as he headed to his
office, and Joe was stuck painting for the next
two hours. After Anomaly closed for the evening, he drove to the police station and read
over the daily report on the Hillard theft. Nothing much in the way of new information since
that morning's roll call. Kevin had met an uni-
dentified woman for lunch at a downtown restaurant. He'd bought party supplies and

stopped at a Circle K for a Big Gulp. Exciting stuff.

Joe reported his conversation with Kevin and let Luchetti know he'd been invited to Kevin's party. Then he grabbed a stack of paperwork off his desk and headed home to Sam.

For dinner, he barbecued some ribs and ate the macaroni salad his sister Debby had left in his refrigerator while he'd been at work. Sam stood on the table next to his plate and refused to eat his bird seeds and baby carrots.

"Sam loves Joe."

"You can't have my ribs."

"Sam loves Joe—braack."

"No."

Sam blinked his yellow-and-black eyes, raised his beak, and mimicked the telephone ringing.

"I haven't fallen for that in months." Joe speared some macaroni with his fork and felt like he was taunting a two-year-old with an ice cream cone. "The vet said you need to eat less and exercise more or you'll get liver disease."

The bird flew to his shoulder, then rested his feathery head against Joe's ear. *"Pretty bird."*

"You're fat." He remained strong during dinner and didn't feed Sam, but when the bird mimicked one of Joe's favorite phrases from a Clint Eastwood movie, he relented and fed him bites of Ann Cameron's cheesecake. It was as good as she'd claimed, so he guessed he owed her coffee. He tried to remember Ann as a kid, and vaguely recalled a girl with wire glasses sitting on one of those emerald green crushed velvet couches at her parents' house, staring at him while he'd waited for her sister, Sherry. She'd probably been about ten, six years younger than him. About Gabrielle's age.

The thought of Gabrielle brought a dull ache to his brow. Joe pinched the bridge of his nose between his thumb and middle finger and racked his brain to figure out what to do about her. He didn't have a clue.

As the setting sun washed the valley in twilight, Joe put Sam in his aviary and plugged *Dirty Harry* into the VCR. Besides Jerry Springer's *Too Hot For Television*, it was about the only tape Sam liked. In the past, Joe had tried to encourage his bird to watch Disney or *Sesame Street* or one of the educational tapes he'd bought. But Sam was a Jerry junkie, and like most parents, Joe gave in a lot.

He drove to the small brick house across town and parked his Bronco next to the curb. A pink porch light glowed above the front door. A few nights ago, the bulb had been green. Joe wondered at the significance but figured he probably didn't want to know.

A pair of squirrels darted across the lawn and sidewalk and skittered up the rough bark of an ancient oak. Halfway up, they paused to glare at him, the ends of their bushy tails snapped. Their agitated chatter filled his ears, reaming him as if somehow he'd been rude enough to steal their stash. He liked squirrels even less than cats.

Joe pounded on Gabrielle's door three times before it swung open. She stood before him wearing a big white shirt that buttoned up the front. Her green eyes widened, and her face flushed a deep red.

"Joe! What are you doing here?"

Before he answered her question, he let his gaze take her in, from the auburn curls falling from the ponytail on top of her head, to the string of beaded hemp tied around her ankle. She'd rolled the sleeves of her shirt up her forearms while the tails hit her about an inch above her bare knees. As far as he could see, she wore little else except multicolored paint smudges. "I need to talk to you," he said, returning his gaze to the increasing flush in her cheeks.

"Now?" She glanced behind her as if he'd caught her in the middle of doing something illegal.

"Yeah, what are you up to?"

"Nothing!" She looked guilty as hell about something.

"The other night I talked to you about interfering in the investigation, but just in case you didn't understand me, I'll tell you again. Quit protecting Kevin."

"I'm not." The light behind her got caught in her hair and shone through the white shirt, outlining her full breasts and slim hips.

"You declined an invitation to his party to-morrow night. I accepted for us."

"I don't want to go. Kevin and I are friends and business partners, but we don't socialize. I've always thought it was best if we don't spend our time away from work together."

"Too bad." Joe waited for her to invite him inside, but she didn't. Instead, she folded her arms, drawing his attention to the black smear across her left breast.

"Kevin's friends are superficial. We won't have a good time."

"We're not going there to have a good time."

"You're going to search for the Monet, aren't you?"

"Yes."

"Fine, but no more kissing."

He rocked back on his heels and looked at her from beneath lowered lids. Her request was perfectly reasonable and irritated more than he would ever admit. "I told you not to take it personal."

"I'm not, but I don't like it."

"You don't like what? Kissing me or not taking it personal?"

"Kissing you."

"Bull, you get all warm and breathless."

"You're mistaken."

He shook his head and said through a smile, "I don't think so."

She sighed. "Is that all you wanted, Detective?"

"I'll pick you up at eight." He turned to leave, but looked back at her over his shoulder. "And Gabrielle?"

"What?"

"Wear something sexy."

Gabrielle shut the door and leaned her back against it. She felt light-headed and queasy, as if she'd conjured up Joe somehow. She took a deep breath and placed a hand over her racing heart. His showing up on her porch at that exact moment in time was some sort of freakish fluke.

Ever since he'd walked away from her booth that afternoon, she'd had an overwhelming desire to paint him again. This time standing within his red aura. Naked. After she'd returned home from a successful day at the Coeur Festival, she'd immediately walked into her studio and prepared a canvas. She'd sketched and painted his face and the hard muscles of his body. With visions of Michelangelo's *David* for inspiration, she'd just started to paint Joe's *parts* when he'd knocked. She'd opened the door and seen him standing there, and for several anxious moments she'd feared he somehow knew what she'd been up to. She'd felt guilty, like he'd caught her peeking at him without his clothes on.

She didn't believe in fate. She believed too strongly in free will, but she couldn't ignore the feeling of foreboding raising the hair on the back of her neck.

Gabrielle pushed away from the door and headed to her studio. She'd meant what she'd told Joe, no more kisses. While she found lying to him easier than she would have imagined a week ago, she couldn't lie to herself. For reasons she could not begin to fathom, standing so close to Joe, his breath whispering across her cheek and his lips brushing her mouth wasn't all that unpleasant. No, it wasn't unpleasant at all.

Gabrielle believed in expressing love honestly and openly, but not in a crowded park, and not with Detective Joe Shanahan. He didn't care for her, and he'd made it real clear that he considered kissing her part of his job. She'd thought about her reaction to his kiss and had come to the logical conclusion that Joe's touch messed up her biorhythm and threw everything out of whack. Kind of a hiccup or a glitch in the life energy connecting her body, mind, and spirit.

If Kevin walked in on them arguing again, or if Joe saw anyone from his past, he was going to have to figure out something else. No more standing close, filling her senses with the scent of his skin. No more impersonal kisses that reached inside and stole her breath away. And there was absolutely no way she was going to dress in "something sexy" for him.

When the doorbell rang the next evening, Gabrielle thought she was ready for Joe this time. No more surprises. She was in control, and if he'd been dressed in worn jeans and a T-shirt, she might have managed it, too. But one look at him and her peaceful center spun off into the cosmos somewhere.

He'd shaved his five o'clock shadow, and his tan cheeks were smooth. His ribbed black polo was made of silk and fit nicely across his wide chest and flat stomach. He'd slipped a woven leather belt through the loops of pleated gabardine pants with razor-sharp creases. Instead of old running shoes or work boots, he wore suede penny loafers. He smelled wonderful and looked better.

Unlike Joe, Gabrielle had purposely put less effort into her appearance. She'd dressed strictly for comfort in a plain white blouse and a shapeless blue-and-white checkered bib jumper that hit her just above the knee. She wore very little makeup and hadn't attempted to do anything different with her hair, just let it curl about her shoulders and down her back like it always did. Her only concession to anything resembling fashion was the pair of silver hoops in her ears and the silver band on the middle finger of her right hand. She'd left her panty hose in her drawer and slipped her bare feet into a pair of canvas sneakers. She figured she looked the antithesis of sexy.

One brow lifted up his forehead telling her he thought so, too. "Where's your little dog Toto?"

Her outfit wasn't *that* bad. "Hey, I'm not the

one who wore my mom's red heels and skipped into a wall."

He leveled his gaze on her. "I was five."

"That's what they all say." She stepped out onto the porch and locked the door behind her. "Besides, I'm sure the party is casual." She dropped her keys into her big macrame handbag and turned to face him. He hadn't moved an inch, and her bare arm brushed across his chest.

"I doubt it." Joe took her elbow as if they were on a real date and led her to the awful beige car she remembered all too well. The last time she'd been cuffed in the backseat. "I've met Kevin, and I doubt he does anything casual, except maybe have casual sex."

The warmth of his palm swept up her arm and down to the tips of her fingers. She forced herself to walk composed by his side, as if his touch didn't make her want to pull away from his grasp. As if she were as calm and unaffected as Joe. She tried to ignore the sensations making her palms sweaty, and she didn't bother to comment on Joe's opinion of Kevin, since what he said was pretty much true. Which made Kevin no better or worse than a lot of other men.

"Last night I thought you were driving a Bronco."

"I was, but Kevin thinks I'm a broke loser. That's what I want him to think," he said and leaned forward to open the passenger door. His chest brushed her arm again, and she took a deep breath through her nose and wondered if his cologne was a combination of ceder and neroli or something else altogether.

"Why do you do that?"

"Do what?"

"Sniff me like I smell bad." He let go of her elbow, and she felt as if she could relax again.

"You're imagining things," she said and slid into the car. Unlike Joe, the interior of the car smelled as awful as it did the day he'd arrested her. Kind of like motor oil, but at least the seats were clean.

The ride to Kevin's took less than ten minutes, and Joe used the time to remind her of the informant's agreement she'd signed. "If Kevin is innocent," he said, "he doesn't need your help. And if he's guilty, you can't protect him anyway."

Cool air brushed her bare legs and arms and the side of her neck. She wished she'd stayed home. She wished she'd been given a choice.

Gabrielle had been to Kevin's house on several occasions, of course, but she really didn't care for it. The two-story contemporary structure hung on the side of a mountain supported by stilts and had a spectacular view of the city. The interior was constructed of lots of marble, hardwood, and steel and felt about as cozy as a museum of modern art.

Gabrielle and Joe walked up the sidewalk together, shoulder to shoulder, barely touching.

"What if one of Kevin's friends recognizes you? What are you going to do?"

"I'll figure something out."

That's exactly what she was afraid of. "Like what?"

Joe rang the doorbell and they stood side by side, staring ahead. "Are you afraid to be alone with me?"

A little. "No"

" 'Cause you look worried about that."

"I don't look worried."

"You look like maybe you don't trust yourself."

"To do what?"

"Keep your hands to yourself."

Before she could respond, the door swung open and the charade began. Joe wrapped his arm around her shoulders, the heat from his palm warming her flesh through the thin material of her blouse.

"I wondered if you two were going to make it." Kevin stepped back, and they moved inside. As always, he looked like he'd just posed for *GQ*.

"I told you I could get her out of the house for a few hours."

Kevin glanced at Gabrielle's bib, and a line appeared across his forehead. "Gabe, this is a new look for you. Interesting."

"It's not that bad," she defended herself.

"Not if you live in Kansas." Kevin shut the

door, and they followed him toward the living room.

"I don't look like Dorothy." Gabrielle glanced downward at her blue-and-white-checked jumper. "Do I?"

Joe pulled her against his side. "Don't worry, I'll protect you from flying monkeys."

She raised her gaze to his eyes, with their rich brown irises and thick, spiky lashes, and it wasn't flying monkeys that had her worried.

"Why don't you let Kevin put that big purse you're packing somewhere?"

"I can put it in the spare bedroom," Kevin offered.

"I want to keep it with me."

Joe snatched it off her shoulder and handed it to Kevin. "You'll get bursitis."

"In my shoulder?"

"Never can tell about bursitis," Joe predicted as Kevin walked off with her purse.

The living room, kitchen, and dining room shared the same large airy space and spectacular view of the city. A small group of guests mingled at the bar, while Mariah Carey sang from hidden speakers, filling the house with every last octave she managed to pull from her vocal cords. Gabrielle didn't have anything against Mariah personally, but she thought the diva would benefit from a lesson in moderation. Gabrielle moved her gaze about the space, from the zebra skin draped over the back of the leather sofa to the African artifacts cluttering the room. Kevin could have used the same lesson.

When Kevin returned, he introduced Joe and Gabrielle to his friends, a tight group of entrepreneurs who were, as far as Gabrielle was concerned, far more worried about the state of their bank accounts than the state of consciousness. Joe kept his arm around Gabrielle as they shook hands with a man and his wife who owned a chain of successful coffeehouses. Others sold vitamins or computers or real estate and apparently did very well. Kevin introduced them to his girlfriend, China, who, Gabrielle could have sworn, was named Sandy the last time they'd met. Whatever her name now, the woman was still petite and blond and flawless, and Gabrielle felt an overwhelming urge to slouch.

Next to China stood her equally beautiful and petite friend, Nancy, who didn't even pretend to be interested in anything Gabrielle might have to say. Her attention was on the man who stood with his hip pressed against Gabrielle. Out of the corner of her eye, she watched pleasure curl the corners of Joe's lips into an appreciative smile. His gaze flickered to Nancy's bosom, and he shifted his weight to his opposite foot. His warm hand slid from Gabrielle's shoulder and across her back, then he shoved his hands into his pants pockets and his touch was gone completely.

She should have been glad. She *was* glad. Only she felt a little deserted and something more. Something uncomfortable that felt like jealousy, but couldn't possibly be jealousy because (a) Joe wasn't her *real* boyfriend; (b) she didn't care about him; and (c) she wasn't attracted to unenlightened men.

Kevin said something Joe must have thought funny, because he tipped his head back a little and laughed, showing straight white teeth and his smooth tan throat. Creases appeared in the corners of his eyes, and the deep mellow sound reached inside her and settled in her chest.

Someone else said something too, and they all laughed. Except Gabrielle. She didn't think there was anything to laugh about. No, there was absolutely nothing funny about the little pang beneath her breastbone, or the white hot anarchy surging through her veins, arousing a physical desire she found impossible to ignore.

Eleven

GABRIELLE BIT INTO AN ASPARAGUS spear and glanced at the silver watch strapped to her left wrist. Nine-thirty. It seemed a lot later.

"If you're not careful, Nancy is going to steal your man."

Gabrielle glanced across her shoulder at Kevin, then returned her gaze to the undercover cop who'd obviously forgotten he was supposed to have a girlfriend, or that he was supposed to be looking for Mr. Hillard's Monet.

Unless Nancy had the painting down her dress, Joe wasn't likely to find it. He stood across the room with his forearm resting on the bar, his hand wrapped around a half empty glass. His head was cocked to one side toward Nancy, as if he couldn't bear to miss one fascinating word uttered from the woman's red lips. "I'm not worried." Gabrielle reached for a slice of toasted Brie on a piece of baguette.

"Maybe you should. Nancy loves to steal

men away from their wives or girlfriends."

"How'd the store do today?" she asked, purposely changing the subject and turning her full attention to Kevin.

"We sold a few garnet pieces, and that big wicker picnic basket. Made about four hundred dollars. Not bad, I guess, for June." He shrugged. "How'd you do with your oils?"

"I sold just about everything. By two o'clock. I only had a few bottles of sunscreen oil. So I packed up and spent the rest of the day at home painting and napping."

She took a bite of the baguette, and her gaze strayed across the room. Now the two were smiling at each other, and she wondered if Joe was secretly making a date to meet Nancy later. They made a good-looking couple. Not only was Nancy petite but she also had that pale, frail look about her, like she needed a man to protect her. A big hunk of man who could throw her over his shoulder and save her from burning buildings. A man like Joe.

"Are you sure you aren't worried about Joe and Nancy?"

"Not at all." To prove it, she turned her back on them, determined to forget about Detective Shanahan. She might have succeeded, too, but his deep, rich laughter rose above the other noise in the room and reminded her of his exact location beside the bar—next to a beautiful little blond in a tiny dress. "Guess who I saw today?" she asked, trying to refocus her attention. "That guy I dated last year, Ian Raney. He's still giving Reiki treatments at the Healing Center. He had a booth at the festival and was healing auras."

"He was an odd one," Kevin chuckled.

"He's gay now." She frowned. "Or maybe he was gay before, and I just didn't know it."

"Really? How do you know he's gay now?"

"He introduced me to his 'special friend,' Brad." She popped the rest of the Brie into her mouth and washed it down with a sip of white wine. "There wasn't a doubt about Brad's sexual orientation."

"A flaming fruit?"

"Flambéed, I'm sorry to say. How could I have gone out with a gay guy and not have known it? Weren't there signs?"

"Well, did he try to get you into bed with him?"

"*No.*"

Kevin put his arm around Gabrielle's shoulders and gave her a comforting squeeze. "There you go."

She looked into his familiar blue eyes and felt herself relax a little. She'd had these kinds of conversations with Kevin in the past. They'd sit in their office on slow days, feet kicked up, ignoring the thousand and one details and demands of running a small business, and they'd talk about anything. "Not all men are like you."

"Yes they are. But most men aren't going to tell you the truth if they think they have a chance to score. I know I don't, so I have nothing to lose."

She laughed and took another sip of her wine. Kevin could be just as superficial as the rest of his friends, but he was never that way with her. She didn't know how he was able to meld his different personalities, but he managed it somehow. He was honest and open and a lot of fun and could almost make her forget about the man across the room and why she was there. "So you're only telling me the truth because we're never going to have sex?"

"That's about it."

"If you thought there was a chance, you'd lie?"

"Like a cheap rug."

"And you think all men are like you?"

"Absolutely. If you don't believe me, ask your boyfriend." He dropped his hand from her shoulder.

"Ask me what?"

Gabrielle turned and looked into Joe's watchful eyes. A knot twisted her stomach, and she tried to tell herself it was the Brie. She didn't want to even think it could be anything other than rich food. "Nothing."

"Gabrielle doesn't want to believe guys lie to women to get them into bed."

"I said not *all* guys," she clarified.

Joe glanced at Kevin, then returned his gaze to Gabrielle. He slid his hand to the small of her back. "This is one of those trick questions, right? Either way I answer, I'm screwed."

A warm tingle swept way up her spine, and she stepped away from his touch. She especially didn't want to think about how easily this one man could affect her with nothing more than a glance or a touch.

"Looks like you're screwed anyway. Maybe you should pay more attention to Gabrielle and less to Nancy," Kevin said, noticing her reaction and misinterpreting it for jealousy. Which it wasn't, of course.

"Gabrielle knows she doesn't have to worry about other women." He took her wine glass and set it on the table. "I have a real fondness for that mole on the inside of her thigh." He raised her hand to his mouth and brushed a kiss to her knuckles. "You might even say I'm obsessed."

He stared at her over the back of her hand. Her fingers trembled, and she tried to remember if she had a mole and couldn't.

"Did you get enough to eat?" he asked against her knuckles.

"What?" Was he really asking about food? "I'm not hungry."

"Ready to go home then?"

Slowly, she nodded.

"Are you two leaving already?" Kevin asked.

"It's our one-month anniversary," Joe explained as he lowered her hand and kept it tight in his grasp. "I'm sentimental about those kinds of things. Let's say good-bye and get your purse."

"I'll get it for you," Kevin offered.

"Thanks, but we'll get it," Joe insisted.

Saying good-bye to Kevin's friends took about three minutes, and most of that was spent trying to convince Nancy that they really did have to leave so soon. Joe wove his fingers through hers, and they walked from the room, palm pressed to palm. If they'd been a real couple, she might have rested her head against his, and he might have turned and pressed a soft kiss to her cheek or whispered something sweet into her ear. But there was nothing soft or sweet about Joe, and they weren't a real couple. They were a lie, and she wondered how anyone looking at them couldn't see behind the facade.

The warm sensation of his touch triggered an even warmer physical desire, but this time her mind and spirit were in control. Just in case, she dropped his hand and kept a few inches of distance between them. She wondered how Kevin was so easily fooled.

Kevin kept his gaze on Gabrielle's back as she and her boyfriend walked from the room. He watched her drop Joe's hand and knew she was upset about something. But whatever it was, Kevin was just as sure her boyfriend could make her forget. Guys like Joe were like that. They could be losers and still get what they wanted handed to them. Not Kevin. He had to take what he wanted.

He glanced around at his young wealthy
guests, eating his food, drinking his booze,
standing in his beautiful house. He'd crammed
his home with wonderful paintings and fine antiques and artifacts. He had one of the best
views in the city, and it hadn't come cheap.
He'd made it to the top of the hill, but one look
at a guy like Joe, and he got that old hunger in
his gut for more and that old pounding in his
head that told him he would never be enough,
never have enough. Enough money, nice
clothes, fancy houses, and fast cars. Enough
beautiful women to make him feel as if he were
different from every other guy walking the
planet. As if he weren't invisible. The hunger
inside was insatiable, and sometimes he feared
there would never be enough.

"Stand right here," Joe ordered once they were
out of sight of Kevin and his friends. "If anyone
comes, talk loud and don't let them in the
room."

"What are you going to do?" Gabrielle asked
as she watched him slip inside the first room
they'd come to. He quietly shut the door without answering, leaving her alone in the hall.

She stood perfectly still, hoping he'd hurry,
trying to hear above the sound of her pounding
heart. She felt like a spy, but not a very good
one. Her hands shook and her scalp grew too
tight. She wasn't cut out to be a Bond girl.
Somewhere else in the house a cabinet door

slammed shut, and Gabrielle jumped like some-one had zapped her with a stun gun. She ran her fingers through her hair and took deep cleansing breaths. She didn't have nerves of steel. She glanced at her wristwatch and waited the longest five minutes of her life.

When Joe appeared again, a deep frown wrinkled his forehead and lowered his brows. Since he didn't look happy and wasn't calling for backup or breaking out the handcuffs, Ga-brielle figured he hadn't found anything. She relaxed a little. Now they would leave.

Joe shoved her purse at her, then moved across the hall and quietly slipped into another room. The door had barely shut when she heard his familiar curse.

"Sweet baby Jesus!"

Everything within Gabrielle stilled. He'd found something. She sneaked inside the room and shut the door behind her, half expecting to see Mr. Hillard's Monet hanging on the wall. What she did see was just as shocking. Mirrors. Everywhere. On the walls, the backs of the doors of the walk-in closet, and on the ceiling. A round bed sat in the center of the room and was covered with a black-and-white sheepskin spread that had a big Oriental symbol in the middle. There were no chests of drawers or nightstands to restrict the view through the mir-rors. Positioned beside the arched doorway leading to the bathroom stood a small pedestal table with an ivory chess set on top. Even from a distance of half the room's width away, Gabrielle could see that the set was antique, Oriental, and, typical of that period, the nude pieces were not quite anatomically proportional. Gabrielle felt as if she'd stepped into a room at the Playboy mansion. Hugh Hefner's babe lair.

"Look at this place. Makes you wonder what kind of action he sees in here," Joe said just above a whisper.

Gabrielle leaned her head back and looked up. "And how much Windex he goes through."

His gaze met hers through the mirrors on the ceiling. "Yeah, that was my second thought."

She hung her purse on her shoulder and watched him walk silently across the room, the thick white carpet muting the sound of his leather loafers. No matter where she looked, she was surrounded by his image. Caught by his dark intent eyes and the sensual lines of his mouth. The profile of his straight nose and the square, stubborn set of his jaw. The curls at the base of his neck, and his wide shoulders outlined perfectly in his ribbed polo. Her gaze moved down his back to the waist of his gabardine trousers, then he disappeared inside the closet, and she was alone with her own image. She frowned at her reflection and stood a little straighter.

So, Kevin was a little perverted, she thought as she pushed her curls behind her ear. It wasn't her business. Covering a bedroom with mirrors wasn't against the law. She ran her hand down the bib of her jumper, tilted her head to one side, and viewed herself with a critical eye. She was nothing like Nancy. She wasn't petite or blond or flirtatious, and once again she wondered what Joe saw when he looked at her.

She saw every little flaw multiplied around the room and couldn't imagine watching herself making love. Totally naked. Obviously Kevin didn't have the same qualm, and that was just a little more information than she wanted to know about him.

She walked to the bathroom, passing the chess set, with its rows of largely endowed and extremely erect pawns. She didn't pause to inspect the other pieces; she really didn't want to know.

The bathroom space was filled with more mirrors, a shower stall, and a big Jacuzzi tub surrounded by tiles. A set of French doors led outside to a small deck and another Jacuzzi. Except for the mirrors, she could visualize herself drawing a bath for a nice relaxing soak, maybe adding some ylang-ylang, definitely lavender and rosemary.

Gabrielle sat on the edge of the Jacuzzi and glanced at her watch. If Joe didn't hurry, she didn't know how they would explain what had taken them so long to retrieve her purse. She tugged the skirt of her jumper down her thighs, then slid it back up to see if she really did have a mole. She leaned forward and saw a perfectly round mole about an inch below the elastic leg of her panties. It wasn't even that noticeable, and she wondered how Joe could possibly have known about it.

"What are you doing?"

She looked up into Joe's face and shoved her skirt down. His brows were pulled together in a straight line across his forehead.

"Looking at my mole. How did you know about it?"

He laughed quietly and lowered to one knee in front of the sink. "I know everything about you," he answered and began a search of the cabinet.

She opened her mouth to tell him she doubted her moles were a matter of police record, but the bedroom door swung open and she recognized Kevin's voice.

"What did you want?" he asked.

Gabrielle's breath caught in her throat, and her gaze found Joe's reflection in the mirror above the sink. He slowly stood and raised a finger to his lips.

The female voice that answered Kevin didn't belong to his girlfriend. "I want to show you something," Nancy answered.

"What's that?" There was a long pause before Kevin spoke again. "Very nice," he said.

"China told me about this room. About the mirrors."

"And you wanted to see for yourself?"

"Yes."

Joe reached for Gabrielle's hand and pulled her with him to the French doors.

"Are you sure? China might find out."

"I don't care." There was a sound like clothes hitting the carpet and Kevin said, "Then come here and say hello to Mr. Happy."

Silently, Gabrielle and Joe slipped outside onto the deck and shut the door behind them. A cool breeze lifted her hair and the bottom of her dress. The last orange and pink rays of the setting sun shot across a mackerel sky, and the lights of the city blinked to life in the valley below. Any other time, Gabrielle might have paused to appreciate the view, but tonight she hardly noticed. Her heart pounded in her ears, and she now knew a few more pieces of information about Kevin that she really wished she didn't. Like he cheated on his girlfriend with her best friend, and he called his penis Mr. Happy.

"Do you think Kevin heard us?" she asked just above a whisper.

Joe walked to the metal railing and looked over. "No. He sounded pretty busy." He straightened and moved to the left corner of the deck. "We can jump from here."

"Jump?" Gabrielle moved to stand beside Joe and looked over the side. The back half of Kevin's house and the whole deck hung from the side of a mountain and were supported by several substantial stilts. The earth below was corrugated with a succession of three-foot-wide terraces and braced with concrete to prevent erosion. "When I signed the confidential agreement, it didn't say anything about jumping off Kevin's deck and breaking my neck."

"You won't break your neck. It's only about ten or twelve feet from over here. All we have to do is climb over the rail, hang from the bottom of the deck, and let go. It'll only be about a four-foot drop."

Her shoulder brushed his as she leaned out a little further. He made it sound so easy. "Unless you miss the terrace you're aiming for, then it's about four more feet." She turned and looked at his profile, bathed in the first shadows of night. "There has to be some other way."

"Sure. We could always go back inside and interrupt Kevin. I imagine things are getting really interesting just about now." He looked across his shoulder at her.

"Maybe we could just wait a bit and then go through the house."

"And what are you going to tell Kevin took us so long to get your purse? He'll think we were knocking boots in the bathroom the whole time."

"He might not think that," she said but didn't really believe it.

"Yes he would, and I'd have to give you a big sucker bite on your neck and mess up your hair just to make sure that's exactly what he'd think." He leaned way over the railing. "It's up to you, though. But if we're jumping, we better do it before it gets any darker out here. I don't want to miss that terrace." He straightened, looked at her, and grinned like he was having a really good time. "You ready?" he asked as if he hadn't just given her a choice between a hickey and jumping to her death.

"No!"

"You're not scared, are you?"

"Yes! Any person with half a brain would be terrified."

He shook his head and swung one leg, then the other, over the rail. "Don't tell me you're afraid of heights?" He stood on the outside edge of the deck, facing her, his hands gripping the metal bar.

"No. I'm afraid of falling to my death."

"You probably wouldn't die." He glanced at the ground below him, then back at her. "Probably could break a leg, though."

"That doesn't make me feel better."

His smile grew. "I was just kidding about that last part."

She leaned forward a fraction and looked down. "This isn't a real good time for jokes."

"You're probably right." He placed a hand beneath her chin and brought her gaze back up to his. "I won't let anything happen to you, Gabrielle. I won't let you get hurt."

They both knew he couldn't promise such a thing, but staring into his intense brown eyes, she almost believed he had the power to keep her safe.

"Trust me."

Trust him? She couldn't think of one good reason why she should trust him, but as she stood there perched above the city, contemplating a leap off the balcony, she discovered that she *did* trust him. "Okay."

"That's my girl," he said with a grin. Then he slid his hands to the bottom rail, lowering himself until all she could see of him was his big hands. Then they were gone too, followed by a heavy thud.

Gabrielle looked down at the top of his head, and he lifted his face up to her. "Your turn," he said, raising his voice just enough to be heard.

She took a deep breath. She could do this. She could climb on the outside of a flimsy rail and dangle ten or twelve feet in the air, then drop and hope she landed on a three-foot-wide terrace. No problem. She slid the strap of her purse over her head and shoulder, then shoved the big bag around to the small of her back. She tried not to think about falling to her death. "I can do this," she whispered and stepped onto the bottom rung of the railing.

"I am calm." She managed to keep her panic at bay as she swung one leg, then the other, over the rail. Another blast of cool air blew up her skirt as she balanced on the edge of the deck, her heels hanging over. The metal bar was cold within her tight grasp.

"That's it," Joe encouraged her from the ground.

She knew better than to glance over her shoulder, but she couldn't stop herself. She looked out at the city lights below, and she froze.

"Come on, Gabrielle. Come on, baby."

"Joe?"

"I'm right here."

She closed her eyes. "I'm scared. I don't think I can do this."

"Sure you can. You're the same woman who knocked me on my ass in the park. You can do anything."

She opened her eyes and looked down toward him, but it was dark and he was hidden in the shadows of the house, and she couldn't see anything but a gray outline.

"Just bend down a little and grab the bottom of the rail."

Slowly she slid her hands down the metal bars until she crouched on the edge, her behind hanging out over the city. She didn't think she'd ever been so terrified in her life. "I can do this," she whispered on a cleansing breath. "I am calm."

"Hurry up before your palms sweat."

Geez, she hadn't thought of sweaty palms, but now she did. "I can't see you. Can you see me?"

His soft, low chuckle rose to her as she crouched with a death grip on the rail. "I have a real nice view of your white panties."

At the moment, Joe Shanahan looking up her

skirt was the least of her problems. She slid one foot from the wooden deck.

"Come on, honey," he coaxed from below.

"What if I fall?"

"I'll catch you. I promise, only you have to let go now, before it gets too dark to see those panties."

She slowly slid her other foot from the deck and dangled above the dark ground below. "Joe," she called out just as her foot contacted with something solid.

"Fuck!"

"What was that?"

"The side of my head."

"Oh, sorry." His strong hands grabbed her ankles, then slid up the backs of her calves to her knees.

"I have you."

"Are you sure?"

"Let go."

"Are you sure?"

"Yeah, let go."

She took a deep breath, counted to three, then released the railing. And she fell, sliding downward within the circle of his big arms. He clasped her to him, and her jumper bunched up around her waist as she slipped down his chest. His hands slid up the backs of her legs, and he held her bare thighs in his grasp. She looked down into his dark face just below hers.

"I did it."

"I know."

"My skirt's up around my waist," she said.

His teeth looked very white when he smiled. "I know." He slowly lowered her until her feet touched the ground, and his palms settled on her behind. "You're not only beautiful, you've got big cojones. I like that in a woman."

Gabrielle could honestly say that no man had ever chosen those exact words to compliment her before. Usually they stuck with more common flattery and commented on her eyes or legs.

"You were afraid, but you went over that railing anyway." His hot hands warmed her flesh through the lace of her underwear. "Do you remember last night when you said I couldn't kiss you anymore?"

"I remember."

"Did you mean on the lips?"

"Of course."

He lowered his mouth and kissed the side of her throat. "That leaves a lot of really interesting spots free," he said as his hands squeezed her bottom.

Gabrielle opened her mouth, then closed it again. What could she possibly say to that?

"Do you want me to find them now or later?"

"Ahh . . . later would probably be better." She tugged at the bottom of her skirt, but Joe's grasp tightened on her behind.

His voice was low and husky when he asked, "You sure?"

Not really. She stood on a terraced mountainside, her butt hanging out of her dress, and she wasn't sure she wanted to be any other place than exactly where she stood. Wrapped in darkness, shoved against Joe's solid chest. "Yes."

He yanked the hem of her jumper and smoothed it over the curve of her bottom. "Let me know."

"I will." She stepped away from the lure of his voice and the warmth of his embrace. "How's your head?"

"I'll live." He turned and hauled himself up to the next level of the terraced retaining wall. She looked up at his outline, and he reached for her hand and pulled her up after him. He hauled her up three more times and made it all seem so easy.

The night had taken on a discernable chill by the time they made it to his old Chevy, and Gabrielle was looking forward to taking a nice warm soak in the tub when she got home. But fifteen minutes later, she found herself sitting on Joe's beige-and-brown sofa, the beady yellow-and-black eyes of his parrot pinning her to the couch. Across the living room Joe stood with his back to her, the cradle of a telephone dangling from one hand, the receiver in the other. He spoke just low enough not to be heard, then walked into the dining room, the long cord trailing after him.

"You've got to ask yourself one question. Do I feel lucky? Well, do ya—punk?"

Gabrielle jumped and turned her full attention to Sam. "Excuse me?"

The parrot flapped his wings twice, then flew to the arm of the couch. He rocked from one foot to the other, then tilted his head to the side and studied her.

"Ahh . . . Polly want a cracker?"

"Go ahead, make my day."

She supposed it made perfect sense that Joe's bird would quote Dirty Harry. She sat perfectly still as the bird walked along the back of the couch, a blue metal band around one scaly leg. "Nice parrot," she said softly and glanced in Joe's direction. He still stood in the dining room, his back to her, his weight resting on one foot. He cradled the receiver between his shoulder and ear and massaged his other shoulder with his opposite hand. For a brief second, she wondered if he'd hurt himself helping her over the retaining walls, but then Sam let out a shrill whistle, and she forgot about Joe. The bird swayed back and forth, then hopped on her shoulder.

"You behave."

"Joe," she called out, keeping her gaze on Sam's black beak.

Sam laid his head against her temple and puffed out his chest. *"Pretty bird."*

Gabrielle had never been around birds before, let alone had one stand on her shoulder. She didn't know what to do or say. She didn't know anything about bird behavior, but she knew she didn't want to make him mad. She'd seen the Alfred Hitchcock classic many times, and the image of Suzanne Pleshette with her eyes pecked out flashed through her head. "Nice parrot," she said and glanced across the room. "Help."

Joe finally looked over his shoulder at her, his now familiar scowl lowering his brows as he spoke a few words into the receiver. After a few terse sentences, he finished the call and walked back into the living room. "Sam, what do you think you're doing?" he asked as he set the telephone on the coffee table. "Get off her."

The bird rubbed his soft head against Gabrielle, but didn't hop from her shoulder.

"Come on now." Joe patted his own shoulder. "Come here." Sam didn't move.

Instead he dipped his head and touched his beak to her cheek. *Pretty bird.*

"Well, I'll be damned." Joe put his hands on his hips and cocked his head to one side. "He likes you."

She wasn't convinced. "Really? How can you tell?"

Joe moved to stand directly in front of her. "He kissed you," he said, then he leaned forward and placed his hand just below Sam's feet. "Lately, he's been in the mood for a mate." Joe snapped his fingers, and the side of his hand brushed her chest through her white blouse. "I guess he thinks he's found a girlfriend."

"Me?"

"Uh-huh." His gaze lowered to her mouth, then returned to the parrot. "Step up, Sam. Be a good bird." Finally Sam obeyed and hopped onto Joe's hand.

"You behave."

"Me? I'm not the guy rubbing my head against a pretty girl and kissing her. I am behaving. Well, I am tonight anyway." He flashed her a smile, then walked to the huge cage sitting in front of a big picture window.

Gabrielle stood and watched him run a careful hand over Sam's feathers before he placed him in the cage. The big bad cop wasn't so big and bad after all. "Does he really think I'm a potential girlfriend?"

"Probably. He's been shredding the newspaper and roosting on his stuffed animals again." Sam hopped on a perch, and Joe closed the wire door. "But I've never seen him behave like he did with you. He usually gets really jealous of the women I bring home and tries to chase them out the front door."

"I guess I lucked out," she said, now wondering how many women he brought to his house, and again, why she should care.

"Yeah, he wants to roost with you." He turned and looked at her. "I can't say that I blame him."

As compliments went, it wasn't great. But for some peculiar reason his words settled near her heart and made her pulse leap. "You suck at flattery, Shanahan."

He just smiled like he knew better and motioned toward the door. "Do you need to stop anywhere on the way home? Maybe run in somewhere and get dinner?"

She stood and followed him. "Are you hungry?"

"No, I thought you might be."

"No, I ate before Kevin's party."

"Oh." He glanced at her across his shoulder. "Oh, okay."

During the drive to Gabrielle's house, her thoughts once again turned to the type of women Joe might bring home. She wondered what they looked like, and if they looked like Nancy. She bet they did.

Joe seemed just as distracted as Gabrielle, and neither of them spoke until she made an attempt at conversation three blocks from her house. "Kevin gives an interesting party." She was sure he'd have a lot to say about that.

He didn't. He just kind of grunted and said, "Kevin's a tool."

She gave up, and they rode the rest of the short way in silence. He didn't say anything as he walked her up the sidewalk or when he took the keys from her hand. The pink porch light caressed his profile and lingered in the soft curls above his ear as he bent forward and opened the door. He straightened and moved his shoulder as if it still bothered him.

"Did you hurt yourself helping me tonight?" she asked.

"I pulled a muscle the other day moving those shelves in your store, but I'll live."

He straightened, and she looked at him, into his tired dark eyes, the beginning of another five o'clock, and the stress creasing his forehead. "I could give you a massage," she suggested before she gave herself time to think better of the offer.

"Do you know how?"

"Of course." Visions of Joe served up in nothing but a towel drifted through her head and warmed the pit of her stomach. "I'm almost a professional."

"You mean, like you're almost a vegetarian?"

"Are you making fun of me again?" She'd taken classes on massage and, although she wasn't a certified masseuse, she considered herself semipro.

His quiet laughter stretched across the still night air and wrapped her up in the depth of the masculine sound. "Of course," he admitted without shame.

At least he was honest. "I bet I could have you feeling better in twenty minutes."

"What do you want to bet?"

"Five bucks."

"Five bucks? Make it ten and you're on."

Twelve

JOE TOOK ONE LOOK AT THE LITTLE towel she offered him and tossed it on the sofa. He preferred the loose-fit freedom of boxers. He liked lots of ball room to give the boys a chance to breathe, and there was no way he was going to run the risk of his goods hoisting that towel into a tepee.

He shifted his weight to one foot and rested his hands on his hips. Hell, he shouldn't even be standing in the middle of Gabrielle's living room. He should be on his way home, to a good night's sleep. He had a briefing at eight the next morning to discuss the stolen antiques he'd seen in Kevin's guest room. He needed to be rested and to have a clear head when he prepared the affidavit he would use to obtain a search warrant. The wording had to be clear and concise and as tight as a virgin's coochie. If not, he'd run the risk of having anything seized during a search thrown out later at trial. There were other things he needed to do tonight, too. He needed to do some laundry, and he needed to call Ann Cameron and tell her he couldn't meet her for coffee tomorrow. He'd stopped by her deli that morning before work, and she'd made him breakfast. She was a real nice lady, and he needed to call and break their date.

Instead, he stood in Gabrielle's house watching her pour oil into a shallow bowl and light candles on the mantelpiece and on different glass tables like she was preparing for a sacrifice. Instead of leaving, he tilted his head to one side and watched her ugly, shapeless dress ride up the backs of her smooth thighs, stopping just short of fantasy land.

She turned down the lights, then flipped the switch next to the fireplace, and orange flame shot from the gas vents and licked at the fake logs. He watched her tie back her long, curly hair with a piece of ribbon, and he debated whether he should tell her that the ivory chess set in Kevin's bedroom, the one with all those little pawns with their wicked little woodies, had been stolen from a house in River Run last month.

Ever since he'd watched her go over that balcony, he'd thought about telling her the truth. He'd thought about it on the drive to his house, while he'd talked to Walker on the telephone, and after he'd hung up. He'd thought about it as he'd stood on her porch with her key in his hand, and as he'd looked into her trusting green eyes. He'd thought about it even as he'd agreed to a massage that he knew was a bad idea.

The captain didn't want Gabrielle informed of anything, but Joe thought she deserved to know the truth about Kevin and about the shelves crammed with many of the antiques recorded as stolen in police central file.

Until about an hour ago, Joe would have been in complete agreement with Walker. But that had been before she'd stood guard outside the guest room door while he'd searched. Before he'd looked into her eyes and asked for her trust. Before she'd gone over that railing for him. Until an hour ago, he hadn't been sure of her innocence, nor had he really cared. It hadn't been his job to care. It still wasn't his job.

"I'll go get my massage table and you can get comfortable."

"I want to sit in a chair. One of those dining room chairs will be good." A hard, *uncomfortable* chair that wouldn't let him relax enough to forget she was his informant, not a woman he wanted to know a whole lot better.

"Are you sure?"

"Oh yeah." But when he'd seen her climb over that railing, clearly terrified, something had shifted within him and changed how he looked at her, what he felt deep down in his core. Watching her dangle above his head, those little white panties filling his view, his heart had lodged somewhere in his throat. As he'd looked up at her hanging above him, he'd known he would have a real hard time catching her if she fell, just as he'd known there was no way in hell he'd let her fall. And in that moment she'd become more than his informant with a killer body, she'd become someone he wanted to keep safe. Someone he wanted to protect.

He'd felt something else, too. As he'd held her in his arms and kissed her neck, he'd felt a sharp tightness in his chest even after the danger had passed. Maybe it had been residual fear or latent stress. Yeah maybe, but whatever it was, he didn't plan to examine it too closely. Instead he chose to focus his attention on Gabrielle's progress as she dragged a wooden chair from the dining room and set it in front of the fireplace.

Even though he believed she deserved to know about Kevin, he couldn't tell her, because she was so extremely readable. Everything she felt showed in her eyes. She couldn't lie without looking like she expected a bolt of lightning to zap her. He couldn't tell her, and he shouldn't stay.

He took a step backward and debated the wisdom of letting Gabrielle rub her hands on him. The debate didn't last long. She tilted her head to the side and looked at him. "Take off your shirt, Joe," she said, and her voice flowed through him like that oil she was warming on a little burner. He guessed he didn't have to leave just yet. He was thirty-five and in control.

It was a massage. Not sex. After he'd been shot, he'd had the knots kneaded from his muscles on a regular basis as part of his therapy. Of course, his therapist had been in her fifties and looked nothing like Gabrielle Breedlove.

Yeah, he could stay. As long as he remembered that Gabrielle was his informant, that screwing around with her would screw up his job. And that just wasn't going to happen. No way in hell.

"Aren't you going to take off your clothes?"

"I'm leaving my pants on."

She shook her head. "I wish you wouldn't. The oil will ruin your pants."

"I'll take my chances."

"I won't peek." The tone of her voice and the frown on her lips told him she thought he was absurd. Then she raised her right hand as if swearing an oath. "I promise."

"Towel's too small."

"Oh." She left and returned a moment later with a big beach towel. She tossed it on the arm of the sofa beside him. "How's this?"

"Great."

Gabrielle paid fascinated attention to Joe's hands as he drew the bottom of his silk polo from his gabardine trousers. Like a maddeningly slow striptease, he pulled the ribbed material just enough to give her a flash of flat stomach and a vertical line of dark hair before he released the shirt and it fell to his waist. She released a breath she hadn't known she was holding and lifted her gaze to his face. She stared into his brown eyes watching her watch him. He raised a hand to grab a fistful of shirt between his shoulders. Then he pulled it over his head and tossed it on the sofa next to the bath towel he'd refused to wear. His hands moved to his belt buckle, and she quickly glanced away.

She turned her attention to the almond oil she'd poured into a shallow lotus bowl and left warming on a vaporizer. Her mouth felt impossibly dry and watery all at the same time. She turned her gaze so he wouldn't catch her staring, but not before she'd seen the fine curls covering the defined muscles of his chest, spreading down his sternum and flat stomach and disappearing beneath the waistband of his trousers. His nipples were a darker brown than in her painting of him, the hair on his chest softer and not as thick.

She added three drops of benzoin and eucalyptus to the almond oil, then placed the bowl and defuser on a small table next to the fireplace. Joe spun the dining room chair to face the fire, straddled the seat, and sat backward. He folded his arms across the top rung and presented her with his smooth back. His tight skin stretched across hard muscle and the indent of his spine that ran between his shoulders to the small of his back. A nicotine patch was stuck to his waist and half hidden by the thick white towel hung low on his hips.

"Don't you think it's going to get too hot sitting so close to the fire?" he asked.

"If your skin isn't warm, your pores will be closed to the healing benefits of the benzoin and eucalyptus." She stood beside him and placed one palm across his forehead and the other at the nape of his neck. "Drop your head a little bit," she said and gently squeezed his knotted neck muscles. "Bring awareness to the tension in your head. Now take a deep cleansing breath and hold it until I tell you," she instructed as she rubbed the pad of her thumb up the top vertebras of his spine and into the fine hair at the base of his skull. She counted to five and slid her thumb back down. "Release your breath, and with it, the tension you feel in your head. Let it go."

"Ahh . . . Gabrielle?"

"Yes, Joe."

"I don't have tension in my head."

The relaxing essence of lavender and geranium filled her living room as she moved to stand behind him. Her hands slid to his temples, and she massaged away the tension he didn't think he had. "Joe, you're so tense you're brittle." She slowly combed her fingers up the sides of his head; his silky hair curled around her knuckles as she entwined them on top of his skull. She applied pressure with her palms and rubbed. "How does that feel?"

He groaned.

"That's what I thought." She spent a bit more

time than usual on his skull and neck, but his hair felt so soft between her fingers that she couldn't help herself. A warm little tingle traveled up her arms and tightened her breasts, and she forced herself to move on, to relinquish the pleasure of touching his hair.

She poured a small measure of the massage oil from the lotus bowl into her palms. "Take a deep cleansing breath and hold it." She placed her hands on the back of each shoulder and rolled and squeezed his muscles. His trapezius and deltoids were tight and knotted, and she moved her hands to the outside edge of his shoulders and down his arms to his elbows. "Feel the tension in the base of your skull. Let it go as you exhale," she instructed even though she had a real good feeling he wasn't using his breathing to relax. She kneaded her way back up. "Visualize the bad stress flowing away from you and replace it with white prana, or clean universal energy."

"Gabrielle, you're scaring me."

"Shhh." She didn't believe anything scared him, especially her. She dipped her fingers into the oil, then slid her palms down, then up his back, preparing and warming his muscles for a deeper massage. She molded her hands to the contours of his flesh, feeling and learning the definition and shape of him. "Is this where it hurts?" she asked as her hands moved to his right shoulder.

"A bit lower."

She kneaded and squeezed and rubbed a drop of black pepper oil onto his aching muscles. The heat from the fire warmed his skin, while the light of the flames chased shadows across his flesh and gleamed in his dark hair. A pleasurable flutter settled in her stomach, and her mind and spirit fought to keep her touch impersonal. She might not be a licensed masseuse, but she knew the distinct difference between a healing massage and a sensual massage.

"Gabrielle?"

"Yes."

"I'm sorry about what happened in the park last week."

"For tackling me?"

"No, I'm not sorry about that. I enjoyed it too much."

"Then what are you sorry about?"

"That you were frightened."

"And that's the only thing you're sorry about?"

"Well, yeah."

She gently sank her fingertips into his flesh. She had a feeling he didn't apologize for anything very often, and she accepted it as his best effort.

"I've got to admit, I've never been mistaken for a stalker before."

"You probably have, just no one has told you the truth before me." She smiled and continued to stroke across his shoulder and down his arms. "You have a very menacing aura some-times. You should work on it."

"I'll be sure to do that."

She slid her hands back up and pressed her thumbs in the bony ridge at the base of his skull. "I'm sorry I hurt your leg."

One of her thumbs brushed his jaw as he glanced over his shoulder at her. His dark eyes looked up at her, firelight casting his face within a golden glow. "When?"

"That day in the park when I got you on the ground. Afterward, you limped to the car."

"That's an old injury. You didn't do that."

"Oh."

"You sound disappointed."

"No." Her fingers fanned outward, and her hands moved to the sides of his rib cage. "Not disappointed exactly. You were so horrible to me, I just liked to think I made you suffer a little bit that day too."

He smiled before he returned his gaze to the fire. "Oh, you did. Every time I walk into the station, I get a raft of shit about you and your hair spray. I'm likely to hear about you for years."

"Once this case is over, everyone will forget about me." Beneath his hard muscles, his ribs tapered to his flat abdomen. "You'll probably forget, too."

"Now, that's never going to happen," he spoke from deep within his chest. "I'll never forget you, Gabrielle Breedlove."

His words pleased her more than she wanted to admit. They settled beneath her breast, next to her heart, and warmed her like the glow of a tea candle. She smoothed her hands down Joe's sides to his waist, up to his armpits, then back down. "Now bring your awareness to your shoulders. Take a deep breath, and hold it." She felt him suck his stomach in, and his muscles turned hard. "You aren't holding a deep breath, are you?"

"No."

"You have to use your breathing if you want to relax completely."

"Impossible."

"Why?"

"Just take my word for it."

"Would a glass of wine help?"

"I don't drink wine." He paused before he spoke again. "There's only one thing that would help."

"What is it?"

"A cold shower."

"That doesn't sound relaxing."

He laughed again, but he didn't sound amused. "Well, there is one other thing I've been sitting here thinking about."

"What?" she asked although she knew.

His words were low and husky when he said, "Never mind. It involves both of us naked, and that can't happen."

Of course she knew it couldn't. They were complete opposites. He upset her universal balance. She wanted a man of enlightenment. He was as enlightened as a caveman. He thought she was crazy, and maybe she was. Less than a week ago, she'd thought he was a stalker; now he sat in her living room while she oiled his body as if he were a Chippendale dancer. Maybe she was crazy. Still she asked, "Why?"

"You're my informant."

Which wasn't a good reason as far as she was concerned. The informant's agreement she'd signed was a piece of paper. A piece of paper that couldn't dictate desire. Now, the fact that they were two totally different people, with totally different beliefs, should have been a very good reason for them to avoid the huge mistake of falling in bed together.

But as she watched the glow of firelight flicker across his smooth back, their differences didn't seem to matter all that much. The movement of her hands turned fluid and soothing and sensual. Joe upset her balance so much that she forgot all about keeping her touch impersonal. She dipped her fingers into the warmed oil, and her touch grew feather light as she caressed his spine. "Bring your awareness into your solar plexus and abdomen. Take a deep breath, then let it go."

She closed her eyes and let her hands slide over the supple contours of his lower back. Then she lightly ran the tips of her fingers up his spine. He shivered even as his muscles bunched beneath his tight, hot skin, and she fanned her thumbs across his smooth flesh. Suddenly, she had an overwhelming urge to moan or sigh or lean forward and sink her teeth into him. "Bring your awareness into your groin."

"Too late." He stood and turned to face her. "It's already there."

She looked up into his heavy-lidded eyes and the curve of his mouth. A bead of sweat slid down his cheek and jaw, down the side of his neck, and settled in the hollow of his tan throat. She lifted her hands and placed them on his flat abdomen. Her thumbs stroked the line of dark hair circling his navel.

Her gaze lowered to his waist and the unmistakable swell of his erection. Her fingers curled against his belly, and her throat felt dry. She licked her lips, and her gaze drifted lower to the scar on his thigh just visible through the split in the beach towel.

"Sit down, Joe," she ordered and pushed until his behind hit the seat. The towel rode up his right thigh, revealing the bottom edge of a pair of black boxers. "Is this where you were shot?" she asked as she knelt between his knees.

"Yes."

She dipped her thumbs into the oil, then circled them over the scar. "Does it still hurt?"

"No. At least not like it used to," he said, his voice rough.

The thought of such violence broke her heart,

and she gazed up into his face. "Who did this to you?"

Looking down at her through lowered lids, he waited so long to answer that she didn't think he would. "An informant named Robby Martin. You probably heard about it. It was in all the newspapers about a year ago."

The name sounded familiar, and it took her a moment to remember. Then a picture of a young blond kid flashed across her memory. The story had been news for a long time. The name of the undercover detective who'd fired the fatal shot had never been mentioned, and she'd forgotten anyone but Robby had been shot. "That was you?"

Again he waited before he answered, "Yes."

Slowly, she slid her thumbs up and down his thick scar and added a little pressure. She remembered it so well, because just like everyone else in the city, she'd talked about it with friends, and she'd wondered if Boise didn't have a few trigger-happy cops running around shooting young men for nothing more than smoking a little pot. "I'm sorry."

"Why? Why would you be sorry?"

"I'm sorry you were forced to do something like that."

"I was doing my job," he said, a hard edge punctuating his words.

"I know." She gently sank her fingertips into his thigh muscles. "I'm sorry you were hurt."

"You don't believe I'm trigger happy?"

She shook her head. "I don't believe you're reckless, or that you'd take someone's life unless you weren't given a choice."

"Maybe I'm as cold-blooded as the papers said. How do you know?"

She answered what she knew to be true in her heart. "Because I know your soul, Joe Shanahan."

Joe looked into her clear green eyes, and he almost believed she could see inside him and know something he didn't know with absolute certainty.

She licked her lips, and he watched the tip of her tongue slide to the corner of her mouth. Then she did something that stopped his heart and sent pure lust slamming into his groin. She bent her head and kissed his thigh.

"I know you're a good man."

His breath caught in his throat, and he wondered if she'd still think he was a "good man" if he asked her to move her mouth a little north and kiss his other, bigger, owie. He stared down at the top of her head, but just as he worked up a real good fantasy involving her face in his lap, she looked up and ruined it. She gazed at him as if she really could look inside his soul. As if she saw a better man than he knew he was.

Joe jumped to his feet and turned his back on her. "You don't know shit," he said as he moved to the fireplace and grasped the mantel.

"Maybe I liked kicking down doors and using my body as a battering ram."

"Oh, I don't doubt that." She came to stand beside him, then she added, "You're a physical guy. What I doubt is that you had a choice."

He glanced across his shoulder at her, then turned to gaze at the little candles burning on the mantel. "I had a choice all right, I didn't have to chase a drug dealer down a dark alley. But I'm a cop, that's what I do. I chase the bad guys, and once I'm committed to something, I see it through. And believe me, I was committed to bringing Robby in." He wanted to shock her. Shut her up. Wipe that look from her eyes. "I was royally pissed off at him. He was my informant, and he'd double-crossed me, and I wanted to get my hands on him." He glanced at her again, but she didn't look shocked. She was supposed to be a pacifist. She was supposed to hate men like him. She wasn't supposed to look at him as if she *felt sorry for him*, for God's sake.

"I saw the burst of fire from Robby's gun," he continued, "and I emptied my clip into his chest before I even knew I'd drawn my weapon. I didn't need to see him to know I'd hit him. Once you hear something like that, you know what it is. And you never forget. Later, I found out that I'd killed him before he'd even hit the ground. And I don't know how I'm supposed to feel about that. Sometimes I feel like shit, and others I'm just damn glad I was the better shot.

It's a hell of a thing to know you've taken away all a man is and all he'll ever be." He pushed away from the mantel. "Maybe I *was* out of control."

"I doubt you've ever been that out of control."

She was wrong. Somehow, she'd gotten him to tell her more about the shooting than he'd told anyone else. All she'd had to do was look up at him through those big eyes like she really believed in him, and he'd babbled like an idiot. Well, he was through talking. For the past half hour, he'd sat on that uncomfortable chair, wondering how her breasts would fit in his palms. He had a raging erection urging him to grab one of those soft hands she'd rubbed all over him and shove it down his boxers so she could stroke something more interesting than his elbow.

He reached for her and covered her mouth with his. He recognized the taste of her full, sweet lips, as if they were lovers. As if he'd known her forever. He slanted his head to one side, and her mouth opened to him, hot and slick and welcoming. He felt her shudder as his tongue touched hers. Her arms twined around his neck, and she clung to him. The front of her bibbed dress brushed his bare chest, while her hips arched toward him, pressing into his rock-hard erection. Joe grasped her waist, and instead of playing it smart and shoving her away, he ground his pelvis up against her. The plea-

sure was exquisite and painful. Throbbing ag-
ony and ecstasy, and he wanted more from her
than a kiss.

His hands moved to the clasp of her overall
straps, and he easily unhooked them. The bib
fell to her waist, and he made quick work of the
buttons closing her white shirt. He pushed
apart both sides of her blouse and finally, finally, filled his hands with full breasts covered
in lace. Her lips trembled and she gasped as his
thumbs brushed back and forth across her hard,
pointed nipples. Then he pulled back and
looked into her face. Her lids fluttered open and
she whispered his name, the sound filled with
the same craving that twisted a painful knot in
his belly. Hunger shone in her eyes, and knowing she wanted him the way he wanted her
made his blood burn in his veins. She was beautiful inside and out. She was passion and long-
ing and fire in his hands, and he wanted to play
with fire for just a bit longer.

Joe took a deep breath and let it out slowly
as his gaze traveled from the auburn hair fram-
ing her beautiful face with wild curls, past her
lips, moist and swollen from his kiss, and down
her throat to his hands filled with her plump
breasts. "Now it's your turn," he said and
looked back up into her face.

Her eyes stared into his as he pushed her
blouse from her shoulders. The white material
slid from her arms and fell to the ground. She
stood before him, her bibbed jumper buttoned

at her hips, and the scalloped edges of her bra cupping her breasts. In the very center, her nipples pushed against the white lace, very hard and pink. He turned slightly at the waist and dipped his fingers into the warm oil. Then he touched the base of her throat and slowly slid his fingertips down her sternum and between the firm swells of her cleavage. Her incredibly soft skin brushed the back of his knuckles as he twisted the center clasp of her bra. It sprang open, and her breasts popped out of the cups. So beautiful and perfect that his throat closed. Joe lifted his hands to her shoulders and slid the lace straps down her arms until the bra fell beside her blouse. Then he reached for the lotus bowl and raised it between them. Slowly, he tilted it until the small amount of remaining oil poured over her white flesh, running down the plump sides and in between her breasts, down her stomach to her navel. Without taking his gaze from her, he emptied the bowl and tossed it on the wooden chair. One clear drop glistened from her nipple, and he touched it with his finger.

He opened his mouth to tell her she had great breasts, but all that came out was a tangle of swear words as he spread the bead of oil across the tip and circled her puckered flesh.

Gabrielle swayed and placed one of her hands on the back of his neck. She pressed her moist lips to his and gently sucked his tongue into her mouth. Joe smeared oil all over soft breasts and smooth belly. He wanted her. He'd never wanted anything like he wanted to give into the aching lust pounding his groin. His palms moved to the sides of her throat, and he pulled back to look at her, at her breasts gleaming in the firelight, the peaks shiny and moist as if he'd kissed her there. He'd never wanted anything like he wanted to shove his boxers down around his ankles and shove Gabrielle up against a wall or down on the couch or on the floor or wherever. He wanted to kneel between her soft thighs, and with the sweet smell of candles and of her filling his head, bury himself deep inside her and stay there for a while. Wanted to pull her nipple into his mouth while he slid in and out of her hot, slick body. She wanted it as much as he did. So, why the hell not give them both what they wanted?

But he couldn't make love to her. Even if she wasn't his informant, he wasn't one of those guys who carried contraception in his wallet, and he almost laughed with relief. "I don't have a condom with me."

"I've been taking birth control for eight years," she said and moved one of his hands back to her slick breast. "And I trust you."

He wished like hell she hadn't confessed that and given him the green light. The ache in his groin throbbed, and before his brain completely descended to his shorts he forced himself to remember who she was and what she was to him. He buried his face in her hair and dropped his hand to his side. He wanted her like he'd never wanted any other woman in his life, and he had to do something fast.

"Gabrielle, honey, can you channel Elvis?" he asked, gasping for breath and grasping at straws.

"Hmm?" Her voice was rough, as if she'd just woken up. "What?"

"Can you channel Elvis Presley?"

"No," she whispered and leaned into him. Her breasts brushed his chest, and the hard tips grazed his own flat nipples.

"Jesus," he wheezed, "can't you try?"

"Right now?"

"Yeah."

She leaned back to look at him through her heavy-lidded eyes. "I'm not psychic."

"So, you can't communicate with the dead?"

"No."

"Damn."

She slid her hand to his shoulder and cleared her throat. "But I have a cousin who communicates with whales."

The corners of his mouth twitched. A cousin who communicated with whales was only a slight distraction, but he would take anything that diverted his attention from Gabrielle's firm breasts. "Really?"

"Well, she thinks she does, anyway."

"Tell me something about whales?" Joe reached behind her and flipped her suspenders back over her shoulders.

"What?"

"Well, what do they think about?" He fastened her suspenders to the bib of her dress and covered temptation as best he could.

"I don't know. Krill or squid maybe?"

Despite his still throbbing groin, Joe walked to the sofa, dropped the towel, and shoved his legs into his pants.

"You're leaving?"

He looked over at her, at the confusion wrinkling her brow, and at the swells of her breasts spilling out the sides of her dress. "I have an early day tomorrow," he said and reached for his shirt. He shoved his arms in the sleeves and pulled it over his head.

Even as Gabrielle watched Joe pull the ends of his polo down his chest, she couldn't believe he was leaving. Not when she could still feel and taste his mouth on her tongue.

"I painted the storage room in your shop today," he said as if she weren't standing there without her shirt. As if her body wasn't humming from his touch. "If this investigation drags into next week, we'll have to think of something else for me to do. Kevin said something about a countertop, but I don't have experience with that sort of carpentry."

She moved behind the dining room chair she'd placed in front of the fire and wrapped her hands around the top wrung. Her knees shook, and she couldn't believe they were talking about his carpentry experience. For the first time since he'd stripped her to the waist, she felt exposed and raised her hands to her breasts. "Okay," she said.

Joe pulled out his keys and headed to the front door. "So, I probably won't talk to you again until Monday. You have my pager number, don't you?"

"Yes." He wouldn't try to call her or see her tomorrow. Maybe it was for the best. A few hours ago she wasn't sure she even liked him, yet now the thought of not seeing him made her feel hollow inside. She watched him walk from her house as if he couldn't get out fast enough, and as soon as the door closed behind him, Gabrielle slid into the chair.

The candles on the mantel flickered, but their scent did nothing to soothe her. Gabrielle's spirits pulled her north and south, yet all her desires seemed to be focused in the same direction—in Joe's direction. It made absolutely no sense. There was no balance in her life when he was around. No peaceful center, but standing so close, feeling the warmth of his naked skin had felt so right. So complete. So whole. He'd confided in her, and she felt as if they'd connected on a more spiritual plane.

They'd known each other for such a short time, and yet she'd let him pour oil on her breasts and touch her as if they were lovers. He made her heart pound and her senses come alive until every part of her body, mind, and spirit focused on him. She responded to him like no man she'd ever known, yet she didn't know him. Her heart pounded as if she recognized him, and there could only be one explanation. She feared what it meant.

Yin and yang.

Darkness and light. Positive and negative. Two complete opposites coming together to make a perfectly balanced whole.

She feared it meant she was falling in love with Detective Joe Shanahan.

Thirteen

THE MIDMORNING SUN THAT POURED through the windows of the police station streamed across Joe's desk and lit up the plastic spring-loaded hula dancer like a religious icon. Joe scanned the form before him, and with little enthusiasm he signed the affidavit requesting a search warrant. He handed it to Captain Luchetti, then tossed his pen on the desk. The blue Bic rolled across the activity report he'd worked on earlier and bumped the hula dancer's bare feet, setting her hips into motion.

"Looks good," the captain uttered as he glanced at the form.

Joe folded his hands behind his head and stretched out his legs. He'd been sitting in the squad room for three hours now discussing the Hillard case with the other detectives. He'd briefed them on what he'd seen in Kevin's house, starting with the stolen antiques in the guest room, continuing with the ivory chess set, and ending with the mirrors in the bedroom. He'd thought he'd have Kevin in custody by now and was disappointed as hell. "Yeah, too bad we can't serve it today."

"That's the problem with you, Shanahan, you're too impatient." Captain Luchetti glanced at his watch and set the affidavit on Joe's desk. "You want everything to wrap up in an hour, like one of those cop shows on television."

Impatience wasn't Joe's problem. Well, maybe just a little, but he had his reasons for wanting the case resolved, and it had nothing to do with patience and everything to do with his redheaded informant.

The captain shrugged into his suit jacket and straightened his tie. "You did good. We'll get our court order to tap Carter's home phone and our search warrant. We'll get him," he said and walked from the room. No matter where he was or what he was doing, Vince Luchetti never missed Sunday mass. Joe wondered who the captain feared more, God, or his wife, Sonja.

He stretched his arms above his head and eyed the affidavit. He'd been meticulous with the language of the document, having learned long ago that defense attorneys thrived on vague or inadequate descriptions and looked for any excuse to claim entrapment. But for all his trouble, he didn't believe his effort would amount to squat. Oh, he'd get his warrant, there was enough probable cause for a judge to authorize a search, but Walker and Luchetti wanted to wait. Since Joe hadn't found the Monet the night before, they weren't convinced a search of Kevin's home would recover the painting, or that Kevin would rat out the collector who the police believed was behind ordering the theft.

So, the warrant would get shoved into the case file. They now had solid evidence that proved Kevin was guilty of fencing stolen antiques, but an arrest would not come of Joe's work from the night before. He'd received a pat on the back and a few high fives. But Joe wanted more. He wanted Kevin sitting in an interrogation room.

"Hey, Shannie." Winston Densley, the only African American detective in property crimes, and one of three detectives assigned to tail Kevin, pulled up a chair next to Joe's desk. "Tell me about those mirrors in Carter's bedroom."

Joe chuckled and folded his arms over his chest. "The room is covered all around, and he can check out his action from every angle."

"Pretty kinky shit?"

"Yeah." And Joe had stood in that kinky room of mirrors, checking out all the angles and images of Gabrielle Breedlove in that shapeless, ugly dress, wondering what she'd look like wearing nothing but one of those Victoria's Secret see-through bras and a pair of matching panties. Or maybe a lace thong so he could grab her bare behind in his palms.

While she'd wondered about Windex, he'd

wondered what she'd look like bare from the waist up. Now he didn't have to wonder. Now he knew. He knew her breasts were larger than he'd imagined, and fit perfectly into his big hands. He knew the soft texture of her skin and the feel of her puckered nipples poking his chest. And he knew other things too, like the sound of her passionate sigh, and the pull of her seductive green eyes. He knew the smell of her hair, the taste of her mouth, and that the touch of her gentle hands made him so hard he could barely think or breathe.

And he knew without a doubt that he'd be a hell of a lot better off not knowing. Joe sighed and ran his hands through his hair. "I want to put this case to bed."

"Case is gonna take as long as it takes. What's your hurry?"

What was his hurry? He'd come within seconds of making love to Gabrielle, and he wasn't so sure it wouldn't happen again. He could tell himself it wouldn't happen, but certain parts of his body weren't listening. He'd come real close to jeopardizing his career with her. If she hadn't come up with a relative who communicated with whales, he might have laid her right there on her living room floor. "Just getting antsy, I guess," he answered.

"You still think like a narc." Winston stood and pushed his chair back across the room. "Sometimes the fun's in the waiting, and we could be at this one a while," he predicted.

Time was one thing Joe didn't have. He needed to get himself reassigned to a different case before he messed up completely and lost his job or got busted to bike patrol. Big problem, though. He couldn't exactly ask for reassignment without a damn good reason, and "I'm afraid I'm going to trade some DNA with my confidential informant" wasn't even a consideration. He had to do something, only he didn't have a clue what that something might be.

He left the report and affidavit on his desk and headed for the door. If he hurried, maybe he'd catch Ann Cameron before her lunch rush. She was exactly the type of woman he always looked for in a girlfriend. She was attractive, one hell of a cook, but more important, she was normal. Uncomplicated. Baptist. Nothing like Gabrielle.

Within half an hour, Joe sat at a small table in Ann's deli, feasting on warm crusty bread and a plate of chicken in creamy pesto. He thought he'd died and gone to heaven—except there was something keeping him from completely enjoying his meal. He couldn't shake the feeling that he was cheating on his girlfriend. Cheating on Gabrielle with Ann. The feeling was totally irrational. But it pecked at him, right at the back of his brain, and wouldn't leave him alone.

Ann sat across the table from him, chatting nonstop about her business and her life and growing up in the same neighborhood. Perfectly normal conversation, yet there was something that didn't feel right about that either.

"I make sure I drink at least three quarts of water, and I walk three miles a day, too," she told him. Her eyes were real bright, as if she were really excited, but he didn't have a clue what was exciting about walking and drinking water. "I remember you used to walk your dog every night," she said. "What was his name?"

"Scratch," he answered, recalling the dog he'd rescued from the pound. Scratch had been a shar-pei pit bull mix and the best dog a boy could own. Now Joe had a bird. A bird who wanted to roost with Gabrielle.

"I have a Pomeranian, Snicker Doodle. He's such a love."

Holy hell. He pushed aside his plate and reached for his glass of iced tea. Okay, he could overlook a little yap-yap dog. She was a great cook and she had nice eyes. There was absolutely no reason why he couldn't see her. He didn't have a girlfriend.

He wondered if Sam would like Ann, or if he would try to chase her out of his house. Maybe it was time to invite her over and find out. And as far as his feelings of guilt, he had absolutely nothing to feel guilty about. Nothing. Nada. Zip.

Gabrielle had planned to spend a quiet morning at home preparing essential oils. Instead, she painted like a crazed Van Gogh. She set the portrait she'd been working on against the wall and began another. Her mother called and interrupted her twice, so she took the telephone off the hook. By noon she'd finished her latest painting of Joe—except for his hands and feet, of course. Like the others, he stood within his aura, but this time she'd taken a bit more creative license with his male package. She didn't think she'd exaggerated. Just sort of guessed, based on the hard length of him she'd felt against her inner thigh the night before.

Just thinking about what had taken place in her living room brought a blush to her cheeks. The woman who'd purposely turned an innocent massage into something erotic wasn't her. She didn't do things like that. There had to be an explanation, like maybe something funky had taken place in the cosmos. Like maybe the full moon had affected the blood flow to her cerebellum, and if there wasn't balance in the cerebellum, there was chaos.

Gabrielle sighed and dipped her brush into red paint. She couldn't quite make herself believe her moon theory, and she was no longer sure of the yin and yang theory either. In fact, she was quite sure now that Joe was *not* her yang. He was not the other half of her soul.

He was only in her life to get back Mr. Hillard's Monet and to pretend to care about her so he could arrest Kevin. He was a hard-living cop who thought her ideals were nutty. He laughed at her and teased her, then consumed her with the touch of his hands and mouth. He certainly didn't kiss her like a man who pretended passion. The night before, he'd shared a part of his past with her, a piece of his life, and she'd thought they'd made a connection.

He'd made her dizzy with wanting, then left her standing alone and dazed. He turned her on, then asked her to channel Elvis, and he called *her* crazy?

Gabrielle rinsed her brushes, then changed out of her painting shirt and into a pair of cutoffs and T-shirt with the name of a local restaurant across the chest. She didn't bother with shoes.

At twelve-thirty, Kevin dropped off a FedEx tube filled with a few antique movie posters he'd purchased from an Internet auction. He wanted her opinion on their value, and the whole time he stood in her kitchen talking appraisal, she expected him to say something about her and Joe jumping from his balcony. But he didn't, and she supposed she should be thankful that he'd been too busy showing Mr. Happy to his girlfriend's best friend. She must have looked guilty, though, because he kept asking her if something was wrong.

After Kevin left, Gabrielle finally took out her boxes of oils and set them next to the small glass bowls and bottles on her kitchen table. She wanted to experiment with facial cleansers and moisturizers, and she blended toners and remedies for broken veins and acne. Just as she was about to mix a face mask of natural powdered clay, hot water, and yogurt, Francis rang her doorbell.

Her friend arrived with a blue denim bra and a pair of matching panties. Gabrielle thanked her, then recruited her for a facial. She wrapped Francis's hair in a bath towel, then made her sit on a dining room chair with her head tilted back.

"Tell me if your skin starts to feel too tight," she said as she smoothed the clay mask on her friend's face.

"It smells like licorice," Francis complained.

"That's because I put fennel oil in it." Gabrielle spread the clay across Francis's forehead, careful not to get it on the towel. Francis had a lot of experience with men, some of it not good, but a lot more than Gabrielle did. Maybe her friend could help her make sense of what had happened with Joe. "Tell me something? Have you ever known a man you don't think you even like, but you can't stop yourself from fantasizing and dreaming about him?"

"Yeah."

"Who?"

"Steve Irwin."

"Who?"

"The Crocodile Hunter."

Gabrielle stared into Francis's big blue eyes. "You dream about The Crocodile Hunter?"

"Yeah, I think he's kind of big and dorky and

could probably use lithium to bring him down a notch, but I love his accent. He looks pretty good in those safari shorts, too. I fantasize about wrestling with him."

"He's married to Teri."

"So what? I thought we were talking about fantasies." Francis paused to scratch her ear. "Are you fantasizing about your detective?"

Gabrielle dipped her fingers into the clay paste and spread it down the bridge of her friend's nose. "Is it that obvious?"

"No, but if he weren't yours, I'd dream up a few fantasies about him."

"Joe isn't mine. He's working in my store, and I find him mildly attractive."

"Bull."

"Okay, he's hot, but he isn't my type. He believes Kevin is involved in selling stolen art, and he probably still thinks I am as well." She spread the clay across Francis's cheeks and chin before she added, "And well, he thinks I'm weird even though he's the one who asked me if I could channel Elvis for him."

Francis smiled and got clay on the corner of her mouth. "Can you?"

"Don't be absurd. I'm not psychic."

"It's not absurd. You believe in other New Age stuff, so I don't think it's all that weird that he would ask you."

Gabrielle wiped her hands on a wet cloth, then bent at the waist and wrapped a towel around her own head. "Well, we were kind of making out at the time," she explained as she straightened.

"Making out?"

"Kissing." She and Francis traded places, and Gabrielle looked up into her friend's face, which was covered, except for her eyes and lips, with white paste. "And stuff."

"Oh, well that is weird." The smooth clay felt wonderful across Gabrielle's forehead, and she closed her eyes and tried to relax. "Did he want you to *be* Elvis, or did he just want to ask the King some questions?"

"What difference does it make? Things were getting pretty hot, and he stopped to ask me if I could channel Elvis."

"There's a big difference. If he just wanted to ask some questions, get a little info, then he's just a bit kinky. But if he wanted you to be the king of rock and roll, then you've got to get yourself a new man."

Gabrielle sighed and opened her eyes. "Joe isn't my man." The edge of Francis's mask and the tip of her nose were beginning to dry. "Your turn," she said and purposely changed the subject. "Why don't you tell me what you did last night." She was more confused than ever and didn't know what had made her think Francis could help her make sense of anything.

After the mask, they tried Gabrielle's toner and conditioning oil. By the time Francis left, both women had clean pores and a healthy glow to their skin. Gabrielle baked a veggie pizza for dinner, and sat down in front of the television to eat. With remote in hand, she surfed the networks looking for an episode of *Crocodile Hunter*. She wanted to see what Francis found so fascinating about a man who wrestled reptiles, but the doorbell rang before she'd had a chance to check out every channel. She set her plate on the coffee table, and moved to the entryway. Just as her hand reached for the knob, Joe stormed in, blowing past her like a funnel cloud. The scent of sandalwood and early evening breeze swept inside with him. He wore a pair of black nylon shorts with a Nike swoosh on the butt. The sleeves had been hacked out of his Big Dog T-shirt, and the armholes hung almost to his waist. His white socks were slightly dingy, his running shoes old. He looked macho and rough around the edges, just like the first time she'd seen him, leaning against a tree in Ann Morrison Park, smoking like a chimney.

"Okay, damnit, where is it?" He stopped in the middle of her living room.

Gabrielle shut the door and leaned back against it. Her gaze moved up his powerful calves and thighs to the scar marring his tan flesh.

"Come on, Gabrielle. Hand it over."

She raised her gaze to his face. He was about three hours past his five o'clock shadow, and he eyed her from beneath lowered brows. At one time, she would have thought him menacing, intimidating, and a big old bully. Not anymore. "Don't you have to have a warrant or writ or something before you can barge into a person's house?"

"Don't play games." He shoved his hands on his hips and cocked his head to one side. "Where is it?"

"What?"

"Fine." He tossed his wallet and key on the table beside her plate, then he proceeded to look behind her couch and in the coat closet.

"What are you doing?

"I leave you alone for one day, and you pull something like this." He sailed by her on his way to the dining room, where he quickly glanced around, then continued into the hall, his words trailing after him. "Just when I begin to think you have a brain, you go and do something so stupid."

"What?" The sound of his steps led to her bedroom, and Gabrielle quickly followed. By the time she got there, he'd opened and closed half her drawers. "If you tell me what you're looking for, I might save you some time."

Instead of giving her an answer, he threw open her closet doors and pushed aside her clothes. "I warned you not to protect him."

He bent at the waist, affording Gabrielle a nice view of his very nice backside. When he straightened, he had a box in his hands.

"Hey, put that back. That contains my personal stuff."

"You should have thought of that earlier. As of right now, you don't have personal stuff. You're in so deep, I don't even think that little weasel of a lawyer you hired can help you." He dumped out the box on her bed, and dozens of bras, panties, bustiers, and merry widows spilled across her duvet. He stared at her lingerie, and his eyes got wide.

If Gabrielle hadn't been so annoyed, she would have laughed.

"What in the hell?" He reached for a pair of black vinyl panties—crotchless, of course. They dangled from his index finger as he inspected them from all angles. "You've got underwear like a hooker."

She snatched the panties from him and tossed them with the others on the bed. " Francis gives me lingerie from her store. I don't really care for most of it."

He picked up a cherry red corset trimmed with black fringe. He looked like a kid with a whole assortment of his favorite candy spread out in front of him. A kid with cheeks tinged blue from a heavy five o'clock shadow. "I like this one."

"Of course you do." She folded her arms beneath her breasts and rested her weight on one foot.

"You should wear this."

"Joe, why are you here?"

Reluctantly, he tore his gaze from the undies

on her bed. "I got a call that Kevin passed you something in a FedEx tube."

"What, is that what all of this is about? He wanted me to see some old movie posters he bought on the Internet."

"So, he was here?"

"Yes. How did you know about that?"

"Damnit." He tossed the corset on the bed and walked past her out of the room. "Why'd you let him in?"

Gabrielle followed close behind, her gaze pinned on the little curls brushing the nape of his neck. "He's my business partner. Why wouldn't I let him in?"

"Gee, I don't know. Maybe because he's a fence and involved in art theft. You figure it out."

Gabrielle hardly heard a word he said. Panic brushed aside all other thought as she followed him past the bathroom to the end of the hall. She grabbed his arm and pulled, but it was like trying to stop a bull. She dashed in front of him and spread her arms, blocking the doorway to her studio. "This is my private room," she said, her heart stopping and her head pounding. "You can't go in there."

"Why?"

"Because."

"Come up with something better."

On such short notice she couldn't. "Because I said."

He grasped her upper arms in his strong

hands and moved her out of his way.

"No, Joe!"

The door swung open. A prolonged moment of silence hung in the air, during which Gabrielle prayed to any god listening that somehow the studio had changed since she'd been in there earlier that day.

"Sweet baby Jesus."

She guessed not.

Slowly he walked into the room, until he stood an arm's length away from the life-sized painting. Gabrielle wanted nothing more at that moment than to run away and hide, but where would she go? She glanced over his shoulder at the canvas, at the early evening sunlight pouring through the sheer curtains, bleaching a patch of light on the hardwood floor, and lighting up the portrait with a sort of ethereal glow. She hoped he wouldn't recognize himself.

"Is that," he asked, pointing at the painting, "supposed to be me?"

There was no hope now. She'd been caught. She might have a problem with proportional hands and feet, but she'd had absolutely no trouble with Joe's penis. There was only one thing to do—brave it out and hide her embarrassment as best she could. "I think it's very good," she said and crossed her arms beneath her breasts.

He looked back over his shoulder at her, his eyes a little glassy. "I'm naked."

"Nude."

"Same damn thing." He turned back, and Gabrielle moved to stand beside him.

"Where are my hands and feet?"

She tilted her head. "Well, I haven't had time to paint them yet."

"I see you had time to paint my dick, though."

What could she say? "I think I did a good job with the shape of your eyes."

"And my balls too."

She tried once again to divert his attention upward. "I captured your mouth perfectly."

"Are those supposed to be my lips? They look puffy," he said, and she supposed she should be grateful he was no longer critiquing his genitals. "And what in the hell is the big red ball? Fire or something?"

"Your aura."

"Uh-huh." He turned his attention to the two paintings leaning against the far wall. "You've been busy."

She bit her top lip and didn't say anything. At least in the painting of him as a demon, he was clothed. The other, well . . .

"Didn't have time to paint the hands or feet on those either?"

"Not yet."

"Am I supposed to be the devil or something?"

"Or something."

"What's with the dog?"

"It's a lamb."

"Oh . . . it looks like a Welsh corgi."

It looked nothing like a Welsh corgi, but Gabrielle didn't argue. First of all, she never explained her art, and second, she could overlook a few tactless comments and blame them on shock. She imagined it might be a bit disturbing to open a door and find a nude portrait of yourself staring back at you.

"Who's that?" he asked, pointing to the painting of his head and David's body.

"Don't you know?"

"That is not me."

"I used Michelangelo's sculpture of David as my model. I didn't know you had chest hair."

"Is that supposed to be funny?" he asked, incredulous, as he shook his head. "I never stand like that. He looks queer."

She hoped he meant queer as in strange, but she doubted it. "He's preparing for his battle with Goliath."

"Damn," he swore and pointed to David's groin. "Look at that. I haven't packed anything that small since I was two."

"You're fixated on your genitals."

"Not me, lady." He turned and directed his finger at her. "You're the one sneaking around painting pictures of my bare ass."

"I'm an artist."

"Yeah, and I'm an astronaut."

She'd been willing to forgive his rude criticism, but only up to a point, and he'd just stepped over the line. "You need to leave now."

He crossed his arms over his chest and shifted his weight to one foot. "Are you kicking me out?"

"Yes."

Undiluted machismo curved the corners of his mouth. "Do you think you're big enough?"

"Yes."

He laughed. "Without your hair spray, little miss bad ass?"

Okay, now she was mad. She shoved his chest and knocked him a step backward. The next time she pushed, he was ready for her and didn't budge. "You can't come in my house and bully me. I don't have to take this from you." She pushed again, and he grabbed her wrist. "You're an undercover cop. You're not my real boyfriend. I would never *ever* have a boyfriend like you."

His smile flatlined as if she'd insulted him somehow. Which was impossible. He'd have to have human emotions to feel insulted. "Why the hell not?"

"You're surrounded by negative energy," she said as she struggled to pull free of his grasp but couldn't. "And I don't like you."

He let her go, and she took a step back. "You liked me enough last night."

She folded her arms, and her gaze narrowed. "Last night there was a full moon."

"What about those naked pictures you painted of me?"

"What about them?"

"You don't paint a guy's dick you don't like."

"My only interest in your ... ah," she couldn't say it. She just couldn't say the D word.

"You can go ahead and call it Mr. Happy," he supplied. "Or penis is good."

"Male anatomy," she said, "is that of an artist."

"There you go again." He placed his hands on her face and cupped her cheeks in his palms. "Creating bad karma for yourself." He lightly brushed one thumb across her chin.

"I'm not lying," she lied. Her breath got stuck in her throat and she thought he would kiss her. But he just laughed, dropped his hands, and turned toward the door. She was caught somewhere between relief and regret.

"I'm a professional artist," she assured Joe as she followed him into the living room.

"If you say so."

"I am!"

"I'll tell you what then," he said as he grabbed his keys from the coffee table, "the next time you feel the urge to paint, give a holler. You dress up in some of your naughty undies, and I'll show you my anatomy. Up close and *real* personal."

Fourteen

AROUND MIDNIGHT, GABRIELLE SHOVED the lingerie Joe had dumped on her duvet to the floor and crawled into bed. She closed her eyes and tried not to think of him standing in her room, his broad shoulders filling out his hacked-up shirt, a pair of crotchless panties dangling from his finger. He was a throwback. A girl's anachronistic nightmare. He made her more angry than any man she'd ever known. She should hate him. She really should. He made fun of her beliefs and now her art, and yet no matter how hard she tried, she couldn't dislike him. There was something about him, some *thing* drawing her to him like the faithful to Mecca. She didn't want to go, but her heart didn't seem to be listening.

If there was one person on this planet Gabrielle knew inside and out, it was herself. She knew what worked for her and what didn't. Sometimes she was wrong, like when she'd thought she'd wanted to become a masseuse only to discover she needed a more creative outlet. Or when she'd taken classes on Feng Shui and learned that planning the design of a room to achieve perfect peace and balance gave her a stress headache.

As a result of the different paths she'd taken in her life, she knew bits and pieces about a lot of different things. Some people might interpret that as flighty or irresponsible, but she saw it differently—more like a willingness to take risks. She was unafraid to change direction midstream. She was open-minded about almost everything. Except the notion that she should allow her heart to become involved with Joe. A relationship between them could never work out. They were too different. Night and day. Positive and negative. Yin and yang.

He would be gone soon, out of her life. The thought of never seeing him again should have made her happy. Instead, it made her feel empty and kept her up most of the night.

The next morning she jogged her usual two miles before she returned home and got ready for work. After her shower, she pulled on a pair of white panties with little red hearts and the matching bra. The set was made of islet and was one of the few items from Francis's store that Gabrielle actually wore. She brushed her hair out, and while it dried, she applied her makeup and hooked a pair of long beaded earrings in her ears.

Mondays were Kevin's day off, and she'd be

alone with Joe until noon, when Mara would arrive. The thought of spending time alone with him scared her even as excited little butterflies fluttered in her stomach. She wondered if he'd spend his time searching Kevin's files again behind the closed office door like he had last week. Or if they'd think of something for him to build or fix. And she wondered if he'd wear his tool belt hung low on his hips.

Gabrielle's doorbell rang, followed by a heavy knock she recognized. She shoved her arms through her white terry cloth robe and tied the belt as she walked to the door. She pulled her hair from beneath the robe and released the deadbolt. Instead of his usual jeans and T-shirt, he wore a navy suit, crisp white shirt, and a burgundy-and-blue tie. Mirrored sunglasses concealed his eyes, and he held a sack from the same deli on Eighth where he'd bought her sandwich Friday. The other hand he'd shoved in the front pocket of his pants. "I brought you breakfast," he said.

"Why, are you feeling bad about making fun of me last night?"

"I've never made fun of you," he said with a completely straight face. "Are you going to invite me in?"

"You've never asked before." She moved aside so he could pass, then shut the door behind him. "You always just barge your way through."

"Your door was locked." He set the paper

sack on the table in front of the couch and pulled out two muffins and two cups of coffee. "I hope you like cream cheese muffins," he said as he reached for his sunglasses and shoved them into the inside pocket of his jacket. Then he glanced up at her through tired eyes and tore the plastic lids from the top of the Styrofoam cups. "Here."

Gabrielle didn't like coffee, but she took it anyway. He handed her a muffin, and she took that, too. For the first time since she'd opened the door, she noticed the tension bracketing the corners of his mouth. "What's wrong?"

"You should eat first. We'll talk in a minute."

"First? How can I possibly eat now?"

He slid his gaze across her cheeks and mouth, then back up to her eyes. "Late last night an art dealer from Portland made contact with Kevin. His name is William Stewart Shalcroft."

"I know of William. Kevin worked for him."

"Still does. At three o'clock this afternoon, William Stewart Shalcroft will arrive on Delta flight two-twenty nonstop from Portland. He and Kevin made plans to meet at a lounge in the airport, exchange the Hillard painting for cash, then Mr. Shalcroft plans to rent a car and drive back to Portland. He'll never make it to the Hertz counter. We'll arrest both of them as soon as they make the exchange."

Gabrielle blinked. "You're kidding me, right?"

"I wish I were, but I'm not. Since the night of

the theft, Kevin has had the painting in his possession."

She heard him. His words were quite clear, yet they didn't make sense. She couldn't have known Kevin for so many years and been so wrong about him. "There has to be a mistake."

"No mistake."

He looked so sure, sounded so adamant, that the first inkling of uncertainty settled in her brain. "Are you absolutely sure?"

"We put a wire on his home phone, and we have him on tape setting up the meeting with Shalcroft."

She looked at Joe, at the exhaustion and strain heavy in his brown eyes. "So, it's all true?"

"I'm afraid so."

And for the first time since he'd cuffed her and hauled her to jail, she allowed herself to believe him. "Kevin stole Mr. Hillard's Monet?"

"He contracted someone else for the actual theft."

"Who?"

"We don't know yet."

She grasped at the answer. "Then isn't it possible that the 'actual' thief is the only thief?"

"No. The theft of a major piece of art like a Monet takes time to plan and a whole underground web of contacts to execute. It starts with a rich collector and works its way on down. We think they've been planning this theft for at least six months, and we don't believe this is the first and only time Kevin and Shalcroft have been involved together. We believe they've been conducting this sort of operation since Kevin worked for Shalcroft in Portland."

Everything Joe said was possible, but incredible to reconcile with the Kevin she knew. "How could he be involved in such a horrible mess?"

"Money. A lot of money."

Gabrielle glanced at the muffin and coffee in her hands. For one confusing moment, she'd forgotten how they'd got there. "Here," she said, setting them on the table. "I'm not hungry." Joe reached for her, but she moved away and slowly sank to the edge of the couch. She sat with her hands in her lap and stared across the room.

Everything in her house looked the same as it had a moment ago. The clock on the mantel silently ticked off the minutes while her refrigerator hummed in the kitchen. An old pickup truck drove past her house, and a dog barked down the street. Normal everyday sounds, yet everything was different now. Her life was different now.

"I let you work in Anomaly because I didn't believe you," she said. "I thought you were wrong, and I built up this whole fantasy in my head where you'd have to come and tell me how sorry you are th—that," her voice cracked, and she cleared her throat. She didn't want to cry or fall apart or make a scene, but she didn't seem to have any control over the tears filling her eyes. Her vision blurred, the printing on the coffee cups smeared and ran together. "That you'd have to apologize for arresting me that day in the park, and for making me betray Kevin. But you weren't wrong about Kevin."

"I am sorry." Joe sat beside her, his feet wide apart, and he closed his big, warm hand over one of hers. "I'm sorry something like this had to happen to you. You don't deserve to be caught up in any of this."

"I'm not perfect, but I've never done anything to earn this kind of bad karma." She shook her head, and a tear spilled down her cheek to a corner of her mouth. "How could I have been so blind? Weren't there signs? How could I be so stupid? How could I not know my business partner is a thief?"

He squeezed her hand. "Because you're like eighty percent of the population. You don't suspect everyone you meet of criminal behavior. You don't walk around suspicious of everyone."

"You do."

"That's because it's my job, and I have to deal with the twenty percent running around like idiots." He brushed his thumb across her knuckles. "I know you probably can't see anything good coming from this right now, but you'll be okay. You've got a real smart lawyer who made sure you'd get to keep your store."

"I don't believe my business can survive this." A second tear slipped from her eyes, then a third. "The theft of that painting is still making news. When Kevin's arrest is reported . . . I'll never be able to recover from something like that." With her free hand, she wiped the moisture from her face. "Anomaly is ruined."

"Maybe not," he said, his deep voice sounding so confident that she almost believed him.

But they both knew her business would never be the same. She would always be tied to the theft of the Hillard painting. Kevin had done that. He'd done that to her, and it was nearly impossible to reconcile Kevin the art fence and the man who'd always brought her rose tea when she hadn't felt good. How could that dichotomy exist in one person, and how could she have thought she knew Kevin so well, yet not really have known him at all? "Do the police think he also has those stolen antiques I was shown the day I was arrested?"

"Yes."

A horrible thought struck Gabrielle, and she quickly looked at Joe across her shoulder. "Do you still think I'm involved?"

"No." He raised a hand and brushed her moist cheek with the backs of his fingers. "I know you aren't involved."

"How?"

"I know you."

Yes, just as she knew him. Her gaze moved over his face, the slight hollow of his cleanly shaved cheeks and smooth jaw. "How could I be so dumb, Joe?"

"He fooled a lot of people."

"Yeah, but I worked with him almost every day. He was my friend, but I guess I never really knew him. Why didn't I feel his negative energy?"

He wrapped his arm around her shoulders and forced her to sit back with him against the couch cushions. "Well, don't feel bad, a person's aura can be real tricky."

"Are you making fun of me?"

"I'm being nice."

A sob caught in her throat, and she looked at him. First Kevin and now Joe. Wasn't anyone who and what she thought? "Why am I always so gullible? Francis tells me all the time that I'm too trusting. It gets me in trouble." She shook her head and tried to blink back the moisture in her eyes. Joe's face was so close she could see his whiskers beneath his tan skin and smell his aftershave. "Some people believe you draw positive or negative events toward you, that you attract the people you deserve."

"Sounds like bullshit to me. If that were the case, you'd only attract aura-seeing, karma-fearing, lapsed vegetarians to you."

"Are you trying to be nice again?"

He smiled. "If you don't know, then maybe I need work."

She looked into his handsome face she knew so well, into his intense eyes with their brows that were usually lowered when he looked at her. At his straight nose and the deep furrow that bowed his top lip. At his smooth skin that would begin a gradual shadow around noon. "My last boyfriend *was* an aura-seeing, karma-fearing vegetarian. Only he wasn't lapsed."

"Sounds like a ball of fire."

"He was boring."

"See, that's because you're a woman who lapses." His thumb swept another tear from her cheek as his gaze moved over her face. "You need a man who appreciates wild, unruly women. I went to parochial school and have a deep appreciation for lapsed girls. In fourth grade, Karla Solazabal used to roll up the waist of her plaid skirt and show me her knees. God, I loved her for that."

And she loved him for trying to cheer her up. "What's going to happen now?" she asked.

His gaze sobered. "Once Kevin is arrested, he'll be booked into—"

"No," she interrupted him. "Am I still your confidential informant until after the trial?"

"No, you're released from the agreement. Since you didn't know anything, I'm sure you won't even need to testify at trial."

His answer settled next to her heart like a hot briquette. She would not ask if he ever intended to see her again, or if he would call now that she wasn't his pretend girlfriend. She wouldn't ask, since she wasn't sure of the answer. "When do you have to go?"

"Not for a while yet."

She slid her hand up his arm, across his

shoulder, to the side of his head. She wouldn't talk about what might happen later, or tomorrow, or next week. She didn't want to think about it. Her fingers brushed his wool collar and combed through his short, spiky hair. A flash of hunger lit his eyes, and he lowered his gaze to her mouth.

"Whatever happened to Karla?" she asked.

He brought a palm up to the sides of her throat and slid his fingers beneath her terry cloth robe. "She's a state legislator." His thumb tipped her chin upward as his lips lowered to brush hers once, twice, three times. He eased her into a soft kiss that seemed to pour through her like sunshine in August, warming her from the top of her head, down her spine, to the pit of her stomach. Hot tingles spread between her legs and thighs, the backs of her knees and the soles of her feet. The inside of his slick mouth tasted of mint and coffee, and he kissed her like she tasted sweet and very, very good to him.

She tilted her head to one side to give him better access, and he drove her against the back of the couch and made love to her mouth with his lips and tongue and hot juices. His warm palm slipped beneath her robe, and he slid his fingertips along the smooth edge of her bra, his touch grazing the swells of her breasts. Her skin grew tight, and she reached for the knot of his tie. He didn't stop her, and she pulled at it until the striped ends hung down his chest. She suckled his tongue as she unfastened the tiny button at his collar. Her fingers worked downward until the dress shirt lay open, then she pulled the ends from his pants. Between their bodies, her hands found his hard abdomen. He sucked in his breath. The fine hair tickled her fingers as she combed them up his stomach and flattened her palms over each male nipple. His muscles hardened beneath her touch, his flesh puckered, and he groaned deep in his chest.

He'd behaved this way the night she'd given him a massage. He'd acted like he wanted her, then he'd asked her about Elvis and he'd left. He'd made leaving look easy. "Do you remember the other night when I gave you the massage?" she asked.

He shrugged out of his jacket and tossed it on the floor. "I'm not likely to forget that massage."

"I wanted you and I thought you wanted me, too. But you left."

"I'm not going anywhere." His gaze met hers as he carefully placed his firearm and holster on the floor by his jacket.

"Why now?"

"Because I'm tired of fighting it. I want you so much I ache, and I'm tired of going home with a killer hard-on that no amount of cold showers can cure. I'm tired of lying awake, picturing you naked like I was sixteen again. Imagining my face in your breasts, and you and me having wild sex. It's time I stopped thinking about it so much and got busy." He flexed his wrists and worked at the buttons there. "You were telling me the truth about those birth control pills, weren't you?"

"Yes."

He tore at the shirt and threw it toward his jacket. "Then it's time I make love to you," he said and came at her, wrapping her in his arms as his mouth swooped to take possession. He ran a hand down her back to her behind, then he gently pushed her to the couch positioning her so that she lay on her back. He knelt on one knee between her thighs, his other foot was planted on her floor, and he pulled back to look down at her with hungry eyes. Gabrielle's robe lay open, exposing her right leg and hip and the slope of her left breast. He untied the belt and moved aside the terry cloth material. His hot gaze touched her everywhere. Lingered on the thin triangle of islet and hearts covering her crotch, then slowly up her abdomen to the stiff underwires of her bra, pushing her breasts together.

"Do you remember the night I walked into your backyard and found you floating in the kiddie pool?"

"Mmm-hmm."

"I wanted to do this." He leaned over her and placed his palms beneath her shoulders. He lifted, then nestled his face in her cleavage. He placed soft kisses between her breasts as she ran her hands across his bare shoulders and down his smooth back. She wrapped one leg around his waist and pressed into him. A low groan rumbled deep in his throat as he pressed back, shoving his hard erection against her crotch. Everything in her consciousness focused on him, the pleasure of his touch, and the dull ache between her legs. His soft kisses made her insane for more, and she arched her back, pressing the fullest part of her breast to his lips. He lifted his gaze to hers and smiled, then he opened his mouth and sucked her through her thin bra. He drove her wild with the slow, undulating rhythm of his hips. Through the narrow strip of her panties and the wool of his pants, he turned her liquid inside. Her skin burned, her nipples tightened, and she dug her fingers into his shoulders and ground against him. He slid his hand from beneath her shoulder and grasped her thigh. Stopping her.

"Slow down, honey, or I'll embarrass myself right here, before the really good part begins."

"I thought this was the really good part."

His quiet laughter filled the space between their lips. "It gets better."

"How?"

"I'll show you, but not on the couch." He stood, drew her to her feet, then pulled her from the room. "I like a bed where I can spread out while I work." They made it as far as the dining room, where she paused to kiss the side of his throat. She tasted his cologne and she slid a hand across his flat abdomen, down the front of his pants, and found the long hard length of him. Then before she knew what he was doing, he picked her up and set her on top of the cool table. Her hand knocked the telephone, and it crashed to the floor. Neither cared.

"The first time I saw you, you jogged past me on the greenbelt, and I thought you had the sweetest legs and ass this side of heaven. I thought you were about the best-looking woman I'd ever seen." He sat in a ladder-back chair and kissed the inside of one calf.

"You thought I was a felon."

"Didn't mean I was opposed to seeing you naked." He pressed his lips to the inside of her knee. "Didn't mean I wasn't looking forward to a strip search. Doesn't mean I don't know what a lucky son of a bitch I am."

Gabrielle's gaze took in his hair and the smile he brushed against her inner thigh. Passion smoldered in his dark eyes as the tip of his tongue touched the mole a few scant inches below the elastic leg band of her panties. Her breath caught in her throat and he held her there, suspended, turning her insides hotter, and making her wonder what he would do next. "Or taste you right here," he said and softly drew her skin into his warm mouth. Every pinpoint of desire in her body intensified and burned, making her jumpy at the same time as it held her frozen in place. His hand slipped up the inside of her thigh to the islet covering her crotch. His thumb brushed her through the thin material, and he lifted his head and looked up at her.

"How does that feel?"

"Good, Joe."

He scooted the chair as close to the table as possible. "This has driven me insane." He wrapped one arm around her waist, then he dipped his head and sucked her shallow navel just below her belly ring. His grip on her upper thigh tightened while his thumb continued to lightly stroke her through her moist panties. She leaned her head back and closed her eyes, shutting out everything but the exquisite pleasure of his hand and his mouth kissing a wet path up her stomach to the inside slope of her right breast. He drew her sensitive skin into his mouth, then pushed aside one cup of her bra and took her nipple into his hot, wet mouth.

Gabrielle moaned and arched her back, lost to the erotic pull of his lips and the smooth texture of his tongue. He slipped two fingers beneath the elastic leg band of her panties and touched her slick flesh, caressing her exactly where she wanted it most, at the place where every sensation pooled and intensified. She tried to close her legs to hold the pleasure of it in, but he stood between her knees. Then cool air brushed across the tip of her moist breast, and she heard him whisper her name. Her eyes fluttered open, and his face was so close that his nose brushed hers.

"Gabrielle," he said again, and then he kissed

her, as soft and sweet as the first. She wrapped her arms around his neck, and he stood with her in his embrace. Looking into his deep brown eyes, her heart swelled with so much emotion she couldn't hide from it anymore. She'd never been very good at hiding anyway.

The hooks of her bra released, and the thin scrap of material fell away. She pressed her naked breasts into his chest and slid one hand down his side and across his smooth back, over the dip in his spine and the hollow of his waist where he'd stuck a nicotine patch. She loved touching him, feeling his flesh beneath her hands. Her fingers slid around his woven leather belt, and she unbuckled and unbuttoned until his pants lay open. Then she pulled back and looked at him. She easily pushed his pants down his thighs and gazed at a pair of white boxers with the words JOE BOXER on the waistband. He kicked his shoes and trousers aside, then tore at his socks until his feet were bare. He took her hand, and this time they did make it to her bedroom.

Her feet sank in the thick white carpet as her gaze moved up his powerful calves to the scar marring his hard thigh. "I can massage it for you," she offered, her voice sounding thick to her own ears as she brushed the scar with the tips of her fingers.

He reached for her hand, moved it up a few inches, and blatantly pressed her palm to the thick ridge of his erection. "Massage this."

"Well, I am almost a professional," she said and slipped her hand beneath the waistband of his shorts and wrapped his hot, hot flesh in her palm. She closed her fist around him and lightly stroked from the base of his rock-hard penis all the way to the smooth, plump head. Her other hand pushed his boxers down his thighs, and she was free to look at him. For the first time to see his powerful body, to view him as an artist who had a deep appreciation for beauty, and as a woman who wanted to make love to the beautiful man who made her heart swell.

She took a step closer, and her nipples brushed his chest. The hot tip of his erection touched her belly, and within her grasp, she rubbed the length of him against her flat stomach and navel. A clear drop of semen smeared her skin as she kissed the hollow of his throat, his shoulder, and the side of his neck. She slid one hand up his chest and looked into his heavy-lidded eyes. "So, when do I get the really good part?"

He nuzzled the side of her throat and groaned, "As soon as you let go of it."

The second she released him, he picked her up beneath the armpits and tossed her on her bed. "Take off those panties," he ordered as he crawled across the duvet to join her in the middle. He helped her pull her underwear down her legs, pausing to kiss her hip, before he pitched her panties over his shoulder, then knelt between her knees. His gaze stared into hers, then lowered to between her thighs. His fingers caressed her belly, her hips, and her slick, sensitive flesh, bringing her close before he stopped and rested his weight on one forearm. "Are you sure you're ready for the really good part?" he asked and brought the broad head of his penis into place.

"Yes," she whispered, and he shoved the long, hard length of him into her. Her eyes widened, her breath caught in the top of her lungs, and she cried out. Then he withdrew and buried himself even deeper.

"Holy Mary mother of God," he groaned and cupped the sides of her face in his palms. He kissed her, his tongue plunging into her mouth as he thrust slowly into her body. She wrapped one leg around his waist, planted her other foot by his knee, and moved with him, matching the rhythm of his pumping hips. She dug her fingers into his shoulders and kissed him back, matching his greed and passion. With each thrust he propelled them closer to climax. And with each thrust, he stroked a place deep, deep inside until she could no longer breathe, and she tore her mouth from his and sucked air into her lungs. The pressure built, and her grasp on his shoulders tightened.

"Joe," she whispered, wanting to tell him how she felt, but there were no words. She wanted to tell him that she'd never felt anything so good and dizzy and hot. She looked up into his tense, strained features as he drove into her, and she wanted him to know she'd never felt so incredible, that he was incredible, and she loved him. That he was her yang, but then he reached beneath her bottom, tilted her pelvis up, and increased the sensation of each thrust, forcing her toward climax. Her heart pounded in her ears, and every ounce of her body, mind, and soul was focused on the slick parts of them where they were joined. She opened her mouth, but all she was capable of uttering was the word yes, followed by a long, satisfied moan.

"That's right, come for me," he whispered, and it was as if the sound of his voice triggered her long, hard fall. Her body tensed and arched as orgasm hit and took over completely. The power of it shook her and squeezed him within her tight body while he plunged harder and deeper. It went on and on, the sensations rolling through her until at last an anguished groan tore from his chest and his harsh breath whispered across her temple. He drove into her one last time, then stilled.

In the aftermath, the only sound was the catching of breath and a siren wailing off in the distance. Every place their skin touched, it stuck together, and a bead of sweat slid down Joe's temple.

A smile slowly curved the corners of his lips.

"That was amazing," she said.

"No," he corrected, pausing to plant a kiss on her mouth, "you are amazing."

Gabrielle unwrapped her leg from his waist.

He grasped her thigh as if he thought she planned to move away and he didn't want her to go. "Do you have someplace you need to be?"

"No."

"Then why don't you just stay where you are, and I'll just stay were I am?"

"Right here? Naked?"

"Uh-huh." He combed his fingers through her hair, and his hip slowly moved. He withdrew, then buried himself, and the sensation all coiled and built again. "I want more of the really good part. How about you?"

Yeah, she wanted more. She wanted a lot more of him, but beyond wanting Joe, she wasn't ready to face the world outside her house. Not yet. She hooked her leg over his waist again, and they started slow, with light, lingering touches, but things turned too hot too quick and somehow they ended up on the floor, rolling around on top of all those naughty pairs of underwear she'd thrown there the night before. She finally landed on top astride his hips.

"Put your hands behind your head," she ordered.

Suspicion shone in his eyes, but he did as she asked. "What are you going to do?"

"I'm going to blow your mind."

"That's a bold statement."

Gabrielle just smiled. She'd taken six months of belly dancing, just enough to know how to roll and undulate real good. She raised her hands high in the air and rotated her hips as she swayed. She closed her eyes and lost herself in the feeling of him touching her deep inside. "You like this?"

"God—d da—mn!"

Her smile grew, and with him buried deep inside, she blew his mind.

"Are you sure I don't smell like a girl?" Joe asked for the third time as he stood in her dining room and pulled his boxers to his waist.

Gabrielle buried her nose in his neck. After they'd picked themselves up off her bedroom floor, she'd dragged him into the shower and revived him with a loofah and a special bar of her homemade lilac soap. He'd stopped complaining about the girly smell when she'd knelt before him and soaped him up real good. "I don't think so," she said as she stepped into her panties, then hooked her bra in place. He smelled like Joe to her.

She folded her arms beneath her breasts, leaned her behind against the table, and watched him button his pants around his waist. The overhead light caressed the russet waves of his wet hair.

"I don't want you to answer the telephone today," he said as he walked into the living room and reached for his shirt and jacket. "At least not until after three. Kevin might try and contact you after his arraignment—I would suggest you don't talk to him." He shoved his arms into his shirt and buttoned the wrists before he worked on the front. "And be sure you eat something healthy. I don't want you getting sick."

What was it with him and food? Gabrielle watched him from the distance of the dining room, loving him so much it hurt. She didn't know how it had happened, but it had. He wasn't the type of man she'd thought she wanted, but he was the man for her. She felt it in the quick beating of her heart and the horrible flutter in her stomach, and she knew it in her soul. It was more than great sex. More than mind-blowing orgasms. He was her male to his female. Positive to negative.

There was only one little spot of potential misgiving on her otherwise blissful euphoria. She wasn't certain if he realized it too.

He shoved one hand into the pocket of his jacket, pulled out his pager, and glanced at the display. "Maybe you should stay with your mother for a few days. Shit. Where's the phone?"

Gabrielle pointed to her feet, where it lay sprawled across the floor. He grabbed his jacket and shoulder holster and walked back into the dining room. With one hand, Joe scooped up the telephone. With his thumb, he pressed the disconnect button, then pushed the seven digits.

"Shanahan," he said as he set his holster and

jacket on the table. "Yeah, my pager was in my car . . . what can I tell you? I just found the telephone off the hook." He shoved the tails of his shirt into his pants, then reached for the jacket. "Tell me you're bullshitting. It's not even noon!" With the telephone cradled between his ear and shoulder, he pushed his arms through the sleeves. "When was that? . . . I'm on my way," he said and dropped the receiver back in the cradle.

"Shit!"

"What?"

He glanced at her, then sat on the ladder-back chair and pulled on his socks. "I *can't* even believe this is happening to me. Not on top of everything else."

"What?"

Joe covered his face with his hands and scratched his forehead as if his skin was way too tight. "Damn," he sighed and dropped his hands. "Carter and Shalcroft changed the meeting time. They were arrested fifteen minutes ago. Dispatch tried to contact me, but couldn't." He stood and shoved his feet into his shoes.

"Oh."

Grabbing his holster, he raced for the door. "Don't talk to anyone until I talk to you again," he said over his shoulder. He yelled a few more obscenities, then ran from her house without even saying good-bye.

Fifteen

JOE CRANKED THE STEERING WHEEL AND
flipped a U in the middle of Gabrielle's
street. The right tire hopped the curb as he tore
at the nicotine patch at his waist and chucked
it out the window. He shoved his sunglasses up
the bridge of his nose and dug around in the
glove compartment until he found a pack of
Marlboros. He lipped a cigarette from the pack
and lit it with his Zippo. A cloud of smoke bil-
lowed toward the windshield, and he took another long pull. His jaws were clenched so tight
his teeth felt as if they would shatter, and he
didn't know how he would explain the new
dent in the Chevy. The dent that was exactly
the size of his foot. He'd love to kick his own
ass, if it were humanly possible.

The biggest arrest of his life, and he'd missed
it. Missed it because he'd been having sex with
his confidential informant. It didn't matter that
maybe technically she hadn't been his informant at the moment of penetration; he'd been

on duty and dispatch hadn't been able to contact him. There would be questions. He didn't have the answers. None that he wanted to give, anyway. Questions like Where the hell have you been, Shanahan?

And what could he say—"Well, Captain, since the arrest wasn't supposed to go down until three, I thought I had plenty of time to have sex with my informant!" Joe scratched his forehead and took another drag. "And hey, she has the most incredible body, after I made love to her once, I got greedy and had to have sex with her again. And that second time was so phenomenal I thought I needed a precoital thump to restart my heart. And captain, you have not had a shower until you've been soaped up and scrubbed down by Gabrielle Breedlove." And if he admitted that, he'd probably have to turn in his badge and become a security guard.

Another cloud of smoke filled the car as Joe exhaled. There was a chance no one would discover his affair with Gabrielle. He certainly didn't feel the need to broadcast the incident or unburden his conscience. But she might, and then he was screwed. When the case went to trial, he could just imagine Kevin's defense attorney grilling him with questions like Isn't it true, Detective Shanahan, that you've had a sexual relationship with your informant, my client's business partner? And isn't this just a case of jealousy perpetrated against my client?

Maybe Kmart needed someone to watch their stores at night.

It took Joe fifteen minutes and another cigarette before he pulled the Chevy into the police lot. He clenched his hands into fists and shoved them in his pants pockets, controlling his anger. The first person he encountered on his way to the booking room was Captain Luchetti.

"Where the hell have you been?" Luchetti barked, but there wasn't a lot of bite behind his words. The captain looked about ten years younger than he had the day before, and he actually smiled for the first time since the Hillard theft.

"You know where I've been." Joe and the other detective had spent hours last night and early this morning poring over every detail and every move the department planned to make. They'd made contingency plans. Plans they'd obviously used without him. "I was at Ms. Breedlove's warning her of Carter's arrest. Where is he?"

"Both Carter and Shalcroft are wrapping themselves in Miranda. Neither are talking," Luchetti answered as they continued down the hall toward the interrogation rooms. For the past week and a half, the air inside the building had been grim and thick with tension. Now everyone Joe passed, from detective to desk sergeant, wore a great big smile. Everyone was breathing again, but not Joe. Not with his ass so close to the wringer.

"Do you smell flowers?" Luchetti asked.

"I don't smell anything."

The captain shrugged. "Dispatch couldn't get a hold of you."

"Yeah, I guess I didn't have my pager on me." Which was basically true. His pager had been in his pants, and his pants hadn't been on him. "I don't know how that could have happened."

"Me either. I don't know how a detective of nine years could get caught without his communication. When we learned Carter changed the meeting time and you couldn't be reached, we sent a patrol unit over to that shop on Thirteenth. The officer reported that he knocked on both front and back doors, but no one answered."

"I wasn't there."

"We sent someone over to her house. Your police vehicle was parked out front, but no one answered the door."

Holy shit. He hadn't heard anyone knocking, but of course, at certain key moments, he wouldn't have heard a marching band passing two feet from his bare ass. "Must have been when we stepped out to get some breakfast," he improvised. "Ms. Breedlove drove."

Luchetti stopped as they entered the division room. "You told her about Carter, and she felt like breakfast? She felt like driving?"

Time to change tactics. He looked the captain in the face and let go of the anger he'd held in reserve. "Are you busting my balls about this? The Hillard theft is *the* most important case the Property Crimes Division has ever seen, bar-fucking-none, and I missed being in on the arrest because I was baby-sitting an informant." Letting out some of the rage felt good—damn good. "I worked hard on this and put in a hell of a lot of overtime. I had to put up with Carter's bullshit every day, and I wanted to slap the cuffs on him myself. I deserved to be there, and the fact that I wasn't just pisses me off. So if you're trying to make me feel like shit, you can forget it. You can't make me feel worse."

Luchetti rocked back on his heels. "Okay, Shanahan, I'll let it drop unless it comes up again."

Joe hoped to God it wouldn't. There was no way he could explain about him and Gabrielle. He couldn't even explain it to himself.

"Are you sure you don't smell flowers?" Luchetti asked and sniffed the air. "Smells like my wife's lilac bushes."

"I don't smell a damn thing." He knew it. He knew he smelled like a girl. "Where's Carter?"

"Number three, but he's not talking."

Joe walked to the interrogation room and opened the door. And there sat Kevin, one hand cuffed to the table.

Kevin looked up, and one corner of his mouth lifted in a sneer. "When one of the cops told me an undercover detective had been working in Anomaly, I knew it had to be you.

I knew from the first day that you were a loser."

Joe leaned one shoulder into the door frame. "Maybe, but I'm not the loser who was caught with Mr. Hillard's Monet, or the loser who filled his house with stolen antiques. I'm also not the loser facing fifteen to thirty in the state pen. That loser would be you."

Kevin's already pale complexion blanched a bit. "My attorney will get me out of here."

"I don't think so." Joe moved aside to let Chief Walker enter the room. "No lawyer alive is that good."

The chief sat across the table from Kevin with a bulky folder filled with paper, some of which Joe knew had nothing to do with Kevin. It was an old police ploy to make a criminal think he had a thick police file. "Shalcroft is being more cooperative than you," Walker began, which Joe figured was just as likely to be a bald-faced lie as the truth. He also figured once Kevin faced the enormity of the evidence against him, he would flip quicker than a dancing poodle. If nothing else, Kevin Carter was an avid self-preservationist. No doubt he'd eventually give the names of the thief he'd used to steal the painting, and everyone else involved.

"You should give some serious thought to co-operating before it's too late," Joe suggested.

Kevin sat back in his chair and cocked his head to one side. "I'm not talking. Screw you."

"Okay, then think about this instead, while you're in a comfy jail cell, I'm going to be at home, grilling up steaks and celebrating."

"With Gabrielle? Does she know who you really are? Or did you use her to get to me?"

Guilt settled in his belly. Guilt and the same wave of protectiveness he'd felt the night he'd watched Gabrielle hang from that balcony. It caught him off guard and pushed him away from the door. "Don't you talk to me about using Gabrielle. You used her for years to give yourself a legitimate front." What he felt churning in his gut was more than just a sense of duty to protect his informant, but he wasn't in the mood to get in touch or get introspective.

Kevin turned away. "She'll be fine."

"When I spoke with her this morning, she didn't seem fine."

Kevin turned back, and for the first time, something besides arrogance and belligerence flickered behind his eyes. "What did you tell her? What does she know?"

"What she knows is none of your concern. All you need to know is that I was in Anomaly to do my job."

"Yeah right," he scoffed. "When you had Gabe shoved up against a wall and had your tongue down her throat, it looked like more than a job to me."

Walker looked up, and Joe forced an easy smile. "Some days were better than others." He shrugged and shook his head, as if Kevin was just spouting off. "I know you're really pissed at me right now, but I'm going to give you some advice. You can take it or tell me to screw myself again, I don't care either way, but here it is: You're not the type of guy who really gives a shit about anyone but you, and now isn't the time to develop scruples. Your ship is going down, my friend, and you can either save yourself or drown with the other rats. I suggest you save yourself before it's too late." He looked Kevin over one last time, then he turned from the room and walked to the holding cells.

Contrary to what the chief had told Kevin, William Stewart Shalcroft wasn't cooperating in the least. He sat cooling his heels in the cell, staring out the bars, the light overhead casting his bald head in a grayish light. Joe watched the art dealer and waited for the adrenaline rush. The surge that always came when it was time to scam a scammer, to get a guy to talk even though you've just told him not to talk or you'll use everything he says against him. The rush didn't come. Instead Joe just felt exhausted. Mentally and physically spent.

The high energy filling the station kept him awake and alert the rest of the day. Listening to the details of Kevin's and Shalcroft's arrest, then listening some more as the story was hashed and rehashed from beginning to end kept his mind occupied and kept him from thinking too much about Gabrielle and what he intended to do about her.

"Did someone bring flowers in here?" Winston asked from across the aisle.

"Yeah, smells like it," Dale Parker, a rookie detective, added.

"I don't smell a damn thing," Joe barked at his coworkers, then buried his nose in paperwork. He spent the rest of the afternoon smelling like a lilac bush and waiting for the ax to fall on his neck. At five o'clock, he grabbed the pile of paper on his desk and headed home.

Sam waited on his perch by the front door. *"Hello, Joe,"* he greeted as soon as Joe walked in.

"Hey, buddy." Joe tossed his keys and the stack of paper on the table in front of his couch, then let Sam out of his aviary. "How was television today?"

"JER—ry JER—ry," Sam screeched as he hopped out of the wire door and flew to the top of the oak entertainment unit.

Joe hadn't allowed Sam to watch Springer for several months. Not since he'd picked up bad language and repeated it at inopportune moments.

"Your mama's a fat hoe."

"Jeezus," Joe sighed and sank down on the sofa. He'd thought Sam had forgotten that one.

"You behave," the mimic perched on the television admonished.

Joe leaned his head back and closed his eyes. His life was headed straight to hell. He'd just about flushed his career, and there was a real possibility that his job was still in jeopardy. He was up to his ass and elbows in paperwork, and his bird had a trashy mouth. Everything was out of control.

Without the distractions of his job, he thought of Gabrielle, of the day he'd first arrested her. His opinion of her had done about a one-eighty in less than a week. He respected her, and he felt real bad that she'd probably been right about her business. Her name and her shop were now connected to the most infamous theft in the state. She probably would have to close it, but thanks to her slick little lawyer, she wouldn't lose everything. At least he hoped she wouldn't.

And then he thought of her soft mouth on his and her hard nipples grazing his chest. Her touch on his back and abdomen. His penis in her hand as she rubbed him across her smooth stomach, back and forth right across that belly ring. He'd almost embarrassed himself right there on her silky skin. He could still see her beaded earrings nestled in her hair as he looked down into her face, still feel the warmth of her body beneath him.

She was beautiful with her clothes on. She was amazing with them off. She'd rocked his world, blown his mind, and if she were any other woman, he'd be trying to figure out a way to talk her out of her clothes again—and again. He'd be in his car, on his way to her house, trying to get her to straddle naked in his lap.

He liked her. Okay, he more than liked her.

He liked her a lot. But liking a woman a lot wasn't love. Even if a relationship with her wasn't as complicated as hell, she wasn't the type of woman he could see himself settling down with. He didn't want to hurt her, but he had to stay away from her.

Taking a deep breath, he combed his fingers through the sides of his hair, then dropped them to his lap. Maybe he had nothing to worry about. Nothing to feel guilty over. She might not expect anything. She was a big girl. A smart girl. She probably knew that making it in her bed, on her floor, and in her shower had been a big mistake. She was probably dreading the thought of seeing him again. They'd made each other feel good for a couple of hours, real good, but it couldn't happen again. She had to know that too. She had to know there wasn't a possibility of any sort of relationship between them.

With the curtains drawn and the lights out, Gabrielle sat alone in her darkened living room and watched the five-thirty local news. The Hillard theft was once again the top story, only this time Kevin's picture flashed on the screen.

"A local man was arrested today in connection with the biggest theft in the state's history. Businessman Kevin Carter . . . ," the newscast began. Film footage showing the front of Anomaly ran as the broadcast continued. It showed police carrying out Kevin's Nagels, his computer, and his files. They'd emptied his desk and had searched the store for stolen property. She knew everything they'd touched, because she'd been there. She'd gotten dressed and driven to her store, and she'd watched them do it. Her and Mara and Francis and her lawyer Ronald Lowman. Standing side by side. Everyone but Joe.

Joe hadn't come back.

The story continued through the first segment and into the second. A photo of William Stewart Shalcroft appeared in one corner, and Kevin in the other, as a police spokesman answered questions. "With the help of an informant," he said, but failed to mention her name and that she was innocent, "we've had Mr. Carter under surveillance for some time . . ." He continued, then the report moved to the human interest side, and Mr. and Mrs. Hillard appeared and thanked the Boise P.D.

Gabrielle pressed the off button on the television remote and tossed it on the couch beside her cordless telephone.

Joe hadn't called, either.

Her life was falling apart in Technicolor for the whole world to see. Her business partner, a man she trusted enough to consider a very close friend, was a thief. The news channels hadn't mentioned her name, but anyone who knew her probably assumed she was guilty by association. She and Ronald had briefly discussed her options, such as closing the store and reopening under a new name, but she didn't know if she had the heart to start over again. She'd think about it once the shock wore off and her head cleared.

The telephone on the couch beside her rang, and her stomach tumbled. "Hello," she answered before it had a chance to ring twice.

"I just saw the news," her mother began. "I'm on my way over."

Gabrielle swallowed her disappointment. "No, don't. I'll come over to your house in a while."

"When?"

"Later tonight."

"You shouldn't be alone."

"I'm waiting for Joe," she said, then she wouldn't be alone. After she hung up with her mother, she ran a bath. She added lavender and ylang-ylang and set the phone beside the tub, but when it rang again, it wasn't Joe this time either.

"Did you watch the news?" Francis began.

"I saw it." Gabrielle hid her disappointment for the second time. "Listen, can I phone you back? I'm expecting Joe to call me."

"Why don't you call him?"

Because she didn't have his home number and he wasn't listed in the telephone book. She'd checked—twice. "No, I'm sure he'll call when he gets off work. Until then, he probably won't be able to talk to me about the case." Or about them. About what would happen now.

After Francis hung up, Gabrielle got out of the tub and dressed in a pair of new khaki shorts and a white T-shirt. She left her hair down because she thought he liked it best that way. She didn't even try to tell herself she wasn't waiting by the phone. No matter how hard she tried, she would never be that good a liar. With each tick of the clock, her nerves wound a bit tighter.

At seven-thirty, a handicapped man selling lightbulbs had the misfortune of calling. "No!" she screeched into the receiver. "I've had a really bad day!" She pressed the disconnect button and sank onto the couch, certain she'd just created the worst karma imaginable. What kind of woman yelled at a disabled man?

The kind of woman whose life was in shreds and who should have been more concerned about her business than her love life but wasn't. The kind of woman whose nerves were raw. The kind of woman who knew in her heart and in her soul that if she could just hold on to Joe, everything would be okay.

She didn't even know his telephone number. If she needed to speak to him, she had to call the police station, or leave a message on his pager. She'd made love to him, and he'd touched her heart like no man had ever touched her before. He'd touched her body and stirred a response like nothing she'd ever experienced. It was more than sex. She loved him, but not knowing what he felt for her tied her stomach in knots. The uncertainty drove her crazy and was worse than anything she'd ever felt in her life.

They'd made love, then he'd run out of her house like he couldn't get out fast enough. And yes, she knew he hadn't had a choice. In the rational part of her mind, she knew leaving the way he had hadn't been his decision, but he hadn't kissed her good-bye. He hadn't even looked back.

The doorbell rang, and she jumped. When she looked through the peephole, Joe stared back at her from behind his mirrored sunglasses. Her breath caught in her throat, and a pain settled in her heart as if she'd swallowed air.

"Joe," she said as she swung the door open. Then she was incapable of uttering another word past the emotion clogging her chest. Her hungry gaze took him in all at once, from the top of his dark hair, black T-shirt and jeans, to the tips of his black boots. She slid her gaze back up to his intensely masculine face, with his characteristic five o'clock shadow and the fine lines of his sensual mouth. A sensual mouth he'd pressed to the inside of her thigh less than twelve hours ago.

"Did you see the news?" he asked, and there was something in his voice, something in the way he stood, that set off warning bells in her head. "Have you talked to your lawyer?"

Finally, she found her voice. "Yes. Do you want to come inside?"

"No, that's not a good idea." He took a step backward to the edge of the steps. "But I did want to talk to you about what happened between us this morning."

She knew what he was going to say before he opened his mouth. "Don't say you're sorry," she warned, because she didn't think her heart could take hearing his regret, as if what they shared together had been a mistake. "Don't tell me that it never should have happened."

"Not saying it doesn't make it right, Gabrielle. What happened was my fault. You were my confidential informant, and there are strict policies and procedures concerning how I treat you. I broke those rules. If you would like to speak with someone in internal affairs, I can give you the name of who to contact."

She looked down at her bare toes, then back up into her reflection in his glasses. He was talking about rules again. She didn't care about rules or policies or speaking to anyone but him. He was talking about what they'd done but not how he felt. He might not love her, but he had to feel the connection between them.

"I was wrong, and I am sorry."

That admission hurt, but she didn't have time to dwell on the pain. If she didn't tell him, he would leave not knowing what was in her heart. If he still left, she wouldn't always wonder whether his knowing would have made a difference. "I'm not sorry. You don't know this about me, but I don't believe in indiscriminate sex. I can hardly expect you to believe that after what happened this morning, but I have to have deep feelings for someone."

His lips formed a straight line, but she'd gone too far to turn back now. "I don't know how this happened," she continued. "Until a few days ago, I didn't even know I liked you very much." With each word she uttered, creases appeared on his forehead. "I've never really fallen in love before. I mean, I thought I was in love several years ago with Fletcher Wiseweaver, but what I felt for him doesn't compare with my feelings for you. I've never felt anything like this."

He took off his sunglasses and massaged his temples and forehead. "You've had a real bad day, and I think you're confused."

Gabrielle looked into his tired eyes, the brown irises like rich, dark chocolate. "Don't treat me like I don't know what I'm feeling. I'm an adult, I don't confuse sex and love. There's only one explanation for what happened today. I'm in love with you."

He dropped his hand, his features turned blank, and an awkward silence filled the air.

"I just told you I'm in love with you. Do you have any reaction to that at all?"

"Yes, but none I think you want to hear."

"Try me."

"There's one more explanation that makes

more sense." He rubbed the back of his neck and said, "We had to pretend to be boyfriend and girlfriend. Things got real hot, real fast, and we got all wrapped up in it. The lines got blurred and confused and we started to believe it. We took things too far."

"Maybe you're confused, but I'm not." She shook her head. "You're my yang."

"Pardon?"

"You're my yang."

He took a step backward down the stairs of her porch. "Your what?"

"The other half of my soul."

He shoved his glasses back on his face and covered his eyes once more. "I'm not."

"Don't tell me you don't feel the connection between us. You have to feel it."

He shook his head. "No. I don't believe in all of that entwining of souls stuff, or seeing big red auras." Taking another step back, he stood on the sidewalk below her. "In a few days you're going to be real glad I'm out of your life." He drew a deep breath into his lungs and let it out slowly. "Take care of yourself, Gabrielle Breedlove," he said and turned away.

She opened her mouth to call to him, to tell him not to leave her, but in the end she held on to the last shred of pride and self-respect she had and stepped into her house, closing the door on the image of his broad shoulders walking away from her and out of her life. Her chest felt as if it were caving in on her heart, and the first sob broke from her throat as she grasped the T-shirt over her left breast. This wasn't supposed to happen. Once she found her yang, he was supposed to know her, recognize her. But he didn't, and she'd never imagined her soul mate wouldn't return her love. She'd never imagined how bad it would hurt.

Her vision blurred, and she leaned her back against the door. She'd been wrong. Not knowing had been better than knowing he didn't love her.

What was she supposed to do now? Her life was in total chaos—real upheaval. Her business was a wreck, her partner was in jail, and her soul mate didn't know he was her soul mate. How was she supposed to go on living her life as if she weren't dying inside? How was she supposed to live in the same city, and know he was out there somewhere and didn't want her?

She'd been wrong about something else too; uncertainty wasn't the worst thing she'd ever felt in her life.

The telephone rang, and she picked it up on the fourth ring. "Hello," she said, her voice sounding hollow and distant in her ears.

There was a short pause before her mother spoke. "What's happened since we spoke last?"

"You're psychic, you tell m-me." Her voice broke, and she sobbed, "When you told me I would ha-have a passionate dark ha-haired lover, why didn't you tell m-me he would break my heart?"

"I'm on my way to pick you up. Throw some things in a suitcase, and I'll drive you up to stay with Franklin. He could use your company."

Gabrielle was twenty-eight, would be twenty-nine in January, but running home to her grandfather had never sounded so good.

Sixteen

GABRIELLE KNELT BESIDE HER GRAND-
father's old leather recliner and rubbed
warm ginger oil into his aching hands. Franklin
Breedlove's knuckles were inflamed, his fingers
gnarled from arthritis. The gentle daily mas-
sages seemed to bring him a measure of relief.

"How's that, Grandad?" she asked, looking
up into his heavily lined face, pale green eyes,
and bushy white brows.

He slowly flexed his fingers as best he could.
"Better," he pronounced and patted Gabrielle
on the head as if she were his old bow-legged
beagle, Molly. "You're a good girl." His hand
slid down her shoulder to the armrest, and his
eyes drifted shut. He did that more and more
often. Last night he'd fallen asleep in the middle of dinner, his fork poised before his lips. He
was seventy-eight, and his narcolepsy was getting so bad that he only wore his pajamas.
Every morning he changed into a clean pair before he headed down the hall to his study. The

only concession he made to the day were the wingtips on his feet.

For as long as Gabrielle could remember, her grandfather had worked in his study until noon, then again late at night, doing what she'd never been quite sure, until recently. As a child she'd been led to believe he was a venture capitalist. But since she'd been home, she'd intercepted calls from men wanting to place five hundred or two thousand on such favorites as Eddie "The Shark" Sharkey or Greasy Dan Muldoon. Now she suspected him of bookmaking.

Sitting back on her heels, Gabrielle lightly squeezed his bony hand. For most of her life, he'd been her father figure. He'd always been abrupt and cantankerous, and he didn't care for other people, children, or pets. But if you belonged to him, he would move the heavens and earth to make you happy.

Gabrielle stood and walked from the room that had always smelled of books, leather, and decades of pipe tobacco—comforting and familiar smells that helped promote healing in her mind-body-spirit since the night a month ago when her mother and Aunt Yolanda had picked her up on the back porch of her house and driven north for four straight hours to her grandfather's home. That night seemed so long ago now, and yet she could remember it as if it had happened yesterday. She could recall the color of Joe's T-shirt and the blank look on his face. She could remember the scent of roses in her backyard, and the cool rush of air blowing across her wet cheeks as she'd sat in the passenger seat of her mother's Toyota. She remembered Beezer's soft fur in her fingers, the cat's steady purr in her ears, the sound of her mother's voice, telling her her heart would mend and her life would get better in time.

She moved down the long hallway to the parlor she'd turned into her studio. Boxes and crates of essential oils and aromatherapies were stacked against the walls, blocking out the September morning sun. She'd kept herself occupied since the day she'd arrived with little more than a bag of clothes and her oils. She'd thrown herself into work, keeping her mind busy, letting herself forget sometimes that her heart was broken.

Since she'd come to stay with her grandfather, she'd traveled to Boise only once to sign papers offering Anomaly for sale. She'd visited Francis, and made sure her lawn was mowed. She'd set her sprinkler system to come to life every morning at four, so she didn't need to worry about her grass dying, but she'd needed to hire a lawn service to mow. The time she'd been in town, she'd gathered her mail, mopped the layers of dust off her furniture, and checked messages on her answering machine.

There hadn't been any word from the one person she wanted to hear from most. Once she'd thought she'd heard the squawk of a parrot, but then the tape had filled with the sound of a telephone ringing in the distance and she'd dismissed it as a prank or a telemarketer.

She hadn't heard from Joe or seen him since the night he'd stood on her porch and told her she'd mistaken sex for love. The night she'd told him she loved him and he'd backed away from her as if she had had an airborne illness. The ache in her heart was a continuous thing, with her when she woke in the morning and when she went to bed at night. Even in her sleep, she couldn't get away from his memory. He came to her in her dreams, as he always had. But now when she awoke, she felt hollow and lonely and without the urge to paint him. She hadn't picked up a brush since the day he'd barged into her house looking for Mr. Hillard's Monet.

Gabrielle walked into the parlor and moved to the worktable where all her bottles of essential and carrier oils sat. The shades in the room were drawn against the damaging rays of the sun, but Gabrielle didn't need to see in order to choose a small bottle of sandalwood from the rest. She took off the cap and held it to her nose. Immediately his image filled her head. An image of his face, his hot, hungry eyes looking at her from beneath lowered lids, his lips moist from kissing her mouth.

Just like the day before, and the day before that, grief rolled through her before she screwed the cap back on the oil and sat it on the table. No, she wasn't over him. Not yet. It still hurt, but maybe tomorrow would be better. Maybe tomorrow she would feel nothing. Maybe tomorrow she would be ready to go back to her home in Boise and face her life again.

"I have your mail," her mother said as she breezed into the parlor. Claire Breedlove had a basket of fresh-cut herbs and flowers hanging from one elbow and a big manila envelope in her hand. She was dressed in a brightly embroidered Mexican dress with a serape thrown over the top to ward off the morning chill and a necklace of worry dolls to ward off misfortune. Sometime during her trip to Mexico, she'd gone nativo and never come back. Her long auburn braid hung to her knees and had liberal streaks of gray. "I received a strong sign this morning. Something good is going to happen," Claire predicted. "Yolanda found a monarch on the lilies, and you know what that means."

No, Gabrielle didn't know what seeing a butterfly in the garden meant, other than the fact that it was hungry and searching for food. Ever since her mother had fated her a dark passionate lover, her psychic predictions were a sore subject. Gabrielle didn't ask about the butterfly.

Claire offered anyway as she handed the envelope to Gabrielle. "You're going to hear good news today. Monarchs always bring good news."

She recognized Francis's handwriting as she took the package from her mother and tore it open. Inside were Gabrielle's monthly utility bills for her home in Boise and various junk mail. Two pieces of mail caught her immediate attention. The first was an engraved envelope with Mr. and Mrs. Hillard's return address scripted on the back. The second was from the Idaho State Correctional Institution. She didn't need to see the address to know who'd sent the letter. She recognized his handwriting. Kevin.

For a few unguarded seconds, joy filled her, as if she were hearing from an old friend. Then just as quickly anger and a spot of sadness replaced her joy.

She hadn't spoken to Kevin since before his arrest, but she'd learned through her attorney that three days after Kevin's arrest, he'd struck a bargain with the prosecuting attorney's office. He'd sung like the proverbial canary, giving information, naming names, and plea bargaining in return for a reduction in the charges against him. He'd named every collector and dealer for whom he'd ever brokered a deal, and he named the thieves he'd used to commit the Hillard theft. According to Ronald Lowman, Kevin had hired two Tongan brothers who'd been out on bail and awaiting trial for some residential burglaries they'd been later found guilty of committing.

For his cooperation, Kevin had been sentenced to five years in prison but would be out in two.

She handed her mother the engraved envelope from the Hillards. "You can read this if you're interested," she said, then took her letter and moved across the hall to the morning room. She sat on a lumpy chaise lounge, and her hands shook as she opened the fat envelope. A four-page letter written on legal paper fell out, and she skimmed the slanted script by the light pouring through the windows.

Dear Gabe,

If you are reading this then there is hope you will give me the chance to explain myself and my actions. First let me say that I am extremely sorry for the pain that I most certainly have caused. It was never my intention, nor did I ever imagine, that my other businesses would impact negatively on you.

Gabrielle paused. *Businesses?* Is that what he called fencing stolen paintings and antiques? She shook her head and returned her attention to the letter. He spoke of their friendship, and how much she meant to him, and the good times they'd shared. She was beginning to almost feel sorry for him when the letter turned in a new and remorseless direction.

I know that a lot of people view my actions as criminal, and perhaps they are right. Receiving and selling stolen property is against the law, but my only TRUE crime is that I have wanted too

*much. I wanted the good things in life. And for
that I am serving a harsher sentence than men
convicted of assault. Wife beaters and child abus-
ers have lighter sentences than me. My purpose
in pointing this out is that when put in perspec-
tive, my crimes seem truly minor in comparison.
Who was hurt? Rich people who are insured?*

Gabrielle dropped the letter in her lap. *Who
was hurt?* Was he serious? Her gaze quickly
skimmed the rest of the letter filled with more
rationalizations and excuses. He called Joe a
few choice names, hoped she'd been wise
enough to realize that Joe had only used her to
get to him, and he hoped that she'd dumped
him by now. Gabrielle was surprised he hadn't
learned of her involvement, and toward the end
of the letter, he actually asked her to write to
him as if they were still friends. She dismissed
the idea, and with the letter in her hand, she
walked into the parlor once again.

"What was in your envelope?" Claire asked
from where she stood at the worktable, blending fresh lavender and roses with a mortar and
pestle.

"A letter from Kevin. He wants me to know
that he's sorry, and that he's not really *that*
guilty. And besides, he only stole from rich people." She paused to drop the letter into the
trash. "I guess the butterfly that told you I'd
hear good news today was full of it."

Her mother looked at her in that calm, composed way she had. Clear of judgement, and Gabrielle felt like she'd just kicked a peace-loving love child.

She guessed she had, but lately she just couldn't seem to help herself. She just opened her mouth, and all the anger she had inside her soul poured out.

Just last week her aunt Yolanda had been raving about her favorite subject, Frank Sinatra, and Gabrielle had snapped, "Sinatra *sucked*, and the only people who didn't think so are women who paint on their eyebrows."

Gabrielle had immediately apologized to her aunt, and Yolanda had seemed to accept and forget about it, but an hour later she'd accidently appropriated a turkey baster from the IGA market.

Gabrielle wasn't herself at all, but she didn't have a real clear sense of her own identity anymore. She used to know, but having her trust and heart broken by two different men on the same day had knocked her belief in herself and her world out of whack.

"The day isn't over yet," Claire said and pointed the pestle at the small engraved envelope on the table. "The Hillards are having a party. The invitation says they want everyone involved in the recovery of their painting to come."

"I can't go." Just the thought of seeing Joe made her stomach feel all fluttery, like she'd swallowed that mystical monarch from her mother's garden.

"You can't hide out here forever."

"I'm not hiding out."

"You're avoiding your life."

Of course she was avoiding her life. Her life was like a black hole, stretching ahead of her and filled with nothing. She'd meditated and tried to visualize her life without Joe, but she couldn't. She'd always been so decisive in her unconstrained life. If something wasn't working, she turned and headed in a new direction. But for the first time, everywhere she turned seemed worse than where she stood.

"You have closure issues."

Gabrielle picked up a sprig of mint and twirled it between her fingers.

"Maybe you should write Kevin a letter. Then you should think about going to the Hillards' party. You need to confront the men who've hurt you so much and made you so angry."

"I'm not all that angry."

Claire simply stared.

"Okay, I'm a little angry."

She'd dismissed the idea of writing to Kevin out of hand, but maybe her mother was right. Maybe she should confront him so she could move on. But not Joe. She wasn't ready to see Joe, to look into his familiar brown eyes and see nothing looking back at her.

When she'd come to stay with her grandfather a month ago, she and her mother and Aunt

Yolanda had talked about Kevin, but mostly she'd talked about her feelings for Joe. She hadn't mentioned that Joe was her yang, though, nor did she intend to. Her mother knew anyway.

Her mother believed that soul mates and fate were intertwined, inseparable. Gabrielle wanted to believe her mother was wrong. Claire had coped with the loss of her husband by changing her life completely. Gabrielle didn't want to change her life. She wanted her old life back, or at least as much as possible.

But maybe her mother was right about one thing. Maybe it was time to go home. Time for closure. Time to pick up the pieces and live her life again.

Joe plugged the tape into the VCR and pushed play. The whir and click of gears filled the silent interrogation room as he leaned his behind against a table and folded his arms across his chest. The film flickered and jumped, then Gabrielle's face filled the television screen.

"I'm an artist myself," she said, and hearing her voice after a month was like feeling sunshine on his face after a long, cold winter. It poured into all the cracks and crevices and warmed him from the inside out.

"Then you can understand Mr. Hillard is quite anxious to get them back," his own voice spoke from off camera.

"I would imagine so." Her big green eyes

were filled with confusion and fear. He didn't remember her looking so scared and trying so hard not to show it. He saw it now because he knew her so well.

"Have you ever seen or met this man?" he asked. "His name is Sal Katzinger."

She bent her head and looked at pictures before shoving them back across the table. "No. I don't think I've ever met him."

"Have you ever heard his name mentioned by your business partner, Kevin Carter?" Captain Luchetti asked.

"Kevin? What does Kevin have to do with the man in the picture?"

The captain explained the connection between Katzinger and Kevin and their suspected involvement in the theft of Hillard's Monet. Joe watched Gabrielle's gaze dart between Luchetti and himself, and every imaginable emotion was right there on her beautiful face. He watched her push her hair behind her ears and get all squinty-eyed as she fiercely defended a man who didn't deserve her friendship. "I would certainly know if he were selling stolen antiques. We work together almost every day, and I could tell if he were hiding a secret like that."

"How?" the captain asked.

Joe recognized the look she gave Luchetti. It was the look she reserved for the unenlightened. "I just would."

"Any other reasons?"

"Yes, he's an Aquarius."

"Sweet baby Jesus," Joe heard himself groan. He heard his exasperation and listened to her explanation about Lincoln being an Aquarian, and this time he laughed. She'd certainly made his head spin that day. Then about every day afterward too. He chuckled as she explained about the time she'd stolen a candy bar but felt so bad that she hadn't really enjoyed it all that much. Then he watched her cover her face with her hands, and his laughter died. When she looked up again, tears swam in her green eyes and wet her lower lashes. She wiped them away and looked into the camera. Her gaze accusing and hurt, he felt as if he'd been hit in the stomach with a nightstick.

"Shit," he said to the vacant room and hit the eject button on the VCR. He shouldn't have watched it. He'd avoided watching it for a month now, and he'd been right. Seeing her face and hearing her voice brought it all to the surface again. All the chaos and confusion and desire.

He grabbed the tape and went home for the day. He needed to take a quick shower, then head over to his parents' house for his father's sixty-fourth birthday celebration. On the way there he planned to stop and pick up Ann.

He'd been spending time with Ann lately. Mostly in her deli. He'd stop by for breakfast, and a few times when he couldn't get away from his desk, she'd bring him lunch. And they'd talk. Well, she would talk.

He'd dated her twice now, and the last time he'd taken her home he'd kissed her. But something hadn't felt right, and he'd ended it almost before it began.

The problem wasn't Ann. It was him. She was just about everything he'd always looked for in a woman. Everything he'd thought he wanted. She was pretty, smart, a great cook, and she would make a great mother for his kids. Only she was so boring that he couldn't stand it. And that really wasn't her fault, either. It wasn't her fault that when he looked at her he wished she would say something really weird that would make the hair on the back of his neck stand up. Something that would set him back on his heels and make him look at things in a whole new light. Gabrielle had done that to him. She'd ruined his view of what he wanted. She'd turned it on its head, and his life and his future were no longer so clear to him. He couldn't shake the feeling that he was just going through the motions. That he was standing in the wrong place, but if he just stood there long enough, waited long enough, everything would click and his life would return to the old, familiar rhythm.

He was still waiting that evening. When he should have been having a great time with his family, he couldn't. Instead, he stood alone in the kitchen staring out at the backyard and thinking about Gabrielle's interrogation tape.

He could still hear her appalled voice when she'd been asked to take a lie detector test. If he closed his eyes he could see her beautiful face and her wild hair. If he let himself, he could imagine the touch of her hands and the taste of her mouth. And when he imagined her body pressed close to his, he could recall the scent of her skin, and it was probably a very good thing she wasn't in town.

He knew where she was, of course. He'd known two days after she'd left. He'd tried to contact her once, but she hadn't been home, and he hadn't left a message. She probably hated him by now, and he didn't blame her. Not after that last night on her porch, when she'd told him she loved him and he'd told her she was confused. Maybe he'd handled everything badly, but typical of Gabrielle, her announcement had shocked the hell right out of him. Coming when it had like that. Right out of the blue on one of the worst nights of his life. If he could go back and handle things differently, he would. He didn't know exactly what he would say, but it didn't matter now anyway. He was fairly certain he was one of her least favorite people these days.

His mother walked through the back door, and the screen slammed behind her. "It's about time for the cake."

"Okay." He shifted his weight to one foot and watched Ann conversing with his sisters. They were probably telling her about the time he'd lit their Barbies on fire. His nieces and nephews ran around the big yard, hosing each other with squirt guns, screaming at the top of their lungs. Ann fit right in, like he'd figured she might.

"What happened to the girl in the park?" his mother asked.

He didn't need to ask what girl. "She was just a friend."

"Hmm." She took out a box of candles and stuck them in a chocolate cake. "Of course, she didn't look like a friend." Joe didn't respond, and his mother continued just as he knew she would. "You don't look at Ann the way you looked at her."

"How's that?"

"Like you could look at her for the rest of your life."

In some respects, the Idaho State Correctional Institution reminded Gabrielle a bit of high school. Maybe it was the speckled linoleum or the plastic chairs. Or maybe it was the smell of pine cleaner and sweaty bodies. But unlike high school, the large room where she sat was filled with women and babies and a sense of depression so suffocating that it pressed down on her chest.

She folded her hands in her lap and waited like the rest of the women. Several times over the course of the past week she'd tried to write Kevin, but each time she'd stopped before she'd written more than a few lines. She needed to see him. She wanted to see his face when she asked him the questions she needed answers to.

A door to her left swung open, and men in prison blue jeans and identical blue shirts filed into the room. Kevin was third from the last, and the minute he saw her, he paused before he continued into the visiting area. Gabrielle stood and watched him walk toward her. His familiar blue eyes guarded, red flushed his neck and cheeks.

"I was surprised you wanted to see me," he said. "I haven't had many visitors."

Gabrielle took her seat, and he sat across the table from her. "Your family hasn't come to see you?"

He looked up at the ceiling and shrugged. "A few of my sisters, but I'm not real big on seeing them anyway."

She thought of China and her best friend Nancy. "No girlfriends?"

"You're kidding, right?" He returned his gaze to her, and a frown wrinkled his brow. "I don't want anyone to see me like this. I almost didn't agree to see you, but I figure you probably have some questions, and I owe you that much."

"Actually, I only have one question." She took a deep breath. "Did you purposely choose me as a business partner to use me as a front?"

He sat back in his chair. "What? Have you been talking to your friend Joe?"

His question and the anger behind it surprised her.

"The day I was arrested he came in and said I'd used you. He actually had the balls to act all pissed off about it too. Then the next day he came to my holding cell, and he goes off on me about how I took advantage of you. Isn't that a laugh, especially when he used you to get to me?"

For a moment she considered telling him the truth about Joe and herself and her part in his arrest, but in the end she didn't. She supposed because she didn't have the energy to discuss it, and it didn't matter now anyway. Nor did she feel she owed him anything. "You didn't answer my question," she reminded him. "Did you purposely choose me as a business partner to use me as a front?"

Kevin tilted his head to the side and studied her for a moment. "Yes. In the beginning, but you're smarter than I originally thought, more observant, too. And I didn't end up doing as much business out of the store as I'd originally planned."

She didn't know what she'd expected to feel. Anger, hurt, betrayal, maybe a little bit of all of those things, but mostly she felt relief. She could move on with her life now. A little older, a bit wiser. And a lot less trusting, thanks to the man sitting across the table from her.

"In fact, I was thinking about going completely legit until the cops stuck their noses in my life."

"You mean after you had the money from the sale of the Hillard Monet?"

He leaned forward and shook his head. "Don't shed any tears for those people. They're rich and they're insured."

"So that made it all right?"

He shrugged without the least bit of remorse. "They shouldn't have had such an expensive painting in a house with such a lousy alarm system."

Stunned laughter escaped her lips. There was no accountability for his own actions, and even in a society that liked to blame lung cancer on tobacco companies and death from handguns on gun manufacturers, blaming the Hillards for the theft of their own painting went beyond superlatively appalling straight to sociopathic. But the truly scary part was that she'd never seen it before.

"You need mental help," she said as she stood.

"Because I don't feel bad that a bunch of rich people get their art and antiques stolen?"

She could try to explain it to him, but she figured her words would fall on deaf ears, and she just didn't care.

"And you didn't come out so bad. The government took everything I own, but you get to keep the shop to do with as you please. Like I said, not bad."

Gabrielle took her keys from the pocket of her

skirt. "Please don't write me or try to contact me in any way."

As she walked through the prison gates, a feeling of freedom brushed her spine that had nothing to do with the chain link and razor wire she'd left behind her. She'd closed one part of her past; now she was ready to start her future. Ready to turn in a new direction and see where life would take her.

She would always regret the loss of Anomaly. She'd loved her store and she'd worked hard to make it succeed, but she had a new idea churning in her brain that woke her up at nights and had her reaching for a legal pad. For the first time in a long time, she was excited and charged with positive energy. Her karma had taken a turn for the better, and it was about time, too. She was real sick of accumulative punishment for past misdeeds.

Thinking of her new life brought her thoughts around to Joe Shanahan. She didn't even try to delude herself. She would never be completely over her feelings for him, but each day got a bit easier. She could look at the paintings of him in her studio without feeling as if her heart had been ripped from her chest. She still felt a bit hollow at times, but the pain had lessened. She could go for hours now without thinking of him. She figured by this time next year, she'd almost be ready to look for a new soul mate.

Seventeen

SILENT WIPERS CLEARED RAINDROPS from the windshield as the last limousine wound its way up the wet mountain road to the Hillard mansion. With each splash of the tires, each inch the vehicle rolled up the ribbon of asphalt, the knot in Gabrielle's stomach twisted. She knew from experience that no amount of visualization, no amount of deep breathing, was going to help. But then, they never had where Joe Shanahan was concerned. It had been one month, two weeks, and three days since she'd told him she loved him and he'd walked away. It was time to face him again.

She was ready.

Gabrielle clasped her hands in her lap and turned her attention to the mansion ablaze with lights. The limousine rolled to a stop in front of the canopy that had been erected from the front door to the drive, and a doorman stood ready to assist Gabrielle.

She was late.

Probably the last to arrive. She'd planned it that way. She'd planned everything, from the loosely tucked braid in her hair, to her black sheath dress that hit her at midthigh. From the front, the dress looked conservative, like something Audrey Hepburn would wear, but seen from the rear, the sheath plunged to the small of her back. Something sexy.

She'd come prepared.

The inside of the Hillards' home somewhat resembled a hotel. The doors to several rooms had been thrown open to create one huge space filled with people. The parquet floors, cornices, arched doorways, frieze and columns were spectacular and overwhelming all at once, but they were nothing compared with The Potato King's view of the valley below. Not that there was ever a doubt—Norris Hillard had the hands-down best panoramic view of the city.

A small band filled the room with soft jazz, and a knot of people danced to the soothing music. From where she stood, Gabrielle could see a bar and buffet against the far wall in a room to her left. She didn't see Joe, and she took a deep cleansing breath, then slowly let it out.

But he was here somewhere. Here with the rest of the detectives and sergeants and lieutenants dressed in suits. Wives and girlfriends hanging on their arms, chatting and laughing as if tonight was just any other party. As if her stomach weren't in knots and she weren't so nervous that she had to force herself to stand perfectly still.

Then she felt his gaze a split second before her eyes locked with his, the man who'd made her love him, then broken her heart. He stood within a small circle of people, and his dark gaze reached down deep inside and touched her battered heart. She'd prepared herself for that treacherous reaction, and for the warm flush drifting across her flesh. She'd known it would happen, and she forced herself to stand there and absorb as much of his face as she could see. Subdued lighting from the ornate chandelier above his head caught in the curls touching his ears. Her gaze moved to his straight nose and the mouth she'd dreamed of kissing her all over. She made herself feel every little flutter of her pulse and hitch in her breath. There were no surprises. She'd expected this would happen.

The crowd parted, and Gabrielle's gaze took in the fit of his dark gray suit and white shirt. The width of his shoulders and his light gray tie. Now she'd seen him. She hadn't died. She'd be okay. She could close this chapter in her life. She could start her future. But, unlike the last time she'd seen Kevin, she didn't feel free of Joe.

Instead of freedom from her anger, it welled up inside. The last time she'd seen him, she'd been so—so desperate for him to love her. So sure that he had to feel *something*. But he hadn't, and all she had left was pain in her heart and anger in her soul. So much for true love.

She let her gaze linger on his face a moment longer, then she turned and headed for the bar. Never again would she love a man more than he loved her. True love sucked.

She'd turned her back on him. She'd walked away, and he felt as if someone had kicked in his chest. His gaze followed her auburn hair as she made her way through the crowd, and with every step that carried her farther away from him, his chest got a little tighter. Yet at the same time, he'd never felt more *alive*. Little pleasure currents zipped along his nerves and raised the hair on his arms. The crowd in the Hillard mansion moved and shifted, their voices a clustered hum in his ears. Everything around him seemed so meaningless and unimportant. Everything but her.

It hadn't happened like the knock-out punch he'd always expected. No bolt of lightning to let him know he wanted her in his life forever. Nothing painful about it. Loving her was more like a cool breeze and warm sunshine on his face. Simple truth. It was like Gabrielle herself. And all he'd had to do to see it was clear away clutter and get out of his own way.

"The son of a bitch was hiding beneath the bed with his girlfriend," laughed a cop from the Uniform Division who'd been the first to respond to Mr. Hillard's call the night his painting had been stolen. The other police and their wives laughed too, but not Joe. His thoughts were occupied across the room.

Gabrielle looked even better than he remembered. Which was near impossible, because he remembered her looking like some sort of sun-worshiping goddess. He'd wondered if she'd come tonight, and until the moment she'd walked in, he hadn't realized he'd been holding his breath, waiting for her.

He excused himself and wove his way through the crowd, nodding to the men he worked with and their wives but keeping his eyes on the redhead with the dress that had no back to it. Keeping track of her wasn't hard. All he had to do was follow the trail of swiveling heads. He remembered the night he'd asked her to wear something sexy to Kevin's party. He'd been half joking, trying to irritate her a little bit, and she'd purposely worn that awful blue checked thing. But tonight she'd definitely worn something sexy. He had an urge to throw his jacket over her shoulders.

His progress was slowed several times as he moved past friends and colleagues who wanted him to stop and chat. By the time he caught up with Gabrielle at the end of the bar, the only other single detective, Dale Parker, had zeroed in and struck up a conversation with her. Normally, Joe didn't have anything against the rookie, but the attention Dale showed Gabrielle's dress irritated the hell out of him.

"Hey, Shannie," Dale said as he handed Gabrielle a glass of red wine. She smiled her thanks to the younger man and, for the first time in Joe's life, jealousy swamped him, grabbed ahold and pulled him under.

"Parker." Joe watched her shoulder stiffen before she glanced across her shoulder at him. "Hello, Gabrielle."

"Hello, Joe."

It had been a lifetime since he'd heard her voice and looked into her green eyes. Not the taped image of her, but her. Hearing and seeing her in person added a few pounds to the heaviness in his chest, and he had that holding-his-breath feeling again. Standing so close, he realized how much he missed her, but looking into her cold, indifferent gaze, he realized something else: it just might be too late.

There had been many times in Joe's life when he'd felt fear tighten the base of his skull. He's felt it most often chasing felons, running them to ground, never knowing what waited at the end. He'd felt it then, and he felt it now. In the past, he'd always been sure of himself, so certain he would win. He wasn't so sure this time. This time the stakes were too high. This was one blind chase he wasn't certain would end the way he wanted, but he had no choice. He loved her. "How have you been?"

"Great. How about you?"

Not all that great. "Okay." He was bumped

from behind and took a step closer. "What have you been up to?"

"I'm thinking of opening a new store."

He stood close enough to smell her skin. She smelled like lilacs. "What are you going to sell?"

"Essential oils and aromatherapy. I did so well at the Coeur Festival that I think I can make a success out of it."

She smelled like that soap she'd rubbed all over him that day in the shower after he'd made love to her. "Are you going to open it in Hyde Park again?"

"No. The demography is better for alternative ventures in Old Boise. I've already looked into a space. The rent is higher than it was in Hyde Park, but once I sell Anomaly, I think I can afford it. I won't have an employee, I have inventory coming out of my ears, and my start-up costs are reasonably low. When I get the lease . . ."

Standing so close without touching her took every ounce of self-discipline he possessed. His gaze lowered to her lips, and he watched her talk, when what he really wanted was to cover her mouth with his. He watched her speak, when what he really wanted was to take her home and keep her all to himself. His mother was right. He could look at her for the rest of his life. All over, from the top of her head to the tips of her toes. He wanted to touch her and make love to her and watch her while she slept.

He wanted to ask her if she still loved him.

"... isn't that right, Shannie?"

He didn't have a clue what Dale was asking. He didn't care, either. "Can I talk to you a minute, Gabrielle?"

"Actually," Dale answered for her, "I'd just asked her to dance when you walked up. She said yes."

Joe had no experience with the jealousy burning like lava in his gut. He looked into her face and said, "Now you can tell him no." The second the words were out of his mouth he knew he'd made a mistake. Her eyes got squinty, and she opened her mouth to let him have it.

"Where's your girlfriend?" Dale asked before she got the chance to tell him to go to hell.

Her mouth closed and she got real still.

Jesus. What had he ever done to deserve this bullshit? "I don't have a girlfriend," he gritted between his teeth.

"Then who is the woman who owns that deli down on Eighth?"

"Just a friend."

"Just a friend and she brings you lunch?"

Joe wondered if the rookie detective would like his nose pushed beneath his left ear. "That's right."

Dale turned to Gabrielle. "Ready?"

"Yes." And without a glance in his direction, she set her wineglass on the bar and headed toward the dance floor. Dale's hand settled in the small of her bare back.

Joe ordered a beer from the bar, then turned to stare through an arched doorway and onto the darkened dance floor in the next room. He didn't need an arrow to point out Gabrielle. With her height, she was easy to spot.

It was a hell of a thing to look at the woman you loved in the arms of another man. Watch the flash of her white smile as she laughed at some stupid joke, and not be able to do a damn thing about it without looking like a jealous ass. He took a pull off the beer without taking his gaze from Gabrielle. He might not have fully realized how much he loved her until he'd seen her walk in the room tonight, but that didn't mean he didn't feel it in every cell in his body. It didn't mean he didn't feel it in every aching thud of his heart.

Winston Densley and his date sidled up to the bar next to Joe, and the two detectives talked shop and discussed the more interesting features of the Hillards' bathroom—the gold toilet with the warm seat. Joe surprised himself and waited a full five minutes before he set his beer on the bar and wove his way onto the crowded dance floor. The kind of Kenny G. saxophone music Joe usually avoided like a flesh-eating disease ended just as he placed his hand on Detective Parker's shoulder. "I'm cutting in."

"Later."

"Now."

"That's up to Gabrielle."

Through the shadowy space that separated
them, her gaze held Joe's and she said, "It's
okay, Dale. I'm going to listen to what he has
to say, and then he's going to leave me alone
for the rest of the evening."

"Are you sure?"

"Yes."

Dale looked at Joe and shook his head.
"You're an asshole, Shanahan."

"Yeah, so sue me." The music started again,
and Joe took her hand in his and wrapped his
other arm around her waist. She stood as stiff
as a statue within his embrace, but just holding
her again was like coming home after an extended absence.

"What do you want?" she asked next to his
ear.

You, he thought, but he figured she wouldn't
be really happy to hear his answer right now.
They needed to clear the air between them before he told her how he felt about her. "I
stopped seeing Ann over a week ago."

"What happened, did she dump you?"

She was hurt. He would make it up to her.
He folded her against his chest. Her breasts
brushed his lapels, and he slid his palm to her
bare back. A familiar ache settled in the pit of
his belly and spread to his groin. "No, Ann was
never really my girlfriend."

"Not again? Were you just pretending with
her, too?"

She was angry. He deserved it. "No. She was

never my confidential informant like you were. I've known her since we were kids." He slipped his hand up her smooth skin and turned his nose into her hair. He closed his eyes and breathed in the scent. The smell reminded him of the day he'd seen her floating in that little pool. "I used to date her sister."

"Was her sister a real or pretend girlfriend?"

Joe sighed and opened his eyes. "You're determined to be mad at me no matter what I say."

"I'm not mad."

"You're mad."

She pulled back and looked at him, and he'd been right. Her eyes were all hot, no longer cold and indifferent. Which he figured was one of those good/bad things, depending on how he looked at it.

"Tell me why you're so angry," he urged, fully expecting to hear how much he'd hurt her that night on the porch, and after she'd poured it all out, he would make everything okay.

"You brought me a muffin from your girlfriend's deli the morning we made love!"

That wasn't quite what he'd expected to hear. In fact, it wasn't anything like what he'd expected. "What?"

She looked somewhere over his left shoulder as if the sight of him hurt too much. "You brought me—"

"I heard you," he interrupted and quickly glanced around to see if any of the other couples had heard her also. She hadn't exactly been quiet. He didn't know what buying a muffin had to do with the morning they'd made love. He'd also brought her a turkey sandwich from Ann's deli. Big deal, but he didn't mention the sandwich because he recognized this was one of those conversations he would never understand and would never win. Instead he brought her hand to his lips and kissed her knuckles. "Come home with me. We can talk there. I've missed you."

"I can feel how much you miss me against my thigh," she said, but still wouldn't look at him.

If she thought his obvious arousal would embarrass him, she would have to think again. "I'm not ashamed of wanting you. And yes, I've missed touching you, and holding you, and I want that again. But that isn't all I've missed about you since you left town." He placed his palms on the sides of her face, bringing her gaze back to his. "I've missed the way you glance around when you think your karma is going to zap you. I miss watching you walk and the way you push your hair behind your ears. I miss the sound of your voice, and that you try to be a vegetarian and can't. I miss that *you* believe you're a pacifist even as you shock me on the arm. I've missed *everything* about you, Gabrielle."

She blinked twice, and he thought she might

be softening. "When I was out of town, did you know where I was?"

"Yes."

She pulled herself from his embrace. "Then how bad did you really miss me?"

He didn't have an easy answer for her.

"Stay out of my life," she said, then walked from the dance floor.

He didn't follow. Watching her walk away from him this time was the purest hell he'd ever suffered, but he'd been a detective for eight years. He'd learned when to back away from the chase until things cooled down.

But he would only wait so long. He'd wasted enough time denying himself the woman he wanted and needed in his life. Dinner every night by six and matching socks wasn't going to make him happy. Gabrielle made him happy. He understood now what she'd told him that night on her porch. She was his soul. He was her soul. He loved her, and she loved him. Something like that didn't disappear, especially in one month.

Joe wasn't a patient man, but what he lacked in patience, he made up for in tenacity. While he gave her time, he'd romance her. True, he didn't have very much experience in that department, but women loved that sort of thing. He was sure he could do it.

He was sure he could romance the hell out of Gabrielle Breedlove.

Eighteen

 AT NINE O'CLOCK THE NEXT MORNING, the first dozen roses arrived. They were gorgeous and pure white, and they were from Joe. He'd scrawled his name across the card, but that was it. Just his name. Gabrielle didn't have a clue what that meant, but she wasn't about to read anything into it. She'd done that once. She'd read too much into the way he'd kissed her and made love to her, and she'd paid.

The second dozen were red. The third dozen, pink. Their fragrance filled her house. She still absolutely refused to look for meaning, but when she realized she was waiting for his call, just as she had the day of Kevin's arrest, she pulled on a T-shirt and running shorts and took off for her jog.

No more waiting. She needed to clear her head. She needed to figure out what to do because she didn't think she could take another repeat of the night before. Seeing him hurt too much. She'd thought she was strong enough to face the other half of her soul, but she wasn't. She couldn't look into the eyes of the man she loved and know he didn't love her. Especially now, when she knew that on the morning he'd made love to her, he'd visited his girlfriend first. Hearing about the woman who owned the deli had been one more stab to her already wounded heart. A deli owner would love to cook. She probably wouldn't mind cleaning the house and doing Joe's laundry, either. The things he'd mentioned were important to him that day in the storage room when he'd pushed her against the wall and kissed her until she could hardly breathe.

Gabrielle jogged past St. John's, a few blocks from her house. The doors were thrown open, and music from the pipe organ floated through the wooden entrance to the old cathedral. Gabrielle wondered if Joe was Catholic or Protestant or atheist. Then she remembered he'd said he'd attended a parochial school, and she figured he was Catholic. Not that it mattered now.

She jogged past Boise High and ran four laps around the school's track before she once again turned toward home. Back to her house filled with the flowers Joe had sent her. Back to the confusion she'd felt since the day she'd met him. She felt it now more than ever. Fresh air hadn't helped at all to clear her head, and there was only one thing she knew for sure. If Joe did call, she'd tell him he had to stop. No more calls or flowers. She didn't want to see him.

She figured the chances of them accidentally running into each other were slim. He was a property crimes detective, and she didn't foresee a burglary in her future. She planned to open a shop selling her oils, and she didn't envision Joe as a potential aromatherapy customer. There was no reason why they would ever see each other again.

Except that he was waiting for her on her front porch, sitting with his feet planted on the step beneath him, forearms resting across his thighs. His sunglasses swung from one hand suspended between his knees. He looked up at her approach and slowly rose. No matter what she told herself, her treacherous heart swelled at the sight of him. Then, as if he thought she meant to say something he didn't want to hear, he held up his hand to stop her. But really, she didn't know *what* to say, since she hadn't formed a coherent thought yet.

"Before you order me off of your porch," he began, "I have something to tell you."

He'd dressed in a pair of khaki pants and a cotton shirt that buttoned up the front. He'd rolled the long sleeves up his forearms. He looked so good she wanted to reach out and touch him, but of course she didn't. "I heard what you had to say last night," she said.

"I don't know what happened last night, but I definitely didn't say everything I needed to."

He shifted his weight to one foot. "Are you going to invite me inside?"

"No."

He stared at her for a moment. "Did you get the roses?"

"Yes."

"Oh. Oh good." He opened his mouth, shut it, then tried again. "I don't know where to begin. I'm afraid of saying the wrong thing again." He paused then said, "I'm sorry I hurt you."

She couldn't look at him and lowered her gaze to her feet. "Is that why you sent the roses?"

"Yes."

The second she heard his answer, she realized she shouldn't have asked the question. She also realized that in a tiny corner of her masochistic heart, she'd held on to the hope that he'd sent the flowers because he loved her the way she loved him. "It's over. I'm over it."

"I don't believe you."

"Believe what you want then." She moved past him, to reach the safety of her house before she burst into tears. The last thing she wanted was for Joe to see her cry.

He reached out and grasped her arm. "Please don't walk away from me again. I know I hurt you the night you told me you loved me and I walked away, but Gabrielle, you've walked away from me twice now."

She stopped. Not because he held her arm

but because there was something in his voice that caught her attention and held her in its grasp. Something she'd never heard before. Something in the way he'd said her name. "When did I ever walk away from you?"

"Last night, and each time I watched you go hurt like a bitch. Like I said, I know that I really hurt you, but don't you think that maybe we can call a truce? Maybe we're even now?" He slid his palm down her arm and grasped her hand. "Don't you think it's time that you let me make it up to you?" He pulled something from his pocket and pressed a metal disk into her palm. "I am the other half of your soul," he said. "And you are the other half of my soul. Together we make each other whole."

Gabrielle opened her hand and looked down at the flat black-and-white pendant suspended from a silver chain. The yin and yang. He understood.

"We belong together." He pressed a kiss to the top of her head. "I love you."

She heard him, but she couldn't speak past the emotions expanding like a balloon in her chest. She stared at the necklace and what it represented. If she believed him, if she trusted him, he'd just given her everything her heart desired.

"And in case you're thinking of telling me to get out of your life again, there's one more thing you should consider. Just think about all the good karma you can create for yourself when you reform me."

She glanced up into his face, and her vision blurred through her tears. "Do you mean it?"

"Yes. You can reform me. Well, you can *try*."

She shook her head as a tear slid down her cheek. "I mean, do you really love me, Joe?"

"With every breath I take," he said without hesitation. "I want to spend the rest of my life making you happy." He wiped her wet cheek with the back of his hand and asked, "Do you still love me, Gabrielle?"

He sounded so uncertain, his eyes so intense, that she couldn't suppress the smile curving her lips. "Yes, I still love you." Absolute relief softened his gaze, and she added, "Although I don't think you deserve me."

"I *know* I don't deserve you."

"Would you like to come inside anyway?"

A whoosh of air escaped his chest. "Yes."

He followed her into the house and waited until she closed the door before he reached for her. His hands grabbed her shoulders, and he pulled her up against his chest. "I've missed you," he said as he planted kisses on her face and her throat. Then he pulled back, looked into her eyes, and swooped in to press his lips to hers. His tongue plunged inside her mouth, and she wrapped her arms around his neck. His hands were everywhere at once. Greedy touches caressing her back, her behind, and cupping her breasts. His thumbs brushed her nipples, and they instantly hardened. She felt totally consumed. Wrapped up in his arms. His embrace. Him. Loving him as much as he loved her.

She pulled back to catch her breath. "I'm sweaty. I have to take a shower."

"I don't care."

"I do."

He pulled air into his lungs and dropped his arms. "Okay, I didn't come here to rush you into anything you aren't ready to do. I know I hurt you, and I know you probably don't feel like making love to me right now. I can wait." He blew out his breath and ran his fingers through his hair. "Yeah, I'll just wait for you. I'll just—" He paused and looked around. "Read a magazine or something."

She tried not to laugh. "You could do that. Or you could join me."

His gaze flew to hers, and Gabrielle reached for his hand. She led him toward the bathroom, and somehow along the way, she lost her shirt and he lost his. He paused to place his open mouth on the side of her neck. She released the hooks of her tight sports bra and freed her breasts into his waiting palms. His deep red aura surrounded them both. Surrounded her with his passion and something that hadn't been there before. His love. It poured over and through her like a heat wave and raised the hair on her arms.

"You're so beautiful to me," he spoke into the

hollow of her throat. "I want to spend the rest of my life looking at you, being with you, making you happy."

Gabrielle kissed him long and hard, her tongue touching and chasing his. He brushed his palms across her tight nipples, then lightly squeezed her breasts. Desire swept across her flesh, and she shoved her hand down the front of his pants and grasped his incredibly hard erection. He was stone covered with satin-smooth skin. She stroked him, running her thumb up and over the head of his hot penis. Feeling him, rediscovering the shape and texture of him until he took a step back and pulled her hand from his pants.

His lids were so low that she could hardly see his shining eyes. "Are you sure you want that shower?" asked an extremely aroused Joe Shanahan.

She nodded, and he practically pulled her out of her shoes. He hauled her willingly into the bathroom, and while she turned on and tested the water, he stripped. Then he stripped her, too, and they stepped into the shower stall. Warm water poured over their heads, and he reached for a bar of lavender soap. He lathered his hands, then rubbed suds all over her body. He paid a lot of attention to her breasts and the peaks of her stiff nipples. He washed her belly and between her thighs. Then he kissed all those places, long, lingering caresses of his tongue and mouth. Her breasts. Her navel. He knelt before her, placed her foot on his shoulder, and grasped her behind in his big hand. He combed his finger through her short pubic hair, then tilted her pelvis toward his mouth and kissed her there. She leaned her head back against the shower wall as the tension inside her built tighter and tighter. Then he stood and she wrapped her legs around his waist. His smooth, hot erection slid against her bottom, and she shivered.

"This is my favorite part," he said, lifting, then lowering her onto his engorged penis, burying himself deep inside. "Touching you where you're all hot and slick. Where it feels so good. Where you feel so good."

"The really good part."

"Yes." He withdrew, then pumped his hips and thrust into her, slowly at first.

"I love you, Joe." He moved harder and faster, and his breath rushed in and out of his lungs as he hammered into her. It didn't take long before both of them shattered in a reeling climax that almost sent Joe to his knees. Her heart pounded in her ears, and it took several long moments for Joe to catch his breath. She didn't realize the water had cooled until he turned it off.

"Sweet baby Jesus," he swore as he withdrew and lowered her to her feet. "That was like trying to run, juggle, and come, all at the same time."

"I appreciate it," she whispered and kissed his neck.

"I wasn't complaining." He grinned and patted her behind. "Do you have anything to eat? Maybe some bacon and eggs? I'm starving after that."

She offered him cornflakes. They sat at her dining room table, wearing nothing but towels and huge smiles. Gabrielle looked beside her at the man she loved and wondered what she'd done so right to deserve everything she wanted. She didn't know, but she figured it was about time her karma started to repay her for the past few months.

That night as she lay in her bed, wrapped in Joe's arms, a feeling of complete balance and utter happiness filled her body, mind, and spirit. She thought perhaps she'd found a bit of nirvana on earth, but she did have one question.

"Joe?"

His hand slid down her ribs to her hip. "Hmm."

"When did you know you loved me?"

"Probably last month, but I didn't know it for sure until you walked into the Hillard party last night."

"What took so long?"

He was silent a moment, then said, "After I was shot, I had a lot of time on my hands to think, and I decided it was time to start a family. I got this picture in my head of what my wife should be like. She'd like to cook and make sure I have clean socks."

"That's not really me."

"I know. You're who I wanted before I knew what I really wanted."

"I think I understand. I always thought I'd fall in love with a man who would meditate with me."

"That's definitely not me."

"I know. *You're* who I wanted before I knew what I really wanted." She pulled back and looked up at him. "Do you still think I'm crazy?"

"What I think," he said and gathered her in his arms, "is that I'm crazy in love with you."

JOE WALKED INTO GABRIELLE'S STUDIO and studied the portrait she was painting of Sam. The subject in question hung upside down from his perch, watching her. The bird on the canvas looked more like a partridge than a parrot, and it had a yellow glow around its head that looked like the sun. He knew it was supposed to be Sam's aura, just as he knew better than to give his opinion.

"Are you sure you don't want to paint me naked instead? I'm willing." Sitting for Gabrielle usually turned into a session of taking those soft little brushes and smearing each other with some non-toxic paint she had. It gave him a whole new appreciation for art.

She smiled as she dipped her brush into a blob of bright yellow. "I have a lot of portraits of your Mr. Happy," she said and pointed toward the stack of canvases against the wall. "I want to paint Sam today."

Damn, he'd been usurped by a bird.

He leaned one shoulder against the wall and watched Gabrielle work. They'd been married for three months, and sometimes he'd catch himself just watching her. His mother had been right about that, he could look at her for the rest of his life, whether she was painting, or making her oils, or sleeping. He especially liked to watch her eyes when he made love to her.

In a week they'd celebrate the day she'd juiced him with a can of hair spray. He really wasn't into celebrating made-up anniversaries, and that was one memory that brought a bigger smile to Gabrielle's lips than his, but he'd celebrate to make her happy.

His gaze lowered to her stomach, and he imagined, if he looked hard enough, that he could see the slight rounding of her belly where his baby grew. They figured she'd conceived the night they'd moved into their new home two months ago. Now *that* had been a celebration.

Sam let out a squawk, then flew from the perch to Joe's shoulder. He puffed out his chest and rocked from one foot to the other.

"You've got to ask yourself one question. Do you feel lucky? Well, do ya—punk?"

Joe gazed at his wife, in her white shirt splattered with paint. Everything he'd ever wanted or would ever need was in this room. He had a beautiful wife he loved so much that it brought an ache to his chest, a baby growing safe and secure in her womb, and a very naughty bird. What more could a guy ask for?

"Yes I do," he said. "I'm one lucky punk."